Stepping Stones

4 vmbo-gt
Textbook

Clair Bellamy Conley

Daniëlle Derkse

Arne van Diemen

Eveline Heij

Eppe Scholtens

Mirjam Versteeg

Eindredactie: Shirley Steinvoort

Native speaker eindredactie: Kate Roberts and Jennifer Purcell

Vijfde editie

Noordhoff Uitgevers

Stepping Stones 4 vmbo-gt bestaat uit:

- *Textbook* = bronnenboek
- *Activity Books 4A* en *4B*
- *Stepping Stones online*, met
  - voor de leerling: onder andere al het audio- en videomateriaal
  - extra voor de docent: onder andere toetsen, tapescripts, uitwerkingen en een presentatietool voor het digitale schoolbord

Wij besteden veel zorg aan de ontwikkeling van onze leermiddelen en doen er alles aan om fouten te voorkomen. Mocht u onverhoopt toch een fout tegenkomen, dan kunt u dit per mail doorgeven aan steppingstones@noordhoff.nl.

Met dank aan Adriënne Buschmann, Elien Cusveller, Sicco Gjaltema, Heleen Kost, Edith van 't Wout

Vormgeving omslag Conceptontwerp: Fabrique, Communicatie en design, Delft / Vertaling Ontwerp De Weijer Design BNO, Baarn
Omslagillustratie De Weijer Design BNO, Baarn
Omslagfoto Imagedock
Vormgeving binnenwerk Bloemvis, Groningen
Illustraties Oirik, Apeldoorn; Geza Illustraties, Heiloo

FSC www.fsc.org MIX Papier van verantwoorde herkomst FSC® C118189

1 / 18

ISBN 978-90-01-83695-5

Table of contents

Theme contents

Theme	Listening/Watching	Reading
1 Just for laughs	A voorbereiden/voorspellen F intensief kijken G globaal luisteren	C oriënterend lezen H voorspellen/voorbereiden
2 Creative minds	A moeilijke woorden F gericht kijken G achtergrond	C globaal lezen H zoekend lezen
3 Going pro	A gericht luisteren F voorbereiden/voorspellen G intensief luisteren	C intensief lezen H structuur
Exam Preparation	1, 2, 13, 14 meerkeuzevragen	3, 4, 15, 16 meerkeuzevragen 5, 18 open vragen 6, 17 citeervragen 7, 19 juist/onjuist-vragen 8, 20 gatenteksten 9, 10, 21, 22 gemengde vragen
4 Can you believe it?	A intensief luisteren G intonatie K moeilijke woorden	C zoekend lezen H gatentekst
5 English around the world	A intensief luisteren G script met gaps K globaal kijken	C tekstdoel H moeilijke woorden

Speaking & Writing	Grammar	Vocabulary	Task
funny experiences recommending something detailed information	past simple, present perfect, past continuous negations (negative) questions	jokes humour stories	A2 Stories from pictures
designing and building opinion instructions	future word order pitfalls	design building	A2 Dragons' Den
application letter talking about yourself job interview	past perfect	work skills personality	A2 B1 Wanted: personal assistant
11 writing about yourself 12 talking about future plans 23 asking for information 24 talking about routines		signal words and phrases	A2 speaking A2 B1 listening, watching,writing A2 B1 B2 reading
finding out how things work making predictions	summary of the tenses 'if' sentences	mind science tricks experiments	A2 B1 Senses survey
facts and convictions comparisons clarification	comparatives and superlatives	language convictions comparisons	A2 My videolog

Show what you know

1 Just for laughs

TABLE OF CONTENTS

ERK

Reading/listening: A2 B1
Speaking/writing: A2

A
LISTENING

What goes around comes around

Hi Jill! Everything is set for tomorrow. I can't wait to see his face ☺

Hey Ahmed, me neither. I think he will go ballistic!

It's probably the only way to teach him a lesson.

How did you find the same one, BTW?

Well, luckily my father has an old one that doesn't work anymore. You really can't tell them apart! Oh, and Mr Walker is in! We just have to find a way to give it to him tomorrow.

Maybe we can give it to him in the staffroom before the lesson?

Great idea! CU tomorrow ☺

B
THEME WORDS

THEME WORDS

to chuckle	to prank	to tease	quirky
foolish	wacky	to crack up	to ridicule
to giggle	to kid	infectious	to smirk
practical joke	mischief	knee-slapper	witty

THE TONIGHT SHOW WITH JIMMY FALLON

***The Tonight Show* is an American late-night talk show that has been on TV since 1954. It is the world's longest-running late-night talk show and it airs every weeknight.**

The Tonight Show has had many hosts since it started and it is considered a big honour to present the show. The current host is Jimmy Fallon. He always kicks off the show with a short monologue in which he jokes about current events. Fallon also has an in-house band; hip-hop group *The Roots*, and in each episode Fallon welcomes a celebrity, with whom he performs a (musical) sketch.

Fallon's sketches

The Tonight Show is known for goofy humour, easy-going interviews, and sketches - like the one in which actress Jennifer Lawrence performed in a funny instructional dance video. Fallon's sketches usually feature celebrities, but sometimes ordinary people are included. Take, for instance, his sketch with unsuspecting strangers at an ice cream shop. To celebrate the fact that he was given his own Ben & Jerry's ice cream flavour, Fallon decided to fool some customers trying out his flavour. In the clip he operated a robot designed to spoon-feed the customers ice cream. Naturally, since Fallon was inside the machine, he made sure the robot arm messed with each person who came along. The customers, of course, didn't have a clue what was going on and most of them were really puzzled by it. Finally, Fallon revealed himself and told them they were being filmed by hidden cameras.

Behind the humour

Fallon, talented as he may be, does not come up with all the material himself. The show actually has 17 staff writers who help make up the jokes and sketches. Seth Meyers is one of them. Meyers used to do sketch comedy himself and explains how important it is to work together: 'The only way you can write a good sketch is to collaborate and be open to other people's ideas. We do that every day at Fallon.'

Every morning, the show's 17 writers are sent four pages of news summaries before their daily 9:45 am meeting. In the writers' room they pitch ideas for sketches inspired by some of those news stories. Fallon has the final say on what ultimately gets chosen. The job requires a thick skin: Meyers estimates that while he writes about 25 or 30 jokes a week, only about one actually makes it on the air. Yes, sometimes it's tough being funny...

Adapted from: bu.edu

D
SPEAKING
WRITING

STONE

1 Talking about funny experiences

Some time ago, / About a month ago,	I was walking in the park / I was on my way home	when	something unexpected happened. / someone caught my attention.

I	saw a man / noticed a young guy	who	was running around in an astronaut costume. / jumped into the pond with his clothes on.

I	didn't have a clue / couldn't understand	what was going on. / why he was acting so odd.

I	felt confused about / was really puzzled by	the whole experience. / this incident.

Believe it or not, / Anyway,	just as I got closer, / I then saw that	the astronaut stepped into a cardboard spaceship. / more people dived into the water.

You	have no idea / should have seen / can imagine	how funny it looked. / what a ridiculous sight it was. / how hard it made me laugh.

To cut a long story short, / It became clear that / It turned out	I had just witnessed a practical joke. / they were filming the event with hidden cameras. / the man was doing this because he had lost a bet.

E GRAMMAR

GRAMMAR

1 Past simple, present perfect, past continuous >> GS 3, 4 and 5, page 137, 138 and 139

Past simple

I **decided** to go to the city centre yesterday. I **noticed** a young guy in a costume. They **shared** their sweets with me. Some time ago, something unexpected **happened**.	Je gebruikt de *past simple* om te zeggen dat iets in het verleden is gebeurd en nu is afgelopen. Vaak staat er een tijdsbepaling in de zin, zoals *last summer*. Je maakt de *past simple* door -ed aan het hele werkwoord toe te voegen. **Let op!** Soms zijn werkwoorden onregelmatig. Zie *GS 25*.

Present perfect

I **have lived** in Nottingham since 2013. We **haven't seen** Harry for two months now. Alli's already **finished** this game. **Have** you **been** to his new house yet? This comedian **has won** the award three times. **I've** never **experienced** anything like it.	Je gebruikt de *present perfect* om te zeggen dat iets in het verleden is begonnen en nu nog aan de gang is, om te te praten over ervaringen en over gebeurtenissen waarvan je nu het resultaat merkt. Je maakt de *present perfect* met *have/has* + voltooid deelwoord. Let op de verklikwoorden, zie *GS 5*.

Past continuous

We **were telling** each other jokes. You **were texting** him all day. They **were filming** the event.	Je gebruikt de *past continuous* om te benadrukken dat iets in het verleden een tijdje aan de gang was. Je maakt de *past continuous* met *was/were* + het hele werkwoord + -ing.
I **was sleeping** while the phone **rang**. They **were talking** when the teacher **walked** in. My sister **called** me when I **was walking** the dog.	Je gebruikt de *past simple* en de *past continuous* samen in een zin om aan te geven dat iets gebeurde terwijl er al iets anders aan de gang was.

F WATCHING

London laughter club

In London, members of a laughter club get together to do laughing exercises. These help to reduce stress and make the body healthier. Also, laughing with a group gives a feeling of togetherness. So don't be shy and laugh!

G LISTENING

A good laugh

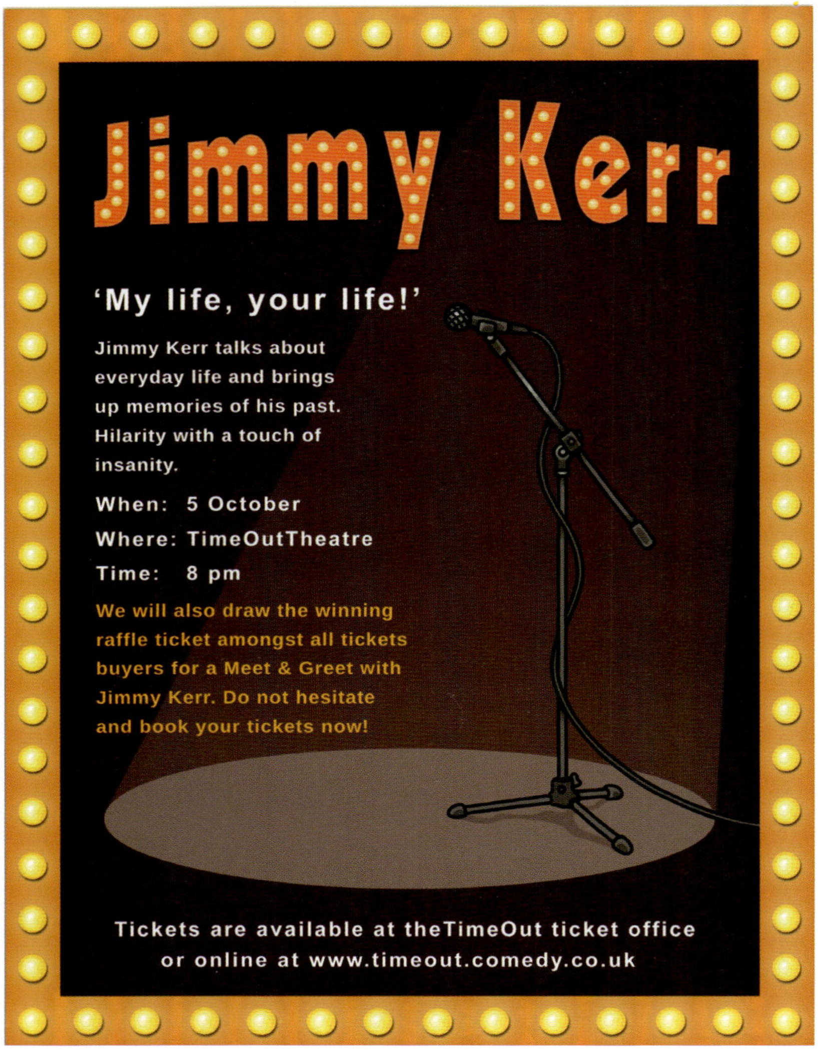

H READING

A PROFESSIONAL PRANKSTER

1 **Sharing the stage with Kanye West? Check! Singing on X-Factor? Check! Training with Manchester City Football club? Check! Comedian Simon Brodkin has made quite a name for himself with his pranks at public events.**

2 Brodkin, who used to be a doctor but quit because it was too exhausting, is an English comedian. He does stand-up shows in which he makes fun of news stories, but he is far better known for something else: he does really surprising stunts. These stunts, often at high-profile events outside the theatre, have attracted a lot of publicity.

3 In 2013, for example, he dressed up as a fictional professional footballer called Jason Bent, with a '9' and 'Bent' on the back of his shirt, and started training with the Manchester City football team. Brodkin himself thought the prank was quite harmless: 'All the players were laughing and smiling. A few of them did seem to think I was a new addition to the team.' A few minutes after he entered the pitch he was arrested for invading a football pitch and he received a caution in court for the incident.

4 **On stage with Kanye West**
Brodkin often plays a character in his performances. In 2015, at the famous Glastonbury Festival, he dressed up as Lee Nelson, another one of his characters, and invaded the Pyramid Stage. For this stunt he put on some baggy trousers, reversed his cap and carried a toy microphone, and ran onstage during one of Kanye West's performances. Brodkin, however, was quickly apprehended by a security guard and didn't manage to rap even one line with the hip hop legend.

5 Brodkin also gained a lot of publicity by stealing one of his own DVDs. Again dressed up as Lee Nelson, he was doing a signing for his DVD at a shop in Oxford Street. As a treat for his fans he 'stole' one of his own DVDs, then was chased around the store by an actor dressed up as a police officer. Somehow they ended up out on the pavement where a real officer got involved, thinking it was a real theft taking place. Eventually, the police officer brought him back into the shop.

On being a doctor

Brodkin loved being a doctor but it was exhausting: 'I remember once being paged, leaping out of bed and running to the ward and realising I was so tired that I'd put my dressing gown on instead of my white coat.'

6 **No more stunts?**
Brodkin recently revealed that he's been banned from doing any more stunts. He explains: 'I've been told absolutely not to do any more. My management and my family have asked me not to.' According to Brodkin his mother was really upset about his recent stunts. 'She said to me "What are you trying to do to me? First you're a doctor, then you give it up to be a comedian, now you're getting arrested. You're going to give me a heart attack."'

7 It remains to be seen, however, if Brodkin can keep his word. 'I'm going to try everything I can to keep myself in check but sometimes, when I get into character, something takes over. So, I don't know if I can make any promises...'

Adapted from: thesun.co.uk

STONE

2 Recommending something

If you like comedies,	you should really check out Comedy Central.
If stand-up comedy is your thing,	I can recommend that new show.

The series	follows the adventures of	an almost-famous rock band on tour.
The story	revolves around	a man who can't remember his past.

You must see her perform	as	her impressions of celebs are brilliant.
I can recommend her show	because	she does really surprising stunts.

I wouldn't	watch	his stand-up show.	It's	silly and annoying.
You shouldn't		the spin-off of this series.		boring and predictable.

3 Asking for and giving detailed information

What kind of jokes	do the performers tell?
	does he play on the audience?

Could you tell me more	about	the topics of the show?
Can you tell me something		the comedian's sense of humour?

Doesn't he	play the lead role	in	the TV series?
Didn't she	make a guest appearance		that sitcom?

The comedian	often plays a character	when he's on stage.
This entertainer	usually involves the audience	in his performances.

It's	a daily talk show.	The host	makes fun of	news stories.
This is	a humorous quiz show.	It	comments on	celebrity culture.

GRAMMAR

2 Negations (*ontkenningen*) >> GS 10, page 144

They **weren't** at home yesterday. Shannon **hasn't got** a baby brother. The show is about a man who **can't** remember his past. We **won't** watch his stand-up show tonight. You **shouldn't** watch the spin-off of this series. I **didn't** have any pets growing up.	Je gebruikt een ontkenning om aan te geven dat iets niet zo is. Je maakt een ontkenning door *not* achter *to be*, *have got*, of hulpwerkwoorden te zetten. Als deze werkwoorden niet in de zin staan, gebruik je *don't* (*do* + *not*), *doesn't* (*does* + *not*) of *didn't* (*did* + *not*) om ontkenningen te maken.

3 Questions and negative questions (*vragen* en *ontkennende vragen*) >> GS 9 and 11, page 143 and 145

Dionne **was** the first to congratulate me. **Was** Dionne the first to congratulate you? You **can** tell me something about the show. **Can** you tell me something about the show?	Vraagzinnen met een vorm van *to be*, *to have got* en hulpwerkwoorden (*can, could, will, should, may, might, must, ought to*) maak je door het (hulp)werkwoord vooraan in de zin te zetten. De rest van de zin blijft hetzelfde.
He **plays** the lead role in this show. **Does** he **play** the lead role in this show?	Bij andere werkwoorden gebruik je *do*, *does* of *did*. **Let op!** Na een vorm van *to do* gebruik je altijd het **hele werkwoord**.
Can't you tell me more? **Isn't** the music too loud? **Didn't she** make a guest appearance in that sitcom?	Je gebruikt ontkennende vragen vaak om te vragen om bevestiging, maar je kunt ze ook gebruiken om ergernis of ongeloof uit te drukken.

Diary comics

In this clip you'll meet James Nash, a comic artist who draws comic strips for a living. He talks about his studies, his inspirations, and the things he does on a typical workday. Follow him around for a day and take a look behind the scenes.

Task

>> TASKCARD

Stories from pictures
Je gaat een komisch verhaal bedenken op basis van foto's.

Taalportfolio
A2 Ik kan zeer kort en elementair gebeurtenissen, activiteiten in het verleden en persoonlijke ervaringen beschrijven.
A2 Ik kan een verhaal vertellen of iets beschrijven.

ERK

Who? What? Where?

Vocabulary

A LISTENING

My father thinks it is not healthy to **be attached to** digital devices.	*gehecht zijn aan*
A professional actor should **be set** to film at any time of the day.	*klaar zijn*
The children enjoy drawing with **chalk** outside in the summer.	*krijt*
If a person robs a bank, the **consequence** is often going to prison.	*gevolg*
They **deserve** to go on holiday, since they have worked hard all year.	*verdienen*
This house is **exactly** what we've been looking for for years now.	*precies*
She didn't want to **face** her friends after such an embarrassing moment.	*onder ogen zien*
You look **familiar**. Have we met before?	*bekend*
If they select you for the TV game show, you could win a small **fortune**.	*fortuin*
My brother will **go ballistic** when he finds out I have ruined his new jumper.	*doordraaien*
Our school has a new **headmaster**, who plans to turn the school around.	*schoolhoofd*
Nathan, stop playing that dreadful music of yours **immediately**!	*onmiddellijk*
Harry has been told not to **overdo** it when it comes to homework.	*overdrijven*
I have decided to play a **prank** on my neighbour on April Fool's day this year.	*grap*
Don't **pretend** you didn't hear me. I know you did.	*doen alsof*
My mum was really **puzzled** as to why the dog ran off so suddenly.	*verbijsterd*
The police are tired of **repeatedly** warning people to use fireworks safely.	*herhaaldelijk*
When you have finished the assignment, come to the **staffroom**.	*personeelsruimte*
It was so lovely to meet you! Shall we **swap** phone numbers?	*ruilen*
The new boy band has been a **target** of the press for the last few weeks.	*doelwit*
I can never **tell apart** Vicky and Lynn. They look almost identical.	*uit elkaar houden*
This tomato soup is a **treasured** family recipe.	*gekoesterd*
Joseph told his trainer that **he wasn't bothered** about frequent training.	*het kon hem niets schelen*

B THEME WORDS

Tim's baby brother started to **chuckle**, like nothing you have heard before!	*grinniken*
Her joke made me **crack up**. It was so funny I couldn't stop laughing.	*in de lach schieten*
It was quite **foolish** of me to leave the door unlocked yesterday evening.	*dwaas*
The new funniest videos show on TV makes me **giggle** every time.	*giechelen*
Stephanie has such an **infectious** laugh, you will soon be joining in.	*aanstekelijk*
I can never **kid** my brother. He is always onto me.	*voor de gek houden*
That joke about the chicken crossing the road is such a **knee-slapper**!	*dijenkletser*
Tom and Anne are always involved in some kind of **mischief**.	*kattenkwaad*
The customer didn't appreciate the **practical joke** the chef played on him.	*poets*
When we **prank** someone, we don't want to hurt anyone's feelings.	*streek uithalen*
Jim is considered to be quite **quirky**. I didn't realise he could be so funny.	*eigenzinnig*
It is unfair to **ridicule** students if they make a mistake. At least they tried.	*belachelijk maken*
Mum said that if we **smirk** at her when she is mad, we're asking for trouble.	*gniffelen*
All brothers and sisters **tease** each other, it's quite normal.	*plagen*
Look at that **wacky** car over there! You wouldn't see me driving in it!	*gek, maf*
Janna is actually quite **witty** once you get to know her better.	*gevat*

C READING

I really want to know when they **air** the next season of *Farland*.	*uitzenden*
If you **collaborate** on a project, you are likely to come up with better ideas.	*samenwerken*
Can you **estimate** how much money you have to save per week to buy the bike?	*schatten*
Gillian keeps trying to **fool** me, but it hasn't worked so far.	*voor de gek houden*
My best friend can be a little **goofy** at times. He thinks he's hilarious.	*maf*
Ordinary people shouldn't **mess with** superheroes or heroines.	*knoeien met*
I love to watch tennis! **Naturally** I support my favourite players.	*uiteraard*
Computers are not actually that hard to **operate**, if you take the time.	*bedienen*
This chair is made completely out of **ordinary** paper, isn't it wonderful?	*gewoon*
Steven had a fantastic idea and had to **pitch** it to the company.	*opwerpen, opperen*
At the beginning of a novel, the author has to **set the tone** first.	*de toon zetten*
Karen missed the main news program, so she watched a **summary** instead.	*samenvatting*
The director of the company always has **the final say** in important decisions.	*het laatste woord*
You can tell me I have a choice, but **ultimately** it's your decision.	*uiteindelijk*
The actors were preparing to play tricks on the **unsuspecting** audience.	*nietsvermoedend*
Eric was never allowed to go to parties or concerts on a **weeknight**.	*doordeweekse avond*

D SPEAKING & WRITING

The assistant was **confused** at the two customers who were double booked.	*verward*
The pirates finally found the gold that was **hidden** beneath the giant X.	*verborgen*
Our teacher found it **odd** that the class was so quiet all of a sudden.	*vreemd*
The scientist was **puzzled** as to why the experiment failed to work.	*verbluft*
If those jeans **turn out** to be too short, I will return them.	*blijken*
Grandad said his surprise party was completely **unexpected**.	*onverwacht*

G LISTENING

When the jury announced their verdict, there was great **anger** in the courtroom.	*boosheid*
She's curious about how we **deal with** exam stress.	*omgaan met*
The team were expected to be in the **dressing room** at 8am sharp.	*kleedkamer*
If they **hesitate** for too long, they might miss the bus.	*aarzelen*
That stand-up comedian can **impersonate** just about any celebrity.	*nadoen*
My neighbour's constant drilling drove me to the point of **insanity**!	*krankzinnigheid*
If life gets a bit **overwhelming**, try to focus on the things that make you happy.	*overweldigend*
Hoverboarding with your friends is the latest **phenomenon** at our school.	*fenomeen*
Perry was thrilled to have won the star prize in the **raffle** at the Spring fayre.	*verloting*
Mrs Brumley decided to **raffle off** the author signed books she had collected.	*verloten*
It was a huge **relief** to hear the flight hadn't been cancelled after all.	*opluchting*
Try not to make everything **revolve around** the test week.	*draaien om*
People who like a YouTube channel can **subscribe** to it.	*abonneren*
In my opinion, the best **tonic** to cheer someone up is a romantic film.	*middel*
Iris had so much work at the office, she asked if she could **work overtime**.	*overwerken*

H READING

This dress will make a great **addition** to my wardrobe.	*toevoeging*
When the police officers **apprehend** the suspect, they will put him in jail.	*aanhouden*
Rappers are generally known to be fans of **baggy** jeans and T-shirts.	*wijde*
The government will **ban** unhealthy food in all schools in the UK.	*verbieden*
The culprit was let off with **caution**. She knows that next time she will be fined.	*waarschuwing*
When I was five I had a beautiful pink and white spotted **dressing gown**.	*ochtendjas*
Being famous must be **exhausting**, with all the concerts and interviews et cetera.	*vermoeiend*
Film producers must make it clear when their characters are **fictional**.	*verzonnen*
There is so much to **gain** when you work hard and do your best.	*behalen, bereiken*
The zoo keeper claimed the snake was **harmless**. I didn't believe her.	*onschuldig*
Laurance asked his mum not to **invade** his personal space.	*binnendringen*
When you make a promise, you have to **keep your word**.	*je aan je woord houden*
Holly had to **leap** out of bed to make the 8 o'clock train.	*springen*
Sometimes in Britain people cycle on the **pavement** if the roads are busy.	*voetpad*
Gregg made a **promise** to his dad that he would pay for the damage.	*belofte*
In the early nineties it was cool to wear your clothing **backwards**.	*omgedraaid*
Rebecca was really **upset** to hear she didn't get in at her school of choice.	*van streek*
Our aunt had an operation, so we decided to visit her on the **ward**.	*ziekenhuiszaal*

I SPEAKING & WRITING

Roald Dahl was utterly **brilliant**. I adore his stories.	*briljant, geniaal*
A good actor should easily be able to get into their **character** in the play.	*personage, typetje*
I cannot miss my show tonight. There will be a special **guest appearance**.	*gastoptreden*
Mel prefers novels that are a little **humorous** and light in content.	*humoristisch*
Judy can do an excellent **impression** of our school dinner lady!	*imitatie*
Liz is so excited to have landed the **lead role** in the latest broadway play.	*hoofdrol*
You are so **predictable**! I knew you would buy that dress we saw yesterday.	*voorspelbaar*

PROVERBS & SAYINGS

To be a barrel of laughs.	*Heel grappig zijn.*
Many a true word is spoken in jest.	*Ware woorden kunnen ook grappig zijn.*
Laughter is the best medicine.	*Lachen is het beste medicijn.*
More fun than a barrel of monkeys.	*Heel vermakelijk zijn.*
To laugh one's head off.	*Kapot gaan van het lachen.*

Grammar overview

Past simple, present perfect, past continuous

past simple	iets is in het verleden gebeurd en nu afgelopen; vaak met tijdsbepaling	I **decided** to go to the city centre yesterday.
present perfect	iets is in het verleden gebeurd en nu nog bezig	I **have lived** in Nottingham since 2013.
	het resultaat is nog merkbaar	I **have broken** my leg, so I can't walk.
	een ervaring	This comedian **has won** the award three times already.
	verklikwoorden	*ever, never, already, yet, before, recently, lately*
past continuous	iets was in het verleden een tijdje aan de gang	You **were texting** him all day.

When the phone **rang**,	I **was sleeping**.
past simple	*past continuous*
iets gebeurde	terwijl iets anders al langere tijd aan de gang is

Negations (ontkenningen)

to be	They **were** at home yesterday.	>	They **weren't** at home yesterday.
to have got	Shannon **has got** a baby brother.	>	Shannon **hasn't got** a baby brother.
can	This man **can** remember his past.	>	This man **can't** remember his past.
hulpwerkwoord	You **should** watch this series.	>	You **shouldn't** watch this series.
to do	I **had** many pets growing up.	>	I **didn't** have any pets growing up.

Questions (vragen)

to be	Dionne **was** the first to congratulate me.	>	**Was** Dionne the first to congratulate you?
to have got	We**'ve got** a new teacher.	>	**Have** we **got** a new teacher?
hulpwerkwoord	You **could** tell me something about the show.	>	**Could** you tell me something about the show?
to do	He **plays** the lead role in this show.	>	**Does** he **play** the lead role in this show?

Negative questions (*ontkennende vragen*)

Was Dionne the first to congratulate you?	>	**Wasn't** Dionne the first to congratulate you?
Have we **got** a new teacher?	>	**Haven't** we **got** a new teacher?
Could you tell me something about the show?	>	**Couldn't** you tell me something about the show?
Does he **play** the lead role in this show?	>	**Doesn't** he **play** the lead role in this show?

2

Creative minds

TABLE OF CONTENTS

ERK

Reading/listening: A2 B1
Speaking/writing: A2

A
LISTENING

Fine design

Send Quote Address Attach Options Spelling Save Security Stop

To: Students' presentation evening
Subject: D.Smith@yahoo.co.uk

Dear parent/guardian,

We are delighted to invite you to our fourth year students' presentation evening. The students have worked on an exam project themed 'Design', under the supervision of Ms Wilkinson, their art teacher.
This project has given students the opportunity to put their skills and talents into practice. Not only have they learned how to think critically and work in teams but also how to solve problems and make presentations. These skills will help them succeed in the future, both in school and in today's work environment.

The students will present their work on February 13th from 7pm.

Please send an email to info@th.secondaryschool.co.uk to let us know whether you will be attending the presentation evening.

Yours sincerely,

Robert Graham
Headmaster

B
THEME WORDS

THEME WORDS

to construct
fabric
one-of-a-kind
blueprint
draft
designer
measurements
modify

to reproduce
trademark
component
depth
handicraft
height
to sculpt
width

WATTS TOWERS: LA'S WEIRD MASTERPIECE

Last week our school visited Watts Towers in Los Angeles. The towers were designed and built by Simon Rodia, an Italian immigrant who worked on the towers for 34 years! This is my report about this architectural wonder.

Rodia arrived in the US at age 15 and worked around the country before settling in LA. He worked full-time his whole life and began working on this monument in his spare time. The Watts Towers, also known as *Nuestro Pueblo* ('our town' in Spanish) are a collection of 17 structures in the area known as Watts in Los Angeles.

Rodia was a cement worker and liked to work with tiles. It is no surprise then that Watts Towers is completely made up of <u>steel-reinforced</u> cement structures which are <u>ornamented</u> with pieces of broken tile. However, he used much more than just cement and tile. He built the structures using recyclable materials and used objects, including soda bottles, seashells, mirrors, and much more. You could say he was the ultimate recycler!

Incredibly, Rodia built the structures using only simple hand tools such as a hammer and chisel. A nearby railway line (now long gone) was his <u>anvil</u>: he placed metal on the tracks and waited for passing trains to flatten it. Can you believe that!

The tour guide said that Rodia bought a triangular plot for his towers so that his work could resemble a ship. The three tallest towers,

which are almost 30 meters high, do indeed look rather like masts. Rodia himself, however, was less open about his influences. Nobody is sure what gave him the inspiration for his massive project. The nearest that Rodia ever came to explaining his masterpiece was to say, 'I had in mind to do something big and I did it.'

After he had completed the towers in 1954, Rodia gave the towers to a neighbour and moved away never to return; the reason is unknown. Nothing happened with the Towers until 1959. The Towers were about to be demolished when people became more interested in Rodia's work and wanted to avoid losing it. The local community is now very proud of the Towers and some even help out by giving tours.

If you ask me, his creations are very artistic and original so I cannot understand why anyone would want to get rid of them. I recommend that everyone visits to marvel at the craftsmanship and hard labour that went into the Towers!

Written by Miguel

steel-reinforced	*met staal versterkte*
ornamented	*versierd*
anvil	*aambeeld, smeedblok*

STONE

4 Talking about designing and building something

We	are going to	design	an inflatable boat.
They	have plans to	construct	a sustainable house.
Some students		make	a wooden chair.

A TV advertisement	gave me the inspiration for	this collection.
A visit to an art museum	helped her develop ideas for	this project.

We	are going to build	the sculptures	using	recyclable materials.
They	will construct	the birdcage		3D printing.

You	have to	assemble	the parts yourself.
	can	cut out	the figures.
It's easy to		secure	the foam pieces.

5 Asking for and giving an opinion

Are you pleased with	the leather bag	I've designed?
Have you got any comments on	the trainers	she's made?
What's your opinion of	these logos	we've sketched?

I'd say that	your idea seems very well thought out.
In my opinion,	the bags have great colours and beautiful patterns.
If you ask me,	your designs always look very artistic and original.
As far as I'm concerned	it's exactly what we're looking for.

Personally, I think	they	are kind of sloppy.
I'm no expert, but	the sketches	look a bit old-fashioned.
I feel	some parts	could use a bit more work.

GRAMMAR

4 Future (*toekomende tijd*) >> GS 7, page 140

They **will construct** the birdcage using 3D printing. Mary-Ann **won't win** the competition. **Will** the film **start** anytime soon?	*will* + het hele werkwoord: om **iets aan te bieden**, bij **beloftes, aankondigingen** en **besluiten**, en bij **voorspellingen** waarvoor je GEEN bewijs hebt.
We **are going to make** an inflatable boat this week. **Is** Sheila **going to go** to the party? Look at the sky. It **isn't going to rain** tonight.	*to be going to* + het hele werkwoord: als iemand iets **in de toekomst van plan is**, of als je een **voorspelling** doet waarvoor je WEL bewijs hebt.
I'**m working** at the supermarket from four till six. They **aren't going** to school on Monday.	*present continuous*: voor **afspraken** in de nabije toekomst waarvan **de tijd en/of plaats al vaststaat**.
The train **departs** at a quarter past five.	*present simple*: tijden volgens een **vast schema.**

5 Word order (*woordvolgorde*) >> GS 12, page 146

He	bought	a	blue	T-shirt.
onderwerp (ow)	*persoonsvorm (pv)*	*lijdend voorwerp (lv)*		
pers. vnw.	*werkwoord (ww)*	*lidwoord*	*bn*	*zn*

Did	he	lose?	|	He	didn't	lose.
hww	*pers. vnw.*	*ww*	|	*pers. vnw.*	*hww*	*ww*

She		always	goes	to her grandparents	on Saturdays.
I	am	usually		at the sports centre	on Fridays.
pers. vnw.	*ww*	*bw frequentie*	*ww*	*plaatsbepaling*	*tijdsbepaling*

A man and his dog

Everybody knows the saying 'a dog is a man's best friend'. That phrase certainly applies to John Dolan and his dog George. After a life of homelessness, crime and drugs, John turned his life around. He picked up a pen and paper and started drawing sketches of George and the buildings around him. John is now a successful artist.

G

LISTENING

Back Forward Stop Refresh Home Search Favorites History Mail Print

www.diply.com

Space colours your place

Think you don't have enough storage in your home? Get creative ideas on how to maximise storage by making the most of your home's existing space.

Store Things On Your Ceiling

If you need more storage space but have no idea where to create it, look up! You'd be surprised at how much unused but usable space is being wasted on your ceiling. All you need to do is bolt some boards where you can slide storage containers into them.

Stairs storage

Shelves and storage spaces under staircases are the best tricks to use the area underneath the stairs. How many of you have thought about using the space under your stairs as a bookshelf?

Murphy bed

A Murphy bed gives you comfort and convenience without sacrificing space. That means more room for you and your family!

H

READING

THE MAN WHO GROWS FURNITURE

Some people like to grow fruits, others prefer to focus on vegetables. Then there is Gavin Munro, who likes to create 'living furniture'. No, he is not a scientist with a crazy idea, but an ordinary man who is living his dream of growing environmentally-friendly chairs!

Gavin Munro, who has named his furniture company *Full Grown*, trains trees to grow into furniture. Growing furniture like chairs is a difficult process. Munro uses custom-made moulds to shape the branches, so that the object grows into one solid piece. 'Then you have to prune the branches at the right time. After it's grown into the shape you want, you nurture the tree as it thickens before harvesting it in the winter. After you're done with this, you wait for the wood to dry. Then you sand the wood until it's smooth,' Munro explains. 'Add the finishing touches and the chair is ready.'

He believes the technique could one day be used to create sustainable furniture on a much larger scale. 'I like to think of it as a kind of organic 3D printing that uses air, soil and sunshine as its source material.' Working together with his wife Alice, Munro mainly uses strong, fast-growing willow for his designs but is also experimenting with other types of wood.

Practical and functional

Munro's creations are more practical and functional than most other furniture: there is no need for nails, fixings and machinery to assemble the chair. More importantly, the designs should last longer than traditionally-made chairs as they don't have the weak points around the joints. Alice explains: 'Just like a broken bone will be a lot stronger where it heals, the points where the wood is grafted are extremely strong.'

The idea of creating 'living furniture' came to Munro at a young age when he noticed a small bonsai tree in his mother's garden that resembled a chair. What attracted Munro to the concept of 'living furniture' was that it would be faster to grow furniture directly rather than chopping a mature tree into bits.

nurture	*voeden, verzorgen*
fixings	*bevestigingen*
grafted	*samengebonden, verenigd*
shoots	*scheuten, boomstengels*

An ancient method

The idea of shaping trees into furniture is not new. The Chinese have been making stools by placing rocks in tree holes for centuries. However, *Full Grown* is the first company that wants to make naturally-grown furniture for the mass market.

Prototypes

It took Munro many years before he could realise his first 'tree furniture'. The first prototypes got damaged when a herd of cows rampaged through a field of young trees. The Munros recovered and they hope to harvest their first big crop next year and sell the furniture in two years' time. Most of the pieces have already been pre-ordered with the chairs selling for £2,500 each and the lampshades priced between £1,000 and £1,500.

Munro adds: 'The whole process takes place over seasons and years - between four and eight years to grow a chair for example. I'm only making 50 or so pieces a year but for every 100 trees you grow there are a 1,000 branches you need to care for and 10,000 shoots you have to prune at the right time. It's an art-form in itself keeping track of everything.'

Munro is currently working on more complex designs, including a bookshelf and a chest of drawers.

Adapted from: dailymail.co.uk

STONE

6 Giving instructions

The first thing you do, is	have a look at your design.
To begin with,	collect your materials.
First,	write down the measurements.

Then,	assemble the pieces and glue them together.
Following this,	sand the wood until it's smooth.
After this,	cut the fabric to size.
Finally,	sew the fabric pieces together.

You have	to	let the glue dry for at least two hours.
It's important		use the correct equipment for the job.
Be sure		work from the top down.

Use the right tools	or else	the wood will split.
Do not screw the bolts in too tightly	otherwise	you'll damage the surface.

After	you've finished,	clean up your workspace.
	you're done with this,	wait for the paint to dry.

Apply a final layer of varnish	and	your chair is finished.
Add the finishing touches		you're done.

GRAMMAR

J
GRAMMAR

6 Pitfalls (*valkuilen*) >> GS 24, page 140

De volgende woorden worden vaak door elkaar gehaald.

This present is from me **to** you. You have **to** let the glue dry. Don't screw the bolts in **too** tightly. He said he would be there **too**.	*To* betekent 'naar', 'aan'. Voor een werkwoord betekent *to* 'om te'. Voor een bijvoeglijk naamwoord betekent *too* 'te'. Aan het einde van een zin betekent *too* 'ook'.
The sequel is even worse **than** the first film. **Then** he scored the winning goal.	*Than* betekent 'dan' (in vergelijkingen). *Then* betekent 'toen', 'dan' (geeft een tijd aan).
First, collect **your** materials. **You're** late. Do get up earlier.	*Your* betekent 'jouw' (bezittelijk voornaamwoord). *You're* is een samentrekking van *you are*.
I parked my bicycle in **its** usual place. **It's** time to go to the dentist.	*Its* betekent 'van het' (bezittelijk voornaamwoord). *It's* is een samentrekking van *it is* of *it has*.
They buy **their** school uniforms online. Do you want to go over **there**? **They're** my best friends.	*Their* betekent 'hun' (bezittelijk voornaamwoord). *There* betekent 'er', 'daar' (plaats). *They're* is een samentrekking van *they are*.
Where did you go on holiday? They **were** very nice to me. **We're** big fans of documentaries.	*Where* betekent 'waar' (vraagwoord). *Were* betekent 'was', 'waren'. *We're* is een samentrekking van *we are*.

K
WATCHING

Passion for fashion

Amsterdam is one of the fashion capitals of the world. It draws students from all over the world to do internships there. Meet Daisy, a design student working in Amsterdam to get inspiration and learn how to design. Her dream is to design an entire collection of her own. Follow her around as she explains what goes into making and designing clothes.

Task

>> TASKCARD

Dragons' Den
Je gaat een ontwerp aanprijzen voor een panel.

Taalportfolio

- (A2) Ik kan uitleggen wat ik leuk of niet leuk vind aan iets.
- (A2) Ik kan een korte presentatie geven over een vertrouwd onderwerp en naar aanleiding van de presentatie duidelijke vragen beantwoorden.

ERK

Back Forward Stop Refresh Home Search Favorites History Mail Print

http://www.bbc.co.uk/programmes/b006vq92

In *Dragons' Den*, entrepreneurs pitch their idea to a panel of rich business people. They do so in order to secure an investment and make their idea happen.

This week, a young man is going to try to persuade the panel to invest in his idea for a telephone helpline. His three-minute pitch, however, does not go as planned...

Apply to enter the Den

If you want to take part in Dragons' Den, download the application form (106KB) and either email or post it as directed in the download.

As part of normal selection process we may approach entrepreneurs, or they may apply direct. In each case all applications are processed in the same way. To be considered all candidates need to submit an application form and these are then subject to the same casting criteria. Final selection for participation in the programme will be decided on a number of factors including the strength of idea and the business plan.

Vocabulary

A LISTENING

The art gallery in Paris has a great **collection** of modern art.	*collectie*
These are the best designs I could **come up with** today.	*verzinnen*
Your project must **contain** your original ideas from class.	*bevatten*
Alison was **delighted** that she had been selected for the show.	*verheugd*
Even though your hair looks crazy now, you will love the **end result**!	*eindresultaat*
An **engineer** will work out how to automate something.	*technicus*
Lyam's legal **guardian** received the letter from the school.	*voogd*
Hopefully my teacher will realise that I have been studying for hours.	*hopelijk*
Jess is going to **invite** all of her colleagues to her big birthday bash.	*uitnodigen*
I have read through your work and I have a question about **line** ten.	*tekstregel*
Many people like to eat fish. I **personally** don't like it.	*persoonlijk*
Gerry's chair is his favourite **piece of furniture** because it is so comfy!	*meubelstuk*
My sister can cook really well and her lasagne is absolutely **superb**!	*geweldig*
The children are old enough to work an hour without **supervision**.	*toezicht*

B THEME WORDS

An architect will create a **blueprint** of his/her idea.	*blauwdruk*
Each **component** of the design must be thoroughly thought out.	*onderdeel*
It can take a year or more to actually **construct** the design.	*bouwen*
Each poem was analysed in great **depth** during the lessons.	*diepte*
My best friend wants to become a famous **designer** in the future.	*ontwerper*
Creating a **draft** is an important part of the process.	*concept*
Tina spent hours figuring out which **fabric** to use for the jacket she designed.	*stof*
Her hobbies are music, reading, knitting and **handicraft**.	*handvaardigheid*
In some countries there is a legal maximum **height** for buildings.	*hoogte*
The **measurements** of this photograph are twelve by twelve centimetres.	*afmetingen*
If they **modify** the plans, they should let me know.	*aanpassen*
My brother is gifted in maths, he's really **one-of-a-kind**.	*uniek*
I love your new living room interior. I'm going to **reproduce** it at home.	*namaken*
When artists **sculpt** a statue, they use many different tools.	*beeldhouwen*
Coca-Cola is most likely the world's biggest **trademark**.	*handelsmerk*
To put up a fence, the **width** and length of the yard must be known.	*wijdte*

C READING

My friend Vlada loves to paint; she's incredibly **artistic**.	*artistiek, kunstzinnig*
A **cement worker** has to get the cement mix just right.	*metselaar*
A **chisel** is used to shape wood, along with a mallet or hammer.	*beitel*
This wooden table is an example of excellent **craftsmanship**.	*vakmanschap*
If they **demolish** this landmark, the villagers will be very upset.	*vernielen, afbreken*
The cooks **flatten** the dough before they roll it.	*platmaken*

My design can only be made with a **hand tool** instead of machinery.	*handgereedschap*
The company first had to calculate how much **labour** was required.	*arbeid, werk*
I just **marvel at** all she has accomplished.	*bewonder*
We may not disturb Mum since she is working on her **masterpiece**.	*meesterwerk*
In my street there is no **passing** traffic, it is always very quiet.	*passerend*
Manchester's best estate agents can't seem to sell the last **plot** of land.	*stuk grond*
The council have recently erected a wonderful **sculpture** in town.	*sculptuur, beeld*
By placing a **seashell** to your ear, you can hear the sea they say.	*zeeschelp*
If they **settle** in the city, they might be surprised by all the noise.	*zich vestigen*
The **tile** in the middle of the wall isn't straight, it needs fixing.	*tegel*
Our garden is a **triangular** shape, which is really unusual.	*driehoekig*

D SPEAKING & WRITING

We have to **assemble** the furniture ourselves.	*in elkaar zetten, monteren*
Uncle Bob bought this **birdcage** from the flea market for his budgie.	*vogelkooi*
If they **cut out** that article, they should buy me a new magazine.	*uitknippen*
There is nothing I enjoy more than to **draw** for several hours.	*tekenen*
Edna was embarassed by the huge **inflatable** crocodile she was given.	*opblaasbaar*
I think I have written my literature essay very **neatly** this time.	*netjes*
The coloured bins are only for things that are **recyclable**.	*recyclebaar*
The artist tried to **sketch** his view from the hotel window.	*schetsen*
I made this fantastic **sketch** of you – isn't it wonderful?	*schets*
Last time the teacher said my work was **sloppy**, but this time it's perfect.	*slordig*

G LISTENING

Rosie was **amazed** to hear that she was selected for the band.	*verbaasd*
You should arrange the cakes in the shop window so that **appeal to** customers.	*aanspreken*
The TV is **attached to** the wall, so it can't be moved easily.	*vastgemaakt aan*
It is important to **bolt** the back of the cupboard to the wall.	*vastschroeven* [verb]
Please remember the stewardesses are here for your safety and **convenience**.	*gemak*
The **function** of this lever is to lift the bucket out of the water.	*functie*
My idea won the contest because it was very **innovative**.	*vernieuwend*
Aunt Brenda would love to have **interior designer** visit her house.	*binnenhuisarchitect*
Always put dirty clothes straight into the **laundry basket**.	*wasmand*
The famous professor visited the university to give a **lecture**.	*lezing*
I love my new **Murphy bed** since it creates more space.	*opklapbed*
The two countries were able to make negotiations **peacefully**.	*vredig*
If they **restyle** my house, I will be very grateful.	*opnieuw inrichten*
This new gadget is **revolutionary**; it will help you to always find your phone.	*revolutionair*
Helen couldn't finish her project because she was missing a **screw**.	*schroef*
In order to complete the bookcase, you need to **screw** the back boarding on tightly.	*vastschroeven*
My parents have got new patio doors that **slide** open and closed.	*schuiven*
The apartment is **spacious**, with three bedrooms, a sizeable lounge and kitchen.	*ruimtelijk*
In the event of an emergency, use the **staircase** and not the lift.	*trap*
Bella has some many books we are running out of **storage** space.	*opbergruimte*
We found the stolen mobile phones in a box **unused**.	*ongebruikt*
My little sister can stay **upside down** on her head for five minutes.	*ondersteboven, op de kop*

This software package is very usable. I would definitely recommend it.	*bruikbaar*
Cheryl really dislikes having to use the vacuum cleaner.	*stofzuiger*
The value of the property has gone up over the last few months.	*waarde*

H READING

Donna spent a great amount of time selecting books for the bookshelf.	*boekenplank*
The removal guys had trouble moving my heavy chest of drawers.	*ladekast*
A good chef can chop vegetables at a great speed in a safe manner.	*kappen, hakken*
Farmers are happy since they were able to produce a good crop.	*oogst*
Check out my new helmet for my moped. It's custom-made!	*op maat gemaakt*
Sam hopes that his leg will heal quickly so he can play football again.	*genezen*
Dad had to stop the car for a herd of cattle that were crossing the road.	*kudde*
That particular joint might need to be tightened every so often.	*verbindingsstuk*
Joanna was bored shopping for a new lampshade for her bedroom.	*lampenkap*
Some movies are for mature audiences, meaning not for children.	*volwassen*
Making the mould is the last part of the manufacturing process.	*mal*
Watch out for that nail on the floor there! That could hurt!	*spijker*
Mrs Corley will be sure to prune her plants once spring time arrives.	*snoeien*
The football team is prepared to rampage since they lost their last match.	*razen*
The charity works hard to realise dreams and wishes of hospital patients.	*realiseren*
It's amazing how much those children resemble their father.	*lijken op*
The last step is to sand the surface of your table until it is smooth.	*schuren*
The scale of the map of Europe was too large to show my village.	*schaal*
The teacher asked the student to place her stool on the table.	*krukje*
We should all use products that are made of sustainable material.	*duurzaam*
Willow is a great type of wood to work with, but it can be expensive.	*wilg*

I SPEAKING & WRITING

A bolt is required to attach the legs on the table securely.	*bout*
The next step is to glue the sequins in a row onto the fabric.	*lijmen*
Each layer of the cake is smothered with buttercream and jam.	*laag*
The surface of this table is made of three types of wood.	*oppervlak*
Coating the wood in varnish gives it a great finish.	*lak*
At home I created my own workspace in the attic where it is quiet.	*werkruimte*

PROVERBS & SAYINGS

To be as useful as a chocolate teapot.	*Behoorlijk nutteloos zijn.*
A picture paints a thousand words.	*Een foto zegt meer dan duizend woorden.*
To make a silk purse out of a sow's ear.	*Iets moois maken van grove materialen.*
To go back to the drawing board.	*Opnieuw beginnen.*
To be state of the art.	*Het neusje van de zalm zijn.*

Grammar overview

Future (*toekomende tijd*)

will	iets aanbieden	I'**ll get** you some tea and a slice of cake.
	beloftes	We **will fix** the bird cage for you.
	aankondigingen	They'**ll be** home at six.
	besluiten	We **won't start** without Lucy.
	voorspelling zonder bewijs	Mary-Ann **won't win** the competition.
be going to	iemand is iets (niet) van plan	We **are going to make** an inflatable boat this week.
	voorspelling met bewijs	Look at the sky. It **isn't going to rain** tonight.
present continuous	afspraken in de nabije toekomst waarvan tijd en/of plaats al vaststaat	I'**m working** at the supermarket from four till six.
present simple	tijden volgens een vast schema	The train **departs** at quarter to seven.

Word order (*woordvolgorde*)

He	bought	a	blue	T-shirt.	
pers. vnw.	*werkwoord (ww)*	*lidwoord*	*bn*	*zn*	
Did	he	lose?	He	didn't	lose.
hww	*pers. vnw.*	*ww*	*pers. vnw.*	*hww*	*ww*
She	always	goes	to her grandparents	on Saturdays.	
	bw frequentie	*ww*	*plaatsbepaling*	*tijdsbepaling*	
I	am	usually	at the sports centre	on Sundays.	
	ww	*bw frequentie*	*plaatsbepaling*	*tijdsbepaling*	

Pitfalls (*valkuilen*)

too: 'te' (voor bijvoeglijk naamwoord) en 'ook' (einde van een zin)	*to*: 'om te' (voor een werkwoord), 'aan', 'naar'	
than: 'dan' (in vergelijkingen)	*then*: 'toen', 'dan' (geeft een tijd aan)	
your: 'jouw' (bezittelijk voornaamwoord)	*you're*: samentrekking van *you are*	
its: 'van het' (bezittelijk voornaamwoord)	*it's*: samentrekking van *it is* of *it has*	
their: 'hun' (bezittelijk voornaamwoord)	*there*: 'er', 'daar' (plaats)	*they're*: samentrekking van *they are*
where: 'waar' (vraagwoord)	*were*: 'was', 'waren'	*we're*: samentrekking van *we are*

TABLE OF CONTENTS

ERK

Reading/listening: A2 B1 B1
Speaking/writing: A2 A2 B1

3

Going pro

A
LISTENING

The right person for the job

B
THEME WORDS

THEME WORDS

to employ	wages	workload	career move
intern	desk job	applicant	qualifications
internship	job hunting	attitude	to resign
promotion	pay rise	entrepreneur	to supervise

Back Forward Stop Refresh Home Search Favorites History Mail Print

http://www.biography.com/news/google-founders-history-facts

How Google started

1 **Google is a multibillion-dollar company nowadays and the most popular search engine in the world, with billions of searches every day. The company is so influential it even originated the verb that most people use for 'to search online' ('to google'). However, even Google had humble beginnings. Its founders, Larry Page and Sergey Brin, started building one of the world's largest IT companies in a garage!**

2 Brin and Page first met when Page visited Stanford University because he wanted to study there. His tour guide was Sergey Brin. Brin and Page didn't immediately hit it off – in fact, their first day together was spent arguing. However, they also found that they had a lot in common, like their skills and passion for computing.

3 Both Brin and Page were really good at solving problems and performed well under pressure. They successfully applied these qualities to a new project they started together. In this project, called 'Backrub,' Brin and Page created, to put it simply, a better way to search the web.

4 At first, they wanted to sell their technology to other web search companies, but these companies didn't offer enough money. Brin and Page therefore decided to start their own company. Starting your own company is a big challenge and they first had to raise $1 million from family, friends and other investors before they could launch their company in 1998. Their first 'office' was a garage they rented from a friend. In this garage they worked day and night to make their company a success.

5 They also agreed that the name 'Backrub' had to go. At first they considered calling their site 'The Whatbox,' but then they came across the word googol (the term for a number with one hundred zeros). With a slight change of spelling, Google.com, which Page considered 'easy to type and memorable', was born. In March 1999, the company moved to Palo Alto, home to several other noted Silicon Valley technology start-ups.

6 Nowadays, Google is the most commonly used search engine in the world and has also launched other useful websites and applications like Gmail, Google+, and Google Drive. Google's story shows that if you are eager to learn new skills and dedicated to your work you can achieve a lot. Brin and Page's story is a great example of how passion, commitment, and courage are often all you need to make your company a success.

STONE

7 Writing an application letter

- I
  - would like to apply for / am very interested in
    - the position of receptionist. / an internship with your company.

- I saw
  - the advertisement / the vacancy
    - in today's newspaper. / on your company's website.

- I am enthusiastic about my work / I am reliable, responsible
  - and I
    - am good at solving problems. / am eager to learn new skills. / perform well under pressure.

- I have a lot of experience / I am experienced
  - in
    - this type of work. / customer service and sales. / maintenance work and repairs.

- At my last job, / In my previous position
  - I helped / I assisted
    - the shop manager
      - with ordering and restocking supplies.
    - customers
      - with their purchases and special requests.

- After
  - I had worked at the shop / I had been an intern
    - for a year, / for six months,
      - I was given more responsibility. / I was offered a part-time contract.

- I look forward to
  - hearing from you soon. / your reply.

- I am available for a personal interview.
- Please find enclosed my CV.

GRAMMAR

7 Past perfect (*voltooid verleden tijd*) >> GS 6, page 140

When I *arrived* at the party Tim **had** already **left**. When we *arrived*, the film **had** already **started**. Sarah **had** just **got** home when I *phoned* her. I **had been** an intern for six months.	Je gebruikt de **voltooid verleden tijd** om aan te geven dat iets eerder is gebeurd dan iets anders. Je maakt de **voltooid verleden tijd** met *had* + voltooid deelwoord.
I *bought* a new watch because I **had lost** my old one. When he *was* thirty he **had** already **written** six books. We *were* really tired because we **had worked** all day.	De **voltooid verleden tijd** staat vaak samen met de *verleden tijd* in een zin. De **voltooid verleden tijd** geeft dan aan wat het eerst gebeurd is.
After I **had eaten** breakfast, I *was* still hungry. As soon as I'**d saved** enough money, I *bought* a ring. Before I *worked* at the youth hostel, I **had** already **gained** work experience at a pet shop. I **had worked** at the shop for a year when I *received* a full-time contract.	In zinnen met de **voltooid verleden tijd** staat vaak een van de volgende woorden: *after*, *before*, *when* of *as soon as*.
Alexis said that she **had**n't **read** the book. Lucas mentioned that he **had bought** a new game. We told you that we **had been** to the amusement park.	Je gebruikt de **voltooid verleden tijd** ook bij de *indirecte rede*. Je geeft dan aan wat iemand anders heeft gezegd.

Safari vet school

Meet some talented veterinary students from the UK. They are sent off to one of the toughest vet schools in the world – the Amakhala Game Reserve in South Africa. Here they will learn to cope with wild and dangerous animals.

G
LISTENING

A speedy job

Speed dating

Have you always wanted to know what a florist does all day? Or what kind of education you need in order to become a pastry chef? And how many times a day a dog walker has to walk dogs? Then 'job speed dating' might be the thing for you!

How does it work?

- choose four professions from the list below
- each session will take exactly ten minutes and will start and end with a ringing bell
- ask as many questions as possible! Think of the upsides and the downsides of certain professions, employment prospects and earnings.

Professions to choose from

- salesperson
- dog walker
- florist
- account manager
- pastry chef
- beautician
- caterer
- vet's assistant
- dental assistant
- mechanic
- nurse
- youth worker

H
READING

JOBS OF THE FUTURE

1 **What will the jobs of tomorrow look like? As the world evolves, so do job trends and job descriptions. What new jobs will emerge and which sectors have the best job opportunities? What kind of qualifications or training do you need to get a job in the future? It's time to find out...**

2 In 10 to 20 years' time the chances are that jobs – and the way people work – will be very different, according to leading futurologist David Morello. He thinks that there will be plenty of new jobs, such as 'urban farmer', and that existing jobs, like fashion designer, will drastically change in nature.

3 **Urban farming**

Morello sees big changes in farming, as food resources will become scarce. He predicts that 'crops will be grown vertically in areas resembling multi-storey car parks to save space. It will be the job of urban farmers to grow these crops and to distribute and sell them locally.' People who are interested in this job should stay up-to-date with the latest developments in renewable energy sources, such as solar and wind power, as farms will most likely be sustainable. Hands-on work will need to be combined with strong organisational skills and the ability to follow strict routines.

4 **High-tech fashion**
According to Morello existing jobs will change as well, mostly due to technological developments. 'Take, for example, fashion design,' he explains. 'It will still be about looking good, but technology will add a functionality factor to clothing. Fashion designers will, for instance, design clothes that can turn sunlight energy into electrical energy. Or they could capture energy generated by walking or running to power mobile phones.'

5 For the fashion designers of the future, a bit of high-tech knowledge may be as essential as knowing how to sew and draw. However, fashion designers will still need to be self-motivated, creative and savvy enough to invent new styles and forms they can put into their designs.

6 **Human skills versus technology**
Morello also argues that the better technology gets, the more people will have to focus on their 'human skills' to survive in the workforce: 'Ultimately, those who can program will create the world we live in. If you can't, find yourself something that computers can't do, such as entertainment, sport, caring and personal services industries.'

7 **Prepared for the future?**
What do teenagers think of these predictions and the new working world? Do they possess the relevant skills for these new jobs? Leah, 17, from Northampton is not worried about her career prospects. 'I'm currently an apprentice at an IT company. The IT and digital technologies industry is constantly changing. I have good computing skills and I'm interested in learning more advanced ones. I think the drive and ability to learn new skills is what employers are looking for.'

8 For some teenagers the jobs of the future sound promising. 'Urban farming? It seems pretty far-fetched to me,' says Oliver, 16, from Wrexham. He is doing an apprenticeship in food and farming. 'I haven't really thought about these new developments. It sounds interesting, though. If this is the future of agriculture I'm all for it. I adapt to new situations easily.'

9 No matter what the jobs of the future will bring, these teenagers show the kind of attitude that will be necessary to make it in tomorrow's job market.

Adapted from: careers2030.cst.org / telegraph.co.uk

futurologist	*toekomstexpert*
food resources	*voedselbronnen*

STONES

8 Talking about yourself

I'm a down-to-earth person / I'm a social person	and I	adapt well to new situations. / enjoy working in a team.

I think I'm / I would describe myself as	a very creative and resourceful person. / hard working, ambitious and well organised.

I have	some basic computing skills / some management skills	and / but	I'm interested in learning more advanced ones. / I'm following courses to learn new ones.

9 Having a job interview

Why	did you apply for this position? / would you be best suited for this position?

What	kind of qualifications do you have? / do you feel are your greatest strengths?

I think	my professional attitude / my ability to work under pressure	sets me apart from other candidates. / makes me a good candidate.

I used to volunteer at the animal shelter, / I've always liked taking care of animals,	so working as a vet's assistant would be amazing. / so the zookeeper internship would suit my interests.

I have studied / I took a course in	graphic design / electrical technology	and I have lots of work experience. / and I have various other qualifications.

I think my strengths are / I'd say my strong points are	reliability / punctuality	and	commitment. / sense of responsibility.

GRAMMAR

J GRAMMAR

8 Used to >> GS 8, page 142

I **used to** volunteer at the animal shelter.
You **used to** call me every weekend.
We **used to** read comics every day.
Gordon **used to** eat meat, but now he's a vegetarian.
There **used to** be a school in this town.
My cousins **used to** go to this school.
They **used to** like this television programme.

Je gebruikt *used to* + het hele werkwoord om te zeggen:
- dat iets in het verleden regelmatig gebeurde (een gewoonte was), maar nu niet meer
- dat iets in het verleden zo was, maar nu niet meer zo is

In het Nederlands zeggen we 'vroeger (altijd)'.

9 *One* and *ones* >> GS 16, page 149

A second-hand car is much cheaper than a new **one**.
Do you prefer the black shoes or the red **ones**?
This pizza tastes better than that **one**.

Je gebruikt *one* (enkelvoud) of *ones* (meervoud) wanneer je een zelfstandig naamwoord verderop in een zin wilt herhalen.

People have big problems and small **ones**.
I have to read a book. Which **one** should I pick?
Do you like westerns? This **one** is a classic.
I like a lot of films, but that **one** is my favourite!
Do you like these muffins? I prefer those **ones**.

Je gebruikt *one* (enkelvoud) of *ones* (meervoud) om een zelfstandig naamwoord te vervangen:
- na een bijvoeglijk naamwoord
- na *which*
- na *this, that, these* en *those*

K WATCHING

My job: TV presenter

Chris Nelson is an experienced presenter, hosting both Formula 1 on live TV and other shows in arenas. He's been doing his job for years, and his shows are watched by millions of people each year. He's eager to share his experiences with you, so watch the clip and you might pick up a trick or two for your next presentation.

Task

>> TASKCARD

Wanted: personal assistant
Je gaat een advertentie schrijven om een persoonlijke assistent aan te nemen.

Taalportfolio
A2 Ik kan informatie van persoonlijke aard vragen en geven.
B1 Ik kan gedetailleerde beschrijvingen geven van bekende onderwerpen binnen mijn eigen interessegebied.

ERK

Back Forward Stop Refresh Home Search Favorites History Mail Print

http://www.personalassistant.co.uk

Are you the personal assistant they're looking for? Apply now!

On this page you will find details of PA vacancies in London. If you apply for one of the PA vacancies, we will forward your application directly to the employer.

Location: London, Paddington
Hourly wage: £ 4.50

Hi I'm Josephine. I'm looking for someone who can help me with some daily chores and other stuff that I just can't find the time to get around to doing...

The following are some of the chores you will be doing:
- Walking the dog at the park, which is just a 5-minute walk away ;-)
- Cleaning up my wardrobe. I'm a bit of slob and I never know what to wear, so my wardrobe is a mess. I could use a hand.
- Since I've mentioned what a mess my wardrobe is; it'd be great if you are a bit fashion-minded. I could use some advice on clothing!
- Vacuuming my room. I'm allergic to dust, well, sort of... ;-)
- If by any chance you'd happen to be able to prepare a tasty hamburger while I'm studying, that would be awesome!

I will need your help for two afternoons a week. Feel free to ask for more information if you are interested.

Vocabulary

A LISTENING

Some people would find a job abroad very **appealing**.	*aansprekend, aantrekkelijk*
Children who are raised to be **bilingual** often find it easy to learn a third language.	*tweetalig*
Sales are **booming** for the latest hover board from China.	*snel groeiend*
The Dutch **branch** of the company has expanded across the country.	*vestiging, tak*
My car didn't start this morning, so I had to **catch the train** to get to work.	*de trein nemen*
You shouldn't **expand** a new business too fast.	*uitbreiden*
My aunt works at a **firm** of accountants in Oxford.	*firma*
I didn't expect anyone to remember my birthday, **let alone** give me a surprise party!	*laat staan*
I really hate my job, but **on the other hand**, I really need the money.	*anderzijds, aan de andere kant*
He cleaned his room **rapidly** to be able to watch the rugby match.	*snel*
The president of the company was absent, so she sent someone to **represent** her.	*vertegenwoordigen*
They needed a new cashier so **urgently** that he started working the same day.	*dringend*

B THEME WORDS

The very first **applicant** turned out to be the best choice for the new position.	*sollicitant*
Making a good first impression is all about **attitude**.	*houding*
They say that changing jobs every five years can be a great **career move**.	*carrièrestap*
Some people prefer a **desk job** and some prefer working outside.	*kantoorbaan*
Our company currently can **employ** over one hundred people.	*in dienst nemen/hebben*
Lance started his own business as a young **entrepreneur**.	*ondernemer*
I want to be an **intern** at a company where I have the chance of getting a job.	*stagiair*
The **internship** that I really want never offers their interns full-time positions.	*stage*
There are many websites available that are dedicated to **job hunting**.	*werk zoeken*
I have been here for two years and I still have not received a **pay rise**.	*loonsverhoging*
Receiving a **promotion** during the first year of a job is very unusual.	*promotie*
The candidate had all the right **qualifications**, but the interview did not go well.	*kwalificaties*
I will **resign** from my job at the supermarket when I finish school.	*ontslag nemen*
A job where the employee must **supervise** others usually earns higher wages.	*toezicht houden*
A person's **wages** should be dependent on the quality and complexity of the work.	*loon*
More **workload** does not always lead to more pay.	*werklast*

C READING

The new **application** I have to download on my computer looks complicated.	*toepassing*
If you can really **apply** yourself to the job, your chances of success will increase.	*toepassen*
My little brothers always **argue** about who gets to use the iPad.	*ruziën*
Joining the army requires **commitment** and determination.	*inzet*
He woke up two hours early because he was so **eager** to get started.	*gretig*
The billionaire started from **humble** beginnings, and worked very hard.	*bescheiden*
The **investor** wanted a guarantee that his money would be well-spent.	*investeerder*

The tech company will **launch** a new tablet next week.	*lanceren*
The main speaker is **noted** for his extensive research in the field of microbiology.	*beroemd*
I usually freeze up when I have to **perform** under pressure.	*presteren*
Jobs that put people under **pressure** often have a high employee turnover rate.	*druk*
To **put it simply**, our product makes your life easier!	*om het simpel te zeggen*
The word 'Google' has become another word for **search engine**.	*zoekmachine*
I asked the waiter to fix a **slight** issue with our bill since we were charged too much.	*klein*
We had an issue with a customer that we had to **solve** quickly and simply.	*oplossen*
Their idea was to create a **start-up** about helping people with a new company.	*beginnend bedrijf*

D SPEAKING & WRITING

A company can lose business if they have poor **customer service**.	*klantenservice*
They had a separate contract to handle **maintenance work** on the equipment.	*onderhoudswerk*
The **position** for which you are applying is no longer available.	*functie*
Are you going to make your **purchase** with cash or credit card?	*aankoop*
I would rather have a car that is **reliable** than fast or cool.	*betrouwbaar*
The **repairs** are going to cost more than my car is worth.	*reparaties*
The staff comes in at night to **restock** all the shelves in the store.	*aanvullen*
Sales of ice cream usually drop during the winter months.	*verkoop*
We need to make sure we keep a good **supply** of candy during Halloween.	*voorraad*

G LISTENING

Working as a trainee means you work **alongside** an experienced professional.	*naast*
One of my strengths is that I can learn new things in a short **amount** of time.	*hoeveelheid*
Sales positions **appeal to** people who are outgoing and who like to talk.	*aanspreken*
One way to learn a trade is to become an **apprentice** to someone with experience.	*leerling*
She has wanted to become a **beautician** ever since she was a little girl.	*schoonheidsspecialist*
There are machines now that take a patient's **blood pressure** automatically.	*bloeddruk*
The **caterer** for this wedding is the same one my parents used for their wedding.	*cateraar*
The manager was watching the new employee **closely** in the beginning.	*nauw*
My boss was **compassionate** when I told him my dog had died.	*meelevend*
The **cons** to working in a fast food restaurant are that I eat too much of the food.	*nadelen*
If you want to be a nurse you have to be able to **cope with** long hours.	*kunnen omgaan met*
Technical professions **demand** a strength and interest in maths and science.	*vereisen*
The **dental assistant** kept asking me questions while she was working on my teeth.	*tandartsassistent*
The university student worked as a **dog walker** to help pay for his tuition.	*hondenuitlater*
The **downside** of living in a big city is all the traffic.	*nadeel*
She asked the **florist** to put one white rose in the middle of the red ones.	*bloemist*
The girl received an **injection** in each leg and didn't shed a tear.	*injectie*
Our school has a **limited** number of computers available.	*beperkt*
When the **mechanic** told me how much it was going to cost, I almost fainted!	*monteur*
While studying to become a **nurse**, she worked nights at a cinema.	*verpleger, verpleegster*
Being a **pastry chef** requires patience and an artistic ability.	*banketbakker*
When deciding where to go on holiday, there were more **pros** for going to France.	*voordelen*
I was not looking forward to the **prospect** of searching for a new job.	*vooruitzicht*
Social work can be **rewarding**, but it doesn't pay well.	*bevredigend, de moeite waard*
I could not believe how rude that **salesperson** was to us!	*verkoper, verkoopster*

A small **sample** of soil was tested for nutrients and acidity.	*monster*
When she lost her job, she received financial **support** from the council.	*steun*
The **surgeon** likes to have jazz music playing while he operates.	*chirurg*
People who **have a sweet tooth** like eating sweet foods, like chocolate.	*een zoetekauw zijn*
The **upside** of living in the city is that there is always something to do.	*voordeel*
We had to raise our prices because our **vendor** started charging more for materials.	*leverancier*
A **vet's assistant** needs to have extensive knowledge of animals.	*assistent dierenarts*
His experience as a **youth worker** helped him to stop the fight between the boys.	*jongerenwerker*

H READING

It is surprising how many people study **agriculture** these days.	*landbouw*
Choosing to follow an **apprenticeship** has become extremely popular these days.	*opleidingsstage*
The **car park** in town is almost always full and it's very pricey.	*parkeergarage*
If you notice black spots **emerge** on the leaves of the roses, take action.	*verschijnen, opkomen*
Languages **evolve** all the time. New words get used and old words disappear.	*veranderen*
I was disappointed with the film. I thought it was too **far-fetched**.	*vergezocht, onwaarschijnlijk*
The goal is to **generate** as much interest in the product as possible.	*opwekken*
Simon is more of a **hands-on** person, he likes practical work.	*praktisch*
Have you seen the new **multi-storey** car park in the city? It's huge.	*met meerdere verdiepingen*
Sandra's interview went well apparently, which is very **promising**.	*veelbelovend*
Jade is computer **savvy**. She knows all there is about computers and technology.	*snugger*
Oil is becoming more **scarce** across the globe, meaning higher prices.	*schaars*

I SPEAKING & WRITING

The technology used by the company is very **advanced**.	*geavanceerd, modern*
Grandad has been on a course to improve his **computing skills**.	*computervaardigheden*
If you want to become an electrician, you need to study **electrical technology**.	*elektrotechniek*
June was a **hard working** girl who never gave up, no matter what.	*hardwerkend*
A **professional** team will train intensively for every match.	*professioneel*
Punctuality has never been her strong point, she is almost always late.	*stiptheid*
When you are looking for a nanny, **reliability** is an essential factor.	*betrouwbaarheid*
Thomas is so **resourceful**! He can always find a solution.	*vindingrijk*
Lorna's **strength** is that she can sell anything to anyone.	*sterk punt*
I think the job you choose should **suit** your interests.	*passen bij*
The summer dance was so **well organised** this year compared to last.	*goed georganiseerd*
I was amazed to hear that Rick has become a **zookeeper** in London.	*dierenverzorger (in dierentuin)*

PROVERBS & SAYINGS

A busman's holiday.	*Vakantie besteden aan werk.*
To learn the ropes.	*Het werk leren doen.*
The tricks of the trade.	*De kneepjes van het vak.*
To have one's work cut out for one.	*Veel werk voor de boeg hebben.*
To take a crash course in something.	*Een spoedcursus volgen.*

Grammar overview

Past perfect (*voltooid verleden tijd*)

		voltooid dw: regelmatig	voltooid dw: onregelmatig
I / you	**had**	visit**ed**	been
he / she / it	**had**	visit**ed**	been
we / you / they	**had**	visit**ed**	been
aangeven dat iets eerder is gebeurd dan iets anders	When we entered the cinema, the film **had** already **started**.		
indirecte rede	Alexis said that she **had**n't **read** the book.		
verklikwoorden	*after, before, when, as soon as*		

One and *ones*

A second-hand **car** is much cheaper than a new **one**.	
Do you prefer the black **shoes** or the red **ones**?	
wanneer?	• na een bijvoeglijk naamwoord
	• na *which*
	• na *this* en *that*

Used to

		used to	infinitief	
gewoonte	We	used to	read	comics every day.
was vroeger zo	There	used to	be	a school in this town.

Herhaling & Verrijking

Theme 1 Just for laughs

Theme 2 Creative minds

Theme 3 Going pro

Understanding laughter

Human beings love to laugh, and the average adult laughs seventeen times a day. Humans love to laugh so much that there are actually industries built around laughter. Jokes, sitcoms and comedians are all designed to get us laughing, because laughing feels good. We've probably all heard the saying 'Laughter is the best medicine', and indeed there is strong evidence that laughter can improve health and help fight disease.

Laughing seems natural, and we know for a fact that all humans laugh. Even deaf people who have never heard a sound still make laughing noises. But what exactly is laughter, and why do we laugh?

What is laughter?

First of all, laughter is not the same as humour. Laughter is the physiological response to humour. Laughter consists of two parts: a set of gestures and the production of a sound. When we laugh, the brain causes us to conduct both those activities simultaneously. When we laugh heartily, changes occur in many parts of the body, even the arm, leg and trunk muscles. Did you know that in your face alone, fifteen different muscles contract when you're laughing?

Contagious

We also know that laughter is contagious. When you step into a room where people are laughing, you will probably start laughing too, even though you haven't got a clue what they are laughing about. And many people will be able to recall an embarrassing situation in which you tried hard to supress your laughter, but laughed anyway.

Robert Provine, a neurobiologist who studies laughter, explains that humans have a 'detector' that responds to laughter by triggering the brain to generate more laughter. This is why laughter is contagious or why it's so hard to supress laughing.

Why do we laugh?

Provine believes that laughter, like the bird's song, functions as a kind of social signal. Other studies have confirmed this theory by showing that people are 30 times more likely to laugh in social settings than when they are alone.

It has become obvious that the purpose of laughter is related to making and strengthening human connections. 'Laughter occurs when people are comfortable with one another, when they feel open and free. And the more laughter there is, the more bonding occurs within the group,' says cultural anthropologist Mahadev Apte. This 'bonding-laughter-more bonding', combined with the common desire not to be singled out from the group, may be another reason why people laugh more when they are together.

Adapted from: science.howstuffworks.com

TINY STREET ART

For most street artists the biggest obstacle to their work is the police; urban artists often have to abandon their work in order to flee from the police. This is not the case for artists Slinkachu and Isaac Cordal, who specialise in 'miniature street sculpture'. For them the biggest dangers are road sweepers and heavy-shoed pedestrians. Since 2006 these two London-based artists have been installing tiny artworks in cities around the world, taking photographs of it and then leaving their work to be kicked or ignored or taken away. No sculpture is more than 5cm in height.

Slinkachu, 31, is a former art director who prefers not to reveal his real name. 'In 2006 I was working at an advertising agency and wanted a creative project outside my day job; I had the idea of leaving miniature train-set figures around London for people to discover, as a way of encouraging interaction with the city. When people think of urban art they often think of graffiti, but I hope that my work will make them see that graffiti is not the only type of street art.'

Slinkachu uses train-set figures for his characters. He cuts them up to change their positions as needed, and paints them with acrylic paints. He also collects lots of objects to use as props – a bottle cap might become a boat, a dead insect could pull a cart, and a tennis ball could be a desert island. For each scene he thinks of a story he wants to tell; 'I can find inspiration anywhere: it could be from a piece of litter. I love playing with scale and imagining how an object would look to a tiny person. A hole in the wall could be a cave, or a puddle could be a lake. I then scout locations and keep a sketchbook full of ideas. I think of each scene as a miniature film set. I use superglue to fix my figures in place, then arrange the surroundings to tell the story.

However, working on the street can be difficult. 'People want to stop me to ask what I'm doing and sometimes the weather ruins my work. I've been told to stop using my camera by security guards or police. But I don't mind all this; it adds an element of uncertainty and surprise that working inside doesn't have.

'I don't hang around to see what happens to the work,' Slinkachu continues. 'I don't want not to know. But there is a strange kind of buzz to abandoning your creations on the street. My work is free to take, if you can find it... No easy task.' His sculptures are almost invisible from walking height. 'One of my pieces, a miniature cash machine with a figure withdrawing money, lasted three months, which I think is probably a record.'

Cordal, 36, doesn't like the thought of the miniature statues being taken away – 'I don't leave them on the street for people to take; street art is for everyone, not just one person.' However, he is realistic about the fact that his art can get damaged or stolen. 'Once art becomes part of the public domain, one of the possibilities is that the work disappears. Most of it disappears very fast. The main predators are cleaning services.'

Because of the fragile nature of the work, both Slinkachu and Cordal have made photography a key part of their method. 'At the beginning I used to take photographs only with the idea of documenting each scene,' says Cordal. 'Then I realised I could use photography to create more complex compositions.' Slinkachu agrees. 'I like to think of the photography as a form of reportage, like I'm recording a small drama. It all started as a hobby, a way to let off steam creatively, but then I became fascinated by the possibilities of telling stories with the figures through photography, and making people feel empathy for these little people. I need to lie down in the street so I can photograph from the little figures' perspective. I shoot at certain times of the day or year because I want the right light or weather conditions. I use a wide depth of field to bring the characters to life, and make them look almost real in their environments, not just like plastic toys.

An important theme in their work is the idea of loneliness and anonymity. Slinkachu: 'I like to think about how people respond to the urban environment, and how the city can be a difficult, lonely place to live. A good example of this is a scene that depicts two figures adrift on what looks like a desert island but is actually a tennis ball floating in a puddle. 'The feeling of being ignored and overlooked, of feeling small, is a universal one,' says Slinkachu. 'It is as easy for us to fall through cracks in the pavement in a big city as it is for the little people.' What happened to the tennis ball island? Slinkachu isn't sure. 'It was quite a visible one so I'm sure somebody spotted it. I like to think some kids found it and took it home.'

Adapted from: theguardian.com

VERRIJKING THEME 3

WHY EVERYONE LOVES TO WORK IN THE UK

The UK is the fifth largest national economy in the world. There are numerous foreign companies in the UK and it is one of the world's biggest manufacturing economies. It attracts a lot of migrants because of its strong economy, high standard of living and good work environment. Let's take a closer look at some of the reasons why the UK is such a popular country to work in.

Science and technology

The British are well-known innovators and many of their inventions have been of major importance to the world of science and technology. Many leading technology industries are located in the UK. The UK is well-known for its aerospace, pharmaceutical and automation industry.

Raj (17, Bangladesh): Last year I had my work experience placement at Rolls Royce UK. The work in Manufacturing Services was varied and no two days were the same. The people I worked with showed me all of the different aspects to the building and testing of a jet engine. I learned a lot about what goes into the building and testing of an engine and the massive amount of support that is required to facilitate this. They also introduced me to the people who are busy designing aero engines. They explained the complicated processes to me and showed me the final component that they had spent months modelling and verifying on a computer. All in all, I enjoyed learning from skilled people and taking part in practical work.

Intercultural environment

In the UK employers have a duty to understand different cultural viewpoints, respect other cultures, and adapt to various cultures. The employers must be open to new ideas and accept differences.

Editha (22, Poland): I work as a production worker at the 2 Sisters Food Group in Glasgow.

I came from Poland two years ago to work in Great Britain and it has been a good experience so far. There are other Polish and Eastern European people working here but I've also made a lot of Scottish friends. The work is good and the 8-hour shifts do not seem so long as I really enjoy my work. Sometimes the language barrier is a problem for my foreign colleagues, because not all of them speak English very well. I'm always happy to help, so I can practise my English even more.

Fashion, commerce and advanced technology

Fashion, commerce and technology are doing extremely well in the UK. There are many events and activities that take place in the UK as it is one of the largest and most advanced economies and they celebrate the development of industries.

Ramona (18, Ireland): I'm working as a sales assistant at Zara in Bristol and my overall experience is really good. However, since I'm a student it is pretty hard balancing work and college life. I normally only work during the weekends and of course those are the busiest days at the shop. What I've learnt at Zara is that you need to be fast, and it is sometimes pretty hard for me to keep up with this fast pace.

On a typical day Saturday I assist in the fitting rooms and this is rather hectic. There are always a lot of clothes left behind in there, so you'll be running up and down the stairs to take them back to the right floor. What I like about this work are my colleagues; they are so friendly and helpful!

Multiple working opportunities

In the UK you can have different jobs at the same time, work double shifts, and work overtime. The earning prospects are very high in the UK. It is part of British culture to work hard for money.

Sarah (19, Canada): I have been working as a waitress on a cruise ship for seven months now. The ship leaves from Southampton every month and sails to the Caribbean, to return to England four weeks later. I chose to work 6 days a week, which is hard work, but I enjoy it a lot. I like dealing with different people and building relationships with guests. You have to work as a team and be very helpful, not only to the guests but also to each other, because you're not just working together in the same place but you're also living together. The most enjoyable part is meeting people from all over the world and the fact that you can visit places that many people can only dream of.

Business

The UK is a great place to start your own business. Private enterprises are very much encouraged. Any individual can instantly become a real company. They can practise trade without any obstacles, in almost any area of business.

Fraser (24, England): I set up my own company SuperJam when I was still a teenager, using my Gran's jam recipes. After selling my produce at farmers' markets I developed a method of producing jam 100% from fruit. I then set up production, created a brand and perfected my recipes. My SuperJam now supplies over 2,000 supermarkets around the world in countries including Australia, Russia, Denmark, Finland and Ireland.

Adapted from: indeed.co.uk / content.wisestep.com

TABLE OF CONTENTS

Exam Preparation

1 LISTENING

Shelter from the Storm

Shelter from the Storm is an emergency night shelter, completely free to guests, providing bed, dinner and breakfast for 44 homeless people every night of the year. Our mission is to house and support the homeless in London whoever they are.
We started with one night in a church hall and now we care for 44 men and women every night, 365 days a year. Each evening they sit down to eat together; a simple ritual for most of us, but for many of them it will be the first time they've done that since they left home.

2 WATCHING

Working life

Peter: I'm talking to Deshi and Amanda, two of our ex-students about the job they got after they left our school. Deshi, you work at a restaurant called Yo! Sushi, I've heard. What exactly is Yo! Sushi?

Deshi: Yo! Sushi specialises in delivering sushi to customers using the conveyor belt method. Our food is prepared in the kitchen. A belt then transports the food to the customers.
I have to sort out the dishes and then put them on the conveyor belt.

Peter: And what about you, Amanda?

Amanda: I am what is called a visual merchandiser or a window dresser.
I am responsible for the appearance of the store, for the shop window installations and the displays around the store.

You did what?

I Walked the Length of the USA

Andy West hiked solo from Canada to Mexico

1 It was a spell of sick leave that finally made Andy West realise that, if he was ever going to achieve his dream of trekking the Continental Divide Trail – the 5,000km north-south route along the Rockies from the Canada/US border to Mexico – he was just going to have to get up and do it. So Andy sold his house, gave up his job and devoted almost a year to planning his mammoth hike, as well as using the challenge to raise money for CHASE hospice care (www.chasecare.org.uk) and the Stroke Association (www.stroke.org.uk).

2 His schedule was exhausting: It took Andy five months, trekking around 32km a day, six days a week, with just one small backpack, to complete his goal. So why did he do it? 'The rewards came from completing a section each day,' explains Andy. 'And being so high up that you could see for miles at a time. My number-one memory is hiking through the snow, high up on a mountain ridge, in the cold air and under beautiful blue skies.' So, what was a typical day on the trail? 'I'd get up early, before dawn, and cook myself some breakfast before setting off. By the end of the day I'd be trekking in the dark with a GPS and a light on my head!'

3 It could be lonely: 'I'd go a long time without seeing anyone – I trekked 650km through Montana and didn't see another person!', Andy admits. But he also met

hunters every now and then and sometimes their prey. 'People often joked that I was going to get shot because "hunters will shoot anything". However, the hunters were really friendly and offered me food and water – which was a life-saver,' Andy recalls. 'And once I saw a grizzly bear, which I scooted around!'

4 Andy had more to contend with than just the odd grizzly. As well as fighting against snow and a trip-threatening leg injury, he also endured a forest fire and the odd lightning storm. Despite these challenges, Andy is not deterred from more trekking adventures and is planning to try the Pacific Crest Trail this year. His advice to anyone thinking of doing their own mega trek? 'Just get on with it!'

For more on Andy's adventure, see www.andywestactive.com.

Cito, vmbo-gl en tl, 2014, tijdvak 2

4 READING

Leaves on the line?

When it comes to delayed trains, commuters have heard nearly every excuse in the book. But it remains something of a novelty to be told that a train is late because the driver has been viciously attacked by a seagull. That's what happened to passengers awaiting the 8.15 from Hastings, East Sussex, to London recently. The rush-hour train was delayed while the driver, who had been struck on the head, was checked over by first aiders. The driver, who had been walking along a platform towards his train's cab at the time, was said to be ruffled, but resumed his duties 15 minutes later.

Liza Donaghue, 63, a mother of four and foster carer, was waiting at Tonbridge station, Kent, when she heard the announcement over the loudspeaker system. She said: 'No one had really taken any notice until that point, then everyone looked and started looking at each other and saying, 'Did he just say what I thought he said?' Then everyone started laughing. People could not believe it.'

A Southeastern Trains' spokesman said: 'This is a rare occurrence. But seagull attacks can be quite serious. They are large birds and people have been knocked to the ground by them.' A spokesman for the Royal Society for the Protection of Birds said that apart from scavenging raids for food, seagulls usually attack people only to protect their young in nearby nests but that it was the wrong time of year for that.

Cito, vmbo-gl en tl, 2015, tijdvak 2

5 READING

Are you our *Hero/Heroine of the Year?*

Calling all superstar brothers and sisters! The search is on to find the pluckiest Mizz reader on the planet… We know you lot are all ace in your own right – but now we've decided to give one lucky reader an extra-special pat on the back. We're launching our Mizz Hero/Heroine of the Year Award. Do you want to know more? Read on.

THE RULES

Okay guys, we're not looking for just anyone because this reader has to be 100% hero/heroine. Maybe you've raised tons of cash for someone who really, really needed it or given a total stranger the 'kiss of life'. Perhaps you beat a serious illness or were a little angel when your best mate was sick. We're looking for the most amazing act of bravery and courage EVER! So, if your story made it to the local paper, make sure you send us a clipping. If not, get an adult to prove that the story is true by signing the form below.

1st PRIZE

The winner will be whisked off to London on an all-expense-paid trip and given a VIP day of five-star treatment. You'll be pampered from head-to-toe in a top salon and, because you deserve it for being so ace, we'll let you bring your best mate along too. You'll also be the star of a feature and get to tell your inspiring story to the rest of us. We'll invite you to a glamorous photo shoot where you'll have your own make up and fashion expert and photographer on hand to turn you into a celebrity for the day.

2nd PRIZE

Four lucky runners-up will also get to share their story at an all-expense-paid *Mizz* photo shoot in London.

<u>How to enter</u>

Closing date for entries is August 26th!

You can nominate yourself or put your mate up for a reward if you reckon he/she deserves it. Tell us why you think this is a hero/heroine story which deserves to win, attach a picture and any newspaper clippings too. Just remember, our judges will be looking for that extra-special something that makes a person 100% hero/heroine. Readers abroad may also compete. Send your entries to:

Ms L. Bennett, Mizz Hero/Heroine of the Year, King's Reach Tower, Stamford Street, London, SE1 9LS England

Name	....
Age	....
Best Mate's name	....
Your address	....
Adult's signature	....

Cito, vmbo-gl en tl, 2012, tijdvak 1

6
READING

Man Eats World's Hottest Curry

Ian Rothwell has become the first person to finish what is believed to be the world's hottest curry, despite suffering hallucinations caused by the dish.

The Widower is a chicken curry which is so dangerous to make that it has to be prepared by chefs wearing goggles and face masks. The dish, which includes 20 naga infinity chillies – the second hottest chilli known to man – is said to cause heart attacks in some people. Therefore, Mr Rothwell had to sign a disclaimer acknowledging his awareness of the risks involved before taking on the challenge. Fighting back tears, Ian Rothwell needed over an hour to eat the chicken dish, washed down with just one bottle of Cobra lager.

Muhammed Karim, chef at the Bindi restaurant said: 'More than 300 people have tackled *the Widower*, but no one has ever been able to finish one. Most manage about seven mouthfuls before they give up. We've had people sweating, crying, shaking and vomiting. We even had to ring an ambulance once. Brave Mr Rothwell had to take a 10-minute break when he started hallucinating, but he managed to swallow every mouthful in the end.'

Cito, vmbo-gl en tl, 2015, tijdvak 2

Rescue the Hitchcock 9

By Kathryn Hadley

The British Film Industry (BFI) has launched a major project to preserve nine of Hitchcock's surviving silent films to their original 1920s versions.

Alfred Hitchcock (1899-1980) directed ten silent films during the 1920s, nine of which have survived and are currently preserved in the air-locked film vaults of the National Film Library in Berkhamsted, Hertfordshire. Most early silent films were destroyed when talkies were introduced at the end of the 1920s. The cellulose nitrate film on which they were produced was often melted down for its silver content. On top of that, they were dangerous to store as the nitrate was very easily flammable. It is remarkable that Hitchcock's silent films have survived – only his second film The Mountain Eagle (1926) has been lost.

The BFI National Archive recently launched a major campaign to keep all nine surviving films in their original versions. The project is the biggest single undertaking in the archive's history. The films will be shown to the public in London in the summer.

Cito, vmbo-gl en tl, 2015, tijdvak 1

8 READING

Drumming: Give it Some Stick

Pounding out your frustrations on the drums is a perfect, healthy family activity, says Lucy Atkins

1 Rock drumming lessons may not seem an obvious family activity, but an hour with teacher Nigel Ralf turns out to be the best entertainment money can buy – not just for adults, but for children too.

2 The benefits of rock drumming are _**1**_. First, there is the simple, therapeutic joy of hitting. Then there are the newly discovered health effects. Researchers recently studied Clem Burke, the drummer from Blondie, and discovered that he burned off up to 600 calories per hour. His fitness, they found, was similar to that of a professional footballer. The researchers now plan to develop rock-drumming programmes in schools as an ingenious way to get either chubby or non-sporty, computer-obsessed children to _**2**_.

3 Ralf, of course, is already doing this. 'Drumming is seen as cool,' he says, 'and although you work up a definite sweat, no child thinks of it as exercise.' They are, after all, still sitting down.

4 There are also many psychological _**3**_. For example, drumming is used to treat depression and other mental illnesses, as well as in drug rehabilitation programmes and as an aid to stop smoking. The idea is that banging a drum activates the brain's pleasure centres, tackles stress, takes you out of your self-obsessed routine and promotes a sense of community.

5 Best of all, it is enormous fun – for all ages. I first discovered this at the school summer fête, where Ralf put on a drumming competition for children. I became hooked. My children may have been _**4**_ to see their mother wildly hitting the drums, but they still agreed to come to a family lesson.

6 Our hour-long session begins with maths. Not a good start – I see my children turn pale – but, says Ralf, 'in drumming, maths is easy'. It is all about recognising multiples of four so you can go at different speeds. We are using electronic drum sets, which are more compact and, _**5**_, have volume control (you can even plug in headphones to avoid upsetting the neighbours).

7 Next, Ralf introduces us to the basic 'four-beat rock rhythm'. This involves a surprising degree of mental flexibility: two hands and a bass-drum foot, each doing something different _**6**_ your brain keeps a one-two-three-four rhythm. It is a brain-aching exercise in coordination, which, he points out, must have knock-on benefits in sport, _**7**_ boosting sluggish brain cells.

8 READING

8 Virtually any child – or adult – can get some sense of achievement from drumming,' says Ralf, who left a job in electronics to teach drumming in primary and secondary schools in Oxfordshire. 'It's also a great way to get people interested in other musical instruments.' Though he offers private lessons, most pupils come to group tutorials after school or to holiday rock schools. 'I get lots of mad mummies wanting a go,' Ralf says. 'The dads are often more **_8_**. Perhaps they don't want to look as if they don't know what they're doing.'

9 It has been brilliant learning something new. All in all, our family rock-drumming lesson is a roaring success. We leave relaxed and smiling, energy spent.

Nigel Ralf runs Drum Beats in Oxford. One-hour private lessons cost £26; group lessons from £8 per child, ages eight and above. (www.drum-beats.co.uk; 07910 433265)

Cito, vmbo-gl en tl, 2014, tijdvak 1

---

9 READING

Why a Safari in Tanzania is Perfect for Solo Travellers

By Patrick Stevensons

1 The honeymooners in expensive Ralph Lauren safari outfits ask which national park I'm going to. Ngorongoro? Serengeti? Neither, I say, Tarangire. They look puzzled. Either the park and its lodge, Oliver's Camp, is second rate or so exclusive they've never heard of it. And on a chilly night in the arrivals hall at Tanzania's Kilimanjaro airport, I'm not sure which is correct.

2 Next morning, waiting for my flight to Tarangire, an American couple argue at the counter about the price of a cappuccino – $4 – and when workers in the coffee plantations next door earn a dollar a day, it does seem a bit rich. Nonetheless, you feel faintly embarrassed. It gets all the more perplexing when an Italian couple start cooing next to me. Everyone is with someone, mostly someone they're in love with. Evidently safaris aren't made for single travellers like me.

3 Messenga is my rescuer. He's formal and hesitant when I land at Tarangire, but as we head for Oliver's Camp in a Land Rover, I'm not yet aware of the stroke of luck I've had. The quality of your guide will make or break your safari. In South Africa and Botswana, I now realise, the guides I've had were competent but unexceptional. They impress Europeans and Americans as they point out a marvel you'd never spot yourself. They are trained to seek what the customer wants (everyone asks for lions) then radio ahead and deliver. Messenga, **_1_**, is different. He grew up in a nearby Masai village and his knowledge of the landscape comes not from books but from a lifetime of observation and devotion to his environment. Tarangire can, just about, do the 'big five' – the lion, elephant, leopard, rhino and buffalo. For Messenga, though, Tarangire is not about the big five but the

'beautiful five' and (his favourites) the 'ugly five'.

4 Travelling on your own with a guide gives you the chance to set your own pace. Mostly we dawdle, spotting a tawny eagle, and having a giggle as a herd of zebras cross our path. I stare and stare at the giraffes, in Tarangire more docile and approachable than any I've encountered. 'Mr Patrick, would you like to move on?' Messenga asks. 'No, I'm OK.' Oliver's Camp is unfenced, a reminder of its exquisite exclusivity; it's the sole encampment within the 1,100square mile park, permitted to exist only if animals are free to roam through it. A security guard walks you back to your tent, assuring you a lion is unlikely to pace past in the night. It's about the only time you wish you weren't alone. But breakfast is your payoff. Silent, alone, a book lazily in hand, a fine cup of coffee, and giraffes lolloping past not more than a couple of hundred metres away. It's fantastically expensive. And worth it, at times like this.

5 Only once is the serenity shattered, when the next day I share a tour. 'No, not that. Only want lions,' barks the fat rude German when Messenga pauses for a beautiful bird, a lilac-breasted roller, while the German's oriental partner, at least 25 years his junior, looks on impassively. When we later find a lion, I want to feed him to it. Who needs company when you have a thousand square miles of safari park to yourself and almost the greatest concentration of wildlife on earth?

Cito, vmbo-gl en tl, 2015, tijdvak 2

No roundabouts, just nine miles of road – and now one speed gun

By Kunal Dutta

1 THE ISLAND of St Mary's in the Isles of Scilly is something of a motoring _1_. With just nine miles of road, no roundabouts or traffic lights, the biggest irony was once that aspiring drivers could take their test there. That was until this week when the island woke up to news that authorities had introduced the island's first-ever speed gun.

2 The move is a milestone for sleepy St Mary's, which until now, was one of few places in Britain where drivers could travel speed-trap free. It is also quite a firm measure for a rural island, that according to the DVLA[1], has only 823 registered vehicles. Most people travel around the island on a bicycle. And the roads are so difficult to navigate by car that it is almost impossible to move beyond second gear and gather speed.

3 Official figures showed that the fastest vehicle clocked by the speed gun since its introduction was a lonely moped whizzing by at a miserable 34mph. Yet police remain determined of the speed gun's necessity. 'There is an element that thinks Scilly isn't in the UK and the laws of the UK don't apply on Scilly,' Sgt Craig argued. 'Sometimes people need reminding that the laws of the land do apply here.' _2_ that it was unlikely that motorists could actually break the speed limit, Sgt Craig justified the purchase of the gun by saying it would be used for gathering evidence of inconsiderate driving in certain areas, particularly the island's main centre in Hugh Town.

4 The reception among islanders remained mild. 'I suppose you do get the odd person driving like a muppet,' said Rhiannon Manning, 34, who works at the island's local taxi office. 'There's a road in the centre of the island, but it winds so heavily if you did try to creep beyond 60mph you'd probably crash. That said, it's probably a good deterrent for dangerous driving in the long-run, wouldn't you agree?' she said, seeking the thoughts of her 56-year-old mother. The response? 'Don't ask me, dear.
I never go beyond 20.'

noot 1 Driver and Vehicle Licensing Agency = Rijksdienst voor het Wegverkeer
Cito, vmbo-gl en tl, 2015, tijdvak 2

11 WRITING

Back Forward Stop Refresh Home Search Favorites History Mail Print

www.interpals.net

Interpals

InterPals is the top site to meet people and make new friends, penpals, language partners, travel buddies!

Make new friends

Learn a language

Discover the world
Meet people everywhere!

What's a penpal? A penpal is a new friend from another corner of the earth whom you get to know through letters... or online messages and chat.
Love to travel? Meet people to show you around!+
Now at 3,507,347 penpals and counting!

12 SPEAKING

13 LISTENING

Back Forward Stop Refresh Home Search Favorites History Mail Print

www.skydive-central.co.uk/forum

Agenda | Restaurants | Drinks | Magazines | Forum

Skydiving

How did you feel when you went skydiving for the first time?

Alice

Posted at 10:12am

You truly feel like you're flying - when are you ever going to get closer to doing so? And it's SUCH a rush, and it's so beautiful all around you, and you have this feeling you're never going to get again – it's not falling... so it must be FLYING! The ground doesn't seem to get any closer for the longest time, and yelling into the wind feels so good. Your clothes are whipping around you with the wind and you're up in the sky. Since your tandem guy's behind you all you can see is the entire beautiful world stretched out below your arms for the first time in your whole entire life.

14 WATCHING

Paralympic skiing

Paralympic cross-country skiing is an adaption of cross-country skiing for athletes with disabilities.

It is one of two Nordic skiing disciplines in the Winter Paralympics; the other is the biathlon. Both Nordic Skiing disciplines are open to men and women. Cross-Country skiers can compete in individual or team, classical or freestyle events ranging from 2.5km to 20km in distance. Skiers with visual impairments compete with a guide, while athletes with a physical impairment compete using either a sit-ski or standing using one or two skis and/or poles.

Adapted from: wikipedia.org

Adventure Playgrounds

(1) Adventure playgrounds to let older children find out about risk will open around the country. Children's Secretary[1] Ed Balls promised to spend extra money for physically challenging play areas aimed at turning 8- to 13-year-olds away from the computer screen. He is worried too many children no longer experience controlled risk which would teach them to take safe decisions in future. It is part of a major government plan to reverse the decline of childhood. This plan also aims at improving drugs and alcohol education in an attempt to tackle increasingly risky behaviour such as binge-drinking. The exposure of children to violent images via the internet or video games will also be tackled.

(2) While the plan will focus on improving children's lives outside school, it will also contain measures aimed at driving up exam performance. Mr Balls will announce a £250 million fund to provide more catch-up classes and one-to-one tuition with the aim of helping struggling pupils and stimulating the gifted. Secondary school pupils who have been expelled from school or are struggling with the curriculum will learn how to run a business at a new breed of 'studio schools' for 14- to 19-year-olds. They will be more like workplaces than schools and pupils will learn teamwork and leadership skills there.

noot 1 Children's Secretary = minister van Gezinszaken

Cito, vmbo-gl en tl, 2013, tijdvak 1

Jellyfish shut down Swedish nuclear reactor

16 READING

It wasn't a tsunami but it had the same effect – a huge cluster of jellyfish forced one of the world's largest reactors to shut down.

Operators of the Oskarshamn nuclear plant in southeastern Sweden had to scramble reactor number three after tonnes of jellyfish clogged the pipes that bring in cool water to the plant's turbines.
The pipes have now been cleared of jellyfish and engineers are preparing to restart the reactor, which is the largest boiling-water reactor in the world.

All three Oskarshamn reactors are boiling-water types, the same technology at Japan's Fukushima Daiichi plant that suffered a catastrophic failure in 2011 after a tsunami breached the facility's walls and flooded its equipment.

Jellyfish are not a new problem for nuclear plants. Last year, California basedDiablo Canyon facility had to shut one of its reactors after gobs of sea salp – a gelatinous, jellyfish-like organism – clogged intake pipes.
Nuclear plants need a constant flow of water to cool their reactor and turbine systems, which is why many are built near large bodies of water.

Cito, vmbo-gl en tl, 2015, tijdvak 2

Dear Mrs Aalbers,

Thank you for booking The London Dungeon for 2 adults and 16 students. You must print this email, bring it with you and hand it in at The Dungeons or you may be refused entry. **Your booking reference is J9AEV** and your booking cost: **£258.10** (including credit card surcharge of £3.00). Please be aware that bookings are non-refundable and check the details below:

By rail/underground: 100 metres from London Bridge Stations: Rail & London underground (Northern & Jubilee lines). 400 metres from Monument/Bank Station: Docklands Light Railway, London underground (District, Circle, Central & Northern Lines)
By bus: services 21, 35, 40, 43, 47, 48, 78, 133, 149, 381, RVI.
Parking: NCP: St Thomas Street and Upper Thames Street.
Coaches: Euro Car Park, Tower Bridge Road
New features: Extremis: Drop Ride to Doom

Lead Name: MRS AALBERS
Booking Reference: J9AEV
Arriving Thursday, May 15, 2011 for the timeslot 15:30-17:29, 2 adults and 16 students
Admission type: **Fast-track**
Time Slot: You can arrive at any time within your specified time slot
Address: **The London Dungeon, 28/34 Tooley Street, London SE1 2SZ**

The London Dungeon

Thank you Mrs AALBERS,
Please keep this e-ticket safe as you will need to exchange it to gain entry to The London Dungeon.

0 76950 45047 9

Your booking reference is: J9AEV

Dungeons.com ticketing is operated and payable by Holiday Extras.
Fast Track Tickets: During peak periods, for example, School Holidays, there may be a queue. However, Fast Track Tickets give you priority entry over the Non Fast Track queue.

Cito, vmbo-gl en tl, 2012, tijdvak 2

18 READING

'Turn Right' into a porta-potty

A German driver took his navigation system's commands a little too literally and ended up in deep doodoo. When he heard the command to 'Turn right now!' from his navigation system he crashed into a small toilet enclosure by the side of the road. Apparently, he turned about 100 feet too soon. The crossing he was supposed to take was another 30 yards down the road.

The 53-year-old driver did not notice the error even after his car went off the road. He continued into a construction site, up a stairway and into the small toilet shack, according to police in the eastern town of Rudolstadt. The incident caused € 2,000 worth of damage to the stairwell, another € 100 in damage to his car, and he was also fined € 35 for reckless driving.

Cito, vmbo-gl en tl, 2015, tijdvak 2

19 READING

The Bramah Museum of Tea and Coffee

Only two minutes from London Bridge Station, is the world's first museum devoted entirely to the history of tea and coffee. It tells the commercial and social 400-year-old history of two of the world's most important commodities since their arrival in Europe from the Far East and Africa.
Since the British played a major role both in the China trade and development of production in India, Ceylon and Africa, the museum naturally tells the story from a British perspective. The museum, through its ceramics, metal ware, prints and displays, answers all those questions that people from around the world ask about British tea and coffee.
The London tea trade has, for generations, conducted the business of unloading ships, marketing, blending and packing on both sides of the Thames close to London Bridge. Although the tea auctions were held north of the river, the South Bank boasted many prestigious warehouses. Also nearby is the George Inn with its original seventeenth century coffee room.
For 200 years the East India Company sailing ships returning from China would unload their cargoes on the Thames.

19 READING

Although the steam ships bringing teas from India, Ceylon and Africa frequently berthed further down river, their cargoes would be brought up by barge as far as London Bridge. Some Clipper sailing ships however, came as far as London Bridge in the 1860s.

Menu
The ceremony of English afternoon tea was popularised throughout the world by the British and is kept alive in our authentic tea room. The five minute wait for the tea to infuse is the heart and soul of English afternoon tea.

Cream Tea
Scones with clotted cream and jam, cake and tea of your choice £7.

Afternoon Tea
Cucumber sandwiches, hot crumpet, tea cake, cake and choice of tea £9.
Guided Tours available.

Pre-Booking
Your table can be reserved for either cream or afternoon tea by emailing us at: bramah@teaandcoffeemuseum.com.

We can accommodate a quiet table for two and groups of up to 45.
Group booking is a specialty.

Cito, vmbo-gl en tl, 2014, tijdvak 1

20 READING

Tuck in ... a quarter of baby food in jars is eaten by adults

Kate Connolly

1 Can't be bothered to chew your food? Too tired to cook and looking for a quick meal? It seems that in such circumstances a growing number of adults may consider opening a jar of baby food. The world's largest baby food manufacturer, Hipp, has said an increasing number of adults are turning to its pre-cooked, pureed meals because they find them _**1**_.

2 About a quarter of those who eat the firm's 100 varieties of pulped meals – from apple and cranberry breakfast to vegetable and

beef hotpot – are adults, it says. Claus Hipp said in recent years it's very popular, particularly among older people, with stewed apple said to be a favourite.

3 Claus Hipp added: 'Not so long ago, we had twice as many births as now, and that, of course, has a knock-on effect. As our society gets ever older, baby food is showing that it has a future in the adult market.' **_2_** birth rates have dropped in most European countries, most notably in Germany, the company's profits rose by € 90m last year to € 500m (£450m).

4 A million and a half jars of baby food come off the Hipp production line every day. Hipp said calorie conscious new mothers saw the meals – which are low in fat, sugar and salt – as a way to help them **_3_** after giving birth and were among new customers it had won in recent years. Sportsmen and women looking for a light meal are believed to favour the jars, too.

5 The company, which recommends its organic meals to babies 'at the start of weaning to three years of age', said it had no intention of relaunching the products for a separate market. 'Older people can often cope with the mashed baby food better than regular meals, but we're not planning to **_4_** ... we want to keep our baby image,' said Hipp, whose father, Georg, started putting baby food in jars in 1960.

6 Eileen Steinbock, of the British Dietetic Association, said pureed food could benefit people whose ability to swallow had been greatly reduced through old age, dementia

or a stroke, and was already in widespread use in care homes. But people who could still chew and swallow should continue to do so for as long as possible,' she added. 'I wouldn't like to see people being given pureed food just because it's easier for a carer to give it to them that way. It should only be given when it's **_5_**,' according to Ms Steinbock.

7 Moreover, the protein content of food declines when it is pureed because extra water is added to help liquify it, leaving it with fewer calories. 'That would be a bad thing because a lot of people who require pureed food find it hard to eat enough and are quite likely to be nutritionally compromised and possibly even malnourished,' she added.

Cito, vmbo-gl en tl, 2014, tijdvak 2

The Truth about Bears

Biologist who befriended animals for BBC film insists they are misunderstood

Suzanne Goldenberg
US environment correspondent

1 Wildlife biologist Lynn Rogers had logged thousands of hours observing North America's black bears. He had shot them with tranquilizers before fitting them with ear tags or radiocollars. He had drawn their blood and mapped their DNA. And he had tracked their movements with pins on maps. None of that had allowed him to really know the creatures. When he did get close to a bear in the wild the animal was usually terrified, caught in a trap in the woods.

2 Rogers realised he had to win their trust. So he abandoned scientific detachment and took the daring and controversial step of forming relationships with his study animals, using food to gain acceptance among an extended bear family in Minnesota. Gaining such trust has given him an insight into their behaviour and social organisation as well as allowing him to explode myths about them.

3 The relationship between Rogers and his research subjects is explored in a BBC film, *Bearwalker of the Northwoods*. The film opens with Rogers – who is 70 – hiking through the woods of north-east Minnesota. Rogers approaches a mother bear and her cubs slowly and deliberately. 'It's me, bear, it's me,' he calls out. The adult female he calls Juliet slaps a few times at the opening of the mud and wood den. Rogers is not alarmed. 'She is not a mean bear. She is just a nervous bear, but she will calm down,' he tells the camera. Within moments, it looks as if Juliet is about to nod off to sleep.

4 Rogers has abandoned just about everything he knew about bears. Contrary to popular belief they do not like honey, and they are not ferocious. Rogers is determined about that. He has never heard a bear roar or growl, and he has never been seriously hurt, even though in his early years he displayed what he calls 'bad bear manners'.

5 Actually, the bears he knows are timid. Defensive postures, such as slapping paws on the ground, are mistaken for aggression. 'In my 42 years of working closely with bears and testing every no-no, I have not found a way of getting a bear to attack. The more I push them the more they try to get away.'

6 It's humans who are the more dangerous animal, he said. 'If you look at the statistics, one black bear out of a million kills somebody. With grizzly bears it's one in 50,000. Among humans it's one person out of 18,000 who kills somebody.'

7 Rogers's methods make him controversial with fellow researchers and he does not have a significant publishing record in academic journals. Tim Ginnett, an American university professor, said feeding the animals runs the risk of changing the behaviour you want to study. 'We want to

understand how they behave and operate in a natural ecosystem, and feeding them – to my way of thinking – kind of disrupts that so it's not an approach we use,' he said.

8 Rogers is no sentimentalist. Even after devoting 40 years of his life to the black bear of Minnesota, he is under no illusion that his interest is felt in return. Even his favourite bear, June, does not really like him, he said. 'If she had feelings I think she would want to seek company like a dog does its master's,' he said, 'but she doesn't think of me in those terms. I'm just the guy that brings her a treat once in a while and she can ignore… that makes her so valuable to science.'

Cito, vmbo-gl en tl, 2014, tijdvak 2

When Posh met Poor

based on an article by Clare Campbell

1 ALICE, 15, lives with her mother, father, sister and little brother in a six-bedroom house in south London. She says: 'I know that my family is well-off. I go to a private school and we live in a large house in a desirable part of London. As a result of my upbringing, I've had a _**1**_ view of life; I was living in a bubble and believed money made you better than other people.

2 Although I'd never met anyone from the council estate[1], I imagined they would all be wearing cheap tracksuits, scraped-back hair and big earrings. I thought Natalie would be the same. _**2**_, when I first saw her, I noticed she was much better-dressed than I'd expected. I really loved her outfit. We liked one another straight away. She was funny and friendly and we were surprised and pleased that I spoke the same slang as her. We talked about everything. Natalie's attitude to boyfriends is very _**3**_. She hates the idea of being tied down. She is used to making her own decisions while I prefer being in a relationship to being on my own. Also, Natalie and her mum have a really good relationship – they're more like sisters. And I was surprised at how cosy and welcoming their flat was. I thought it would be much smaller and pokier.

3 Meeting Natalie has changed me a lot. I feel really guilty about what I was like before, and I no longer think public school kids are better than everyone else. Natalie and I now chat online several times a week. I feel so much respect for what she and her mother have been through and how they've tried to help themselves. Natalie's really bright and I know she'll make something of herself, and we got on so well I'm sure we'll stay friends.'

4 NATALIE, 17, lives with her 38-year-old mother, Vicky, and five-year-old brother, Gabriel, in a two-bedroom council flat on a south London estate. She says: 'I've lived on this estate all my life. My dad died when I was six. All I can remember about him was that he was always loving and affectionate. Mum can't work because she suffers from depression, so I take care of my brother, Gaby, who has a speech problem.

5 We live on benefits of £165 a week, which is sometimes not enough, so my mum has to borrow money. I dropped out of school when I was 15, mainly because I had to take care of my mum and brother. I feel I've been through more in my life than the average 40-year-old woman. Sometimes I feel resentful for the way my life is. It shouldn't be my task to get Gaby to school, but there's no one else to do it.

6 Still, recently I've gone back to college. I've always been ambitious and I made up my mind that I wasn't going to grow up to be another single mother living on benefits all my life. I knew Alice's life would be very different to mine, that she might not understand. I didn't want her judging, or feeling sorry for me, however. We may be poor, but we're not tramps.

7 I really liked the skirt Alice was wearing when I saw her the first time. She smiled, and I knew we'd be okay. Her house was really beautiful and her family made me feel welcome too. I didn't feel as out of place as I thought I would. But it also seemed to me that Alice was not as close to her mum as I am to mine. If that's what having more money does to a family, I don't want it.

8 Alice and I are constantly in touch with one another, but I'm so busy with college, as well as trying to get a part-time job, that we haven't managed to meet up again recently. Still, I know we'll stay friends. Alice is an okay girl.'

noot 1 council estate = een wijk met goedkope huurwoningen

Cito, vmbo-gl en tl, 2015, tijdvak 2

Volunteer opportunities

23 WRITING

Back Forward Stop Refresh Home Search Favorites History Mail Print

http://www.safehavenhumane.org/volunteer-opportunities-kids

We are pleased to offer a variety of volunteer opportunities for kids under the age of 18. Youth volunteer opportunities in our animal shelters include:

Dog/Cat Socialization – The shelter environment may be stressful for an animal. To help overcome this stress, we depend on volunteers to help give the animals extra attention needed to feel happy!

Fundraising and Events – We receive no public funding, and rely heavily on donations and fundraising efforts to keep our shelter running. Volunteers make these fundraising events a success!

For more information about our youth volunteer program, please call us at 541.928.2789 or email volunteer@safehavenhumane.com.

My daily routines

24 SPEAKING

Abby McDermott about her daily routines

- Lay in bed for about ten minutes after waking up, get up, get uniform, go upstairs and shower (my room's in the basement), get changed, brush teeth, grab a nutrigrain bar (or whatever breakfast snack we have), and go to catch the bus for 6:30-6:40 (depending).

- My classes this semester: Maths, science, textiles, multimedia, P.E., French, history, English

- I usually do my homework after dinner, so around 5:30pm. And it usually takes me to about 6:30-7:00, so then I can relax and play games on my laptop for a while.

- Eat snack maybe, make sure all my homework and school stuff is back in my bag (I have a bad habit of forgetting things), make sure I have a clean uniform for the next day and if I don't I need to wash it I crawl into bed and watch some TV.

- I usually try to go to bed around 10:00pm, but I tend to get distracted by online things, so I usually crawl into bed around 11-11:30.

Adapted from: au.answers.yahoo.com

Vocabulary

OPSOMMING/TOEVOEGING

The boy is **also** very good at sport.	*ook*
He was late **and** he forgot his homework.	*en*
We were wet, **as well as** very cold, after our walk.	*evenals*
I don't mind that you're late. **Besides,** it's not your fault!	*bovendien, daarnaast*
The book is **both** funny **and** scary.	*zowel ... als ...*
By the way, have you thought about my ideas?	*trouwens*
The house **even** has a swimming pool.	*zelfs*
First, turn on the computer. **Secondly**, click 'start'. **Thirdly**, start the programme.	*(als) eerste, tweede, derde*
First of all I would like to welcome you all to the tenth annual tennis grand slam.	*ten eerste*
For starters, I don't like getting up early.	*om te beginnen*
The birthday cake is beautiful. **Furthermore**, it tastes good!	*bovendien*
Our holiday was fun. **In addition**, I made some new friends.	*bovendien*
In conclusion, I don't like this book at all.	*concluderend*
Gary did **indeed** leave his bag at the security check at the airport.	*immers*
If you buy this laptop, we'll throw in a free mouse. **In fact,** we'll give you a free case too!	*sterker nog*
I like this film. There are lots of stunts. **Moreover**, the hero is good-looking.	*bovendien*
Neither Mum **nor** Dad knew the answer to my question.	*noch ... noch ...*
The **next** step is putting the cake in the oven.	*volgende*
Not only did I finish my homework **but** I **also** cooked dinner.	*niet alleen ... maar ook ...*
Would you like some dessert **too**?	*ook*
The present was nice, and **what's more** my friend made it herself.	*bovendien*

TEGENSTELLING

He was there, **although** he was a bit ill.	*(al)hoewel*
I have no other pets **besides** my dog.	*behalve, anders dan*
I like swimming, **but** I hate diving.	*maar*
Our cat loves to sleep all day. **By contrast**, our dog never sits still.	*daarentegen*
Our holiday was fun **despite** all the rain.	*ondanks*
The dress is still available in **either** black **or** white.	*ofwel ... of ...*
Everybody was there, **except** John.	*behalve*
She says she's telling the truth. **Even so**, I don't trust her.	*toch, desondanks*
I love my brother, **even though** he can be annoying at times.	*hoewel*
The weather was good. **However**, I did wear a scarf.	*echter, maar*
The water isn't clean. **In fact**, it is very dirty.	*feitelijk, eigenlijk*
I was really cold **in spite of** the sun.	*ondanks*
Would you like to go out for lunch **instead of** dinner?	*in plaats van*
The film was scary but I watched it **nevertheless**.	*desalniettemin*
Don't say you can't finish your presentation in time; **of course** you can!	*natuurlijk*
On the one hand, the food was great. **On the other hand**, it was a bit too expensive.	*enerzijds, anderzijds*
Would you like pizza **or** pasta for dinner?	*of*
I would **rather** go to a concert **than** to the cinema.	*liever ... dan ...*

I know it's late but shall we **still** go for a walk? — *toch*
Sure, you could spend all your pocket money, but why not save it? — *zeker, natuurlijk*
This house is much bigger **than** that house. — *dan*
I agree that cricket is fun. **Then again** the matches are very long. — *aan de andere kant*
I don't think I'll be able to get tickets for the concert **unless** I win some by chance. — *tenzij*
Stephanie always makes sure her homework a priority, **unlike** her brother. — *in tegenstelling tot*
He earns a lot, **whereas** she doesn't earn much at all. — *terwijl*
It was raining hard. **Yet**, we still went hiking. — *toch*

VERGELIJKING

They stared at me **as if** I was crazy. — *alsof*
I am taller when **compared to** my sister. — *vergeleken met*
The apple is tasty. The orange is **equally** nice. — *evenzeer, evenzo*
My brother plays football, **just like** my dad. — *net zo (als)*
I wish I could dance **like** Beyoncé! — *zoals*
Hilda said to have a wonderful spring break. I told her **likewise**. — *hetzelfde*
The twins were **similarly** dressed. — *op dezelfde manier*

OORZAAK/GEVOLG

They left too late and **as a result**, they missed their train. — *daarom, als gevolg van*
By swimming so fast, the swimmer has set a new world record. — *door*
We didn't have a map, **consequently**, we got lost. — *met als gevolg, waardoor*
We're a bit late, **so** we have to hurry. — *dus, daarom*
Let's go by car, **so that** we will be there earlier. — *zodat*
He hurt his arm. **Therefore** he won't be at school tomorrow. — *daarom*

REDEN

As you didn't answer your phone, I left a message. — *daar, omdat*
I can't come, **because** I have another appointment. — *omdat, want*
The event was cancelled **because of** the storm. — *vanwege*
We listened carefully, **for** he had some great ideas. — *want*
Let's have a picnic **since** it's such a nice day. — *aangezien*
Susan broke her leg. **That's why** she's in hospital. — *daarom, dat is (de reden) waarom*
He can't attend the party. **The reason being** that he's ill. — *de reden daarvoor is*

CONCLUSIE

My dad deserves a pay rise. **After all**, he works hard. — *tenslotte*
In short, the film is about friendship. — *kortom*
You're right. He was very rude **indeed**. — *inderdaad*
Everyone applauded. **This shows** that the concert was good. — *dit laat zien*
Our team scored the most goals, **thus** we won the game. — *dus, zo, op die manier, samenvattend*

VOORWAARDE

If I go to the party, will you come too?	*als, indien*
In case you missed the show, here's a recap of last night's episode.	*in het geval dat*
Provided you study hard, you should pass the test.	*mits, op voorwaarde dat*
I will be there at 9am unless the bus is late.	*tenzij*

VOORBEELDEN

I like animals, horses for example.	*bijvoorbeeld*
I like to listen to music, like techno, for instance.	*bijvoorbeeld*
I prefer going to warm countries like Spain.	*zoals*
I can speak two foreign languages, namely French and English.	*namelijk*
She likes sports such as football and tennis.	*zoals*

TIJD/VOLGORDE

After we had dinner, we went to the cinema.	*nadat*
Would you like a biscuit before I eat them all?	*voor(dat)*
The family arrived at the airport earlier than planned.	*vroeger*
We got lost but we made it home eventually.	*uiteindelijk*
Finally, you have to print out the document.	*tenslotte*
Who would like to go first?	*eerst*
The plane was initially supposed to land this morning.	*aanvankelijk*
My best friend has always kept her promises in the past.	*in het verleden, vroeger*
I'll finish my homework later.	*later*
I am cleaning the house, meanwhile my brother is playing video games.	*ondertussen*
Mum says I have to do the dishes now.	*nu*
Once the cake was ready, she took it out of the oven.	*zodra, toen eenmaal*
We had lunch, then we went shopping.	*toen*
Please wait here until the teacher is ready to see you.	*totdat*
The telephone rang while we were having dinner.	*terwijl*

TABLE OF CONTENTS

ERK

Reading/Listening: A2 B1
Speaking/writing: A2

4

Can you believe it?

A
LISTENING

Quiz What kind of learner are you?

In order to define your learning style, look at the problem below and see what kind of learner you are.

1 Your bicycle has a flat tyre. You have to fix it, but you have never done it before. What would you do?

A I call a family member or friend or someone else who knows how to fix a tyre. He/she can give me instructions.

B I watch instruction videos online and/or go to the nearest bicycle shop and watch them fix a tyre.

C I buy all the supplies I need and start repairing my tyre. Eventually I'll figure out how to do it.

RESULTS

A: Listening learner
B: Seeing learner
C: Experience learner

B
THEME WORDS

THEME WORDS

to be flabbergasted	to grasp	senses	optical illusion
behaviour	intuition	to conceal	psychology
confusion	magician	disguise	to react
imagination	to manipulate	distraction	trickery

RISING STAR: TROY VON SCHEIBNER

Mixing mind-bending stunts and mischievous tricks, Troy Von Scheibner is the latest rising star in the magician community. Von Scheibner is nothing like old-fashioned magicians. He wears tattoos, gold watches and baseball caps instead of top hats and a cape. He's an urban magician and has made magic 'hip' again for young people. We all know his tricks aren't real, but we like to be surprised by them nevertheless.

I am at the Parlour Skate Store in Mile End, where he is filming the second series of his show, *Troy*.

He shows us around and answers my questions. Troy, 26, from South London, became interested in magic when he saw David Blaine on television. 'I saw him on TV when I was 12. Back then we thought of magicians as old-fashioned, but Blaine made it cool, modern and fresh again.'

Troy really got started doing magic tricks when his father signed him up for a magicians' club where he won *Young Magician of the Year* at the age of 15. At school he was known as 'Magic Boy.' 'I stopped performing for people at university because everyone wants you to do tricks all the time. Sometimes I just want to chill.' Nowadays, however, he tells me he always has a pack of cards on him because he is famous and people expect him to perform a trick wherever he goes.

Maybe this is the right time for me to ask him to do a trick. I've always wanted to find out how these card tricks work. Taking a fresh pack he unwraps it, shuffles it and asks me to pick a card, write a number on it, remember it carefully and put it back. I hold the pile of cards, he puts his hands on top. When I open my hands, the loose stack of cards has been replaced by a wrapped box. It kind of bothers me I failed to notice the trick he has performed. Of course he played a visual trick and my mind couldn't process it.

Troy explains that what he does is more than just tricks. Social skills are also crucial: 'A lot of magicians tend to be a bit socially awkward because they've spent so many hours practising in front of the mirror, so when you have to go out and show people it can be quite daunting. Good social skills help you connect with people better, and if people like you they'll automatically like what you do.'

Von Scheibner is a likeable guy indeed. I have just experienced it myself. Maybe his charm is part of the trick he pulled on me.

Adapted from: standard.co.uk

STONE

10 Finding out how things work

I wanted	to find out	how his card tricks work.
Our aim was	to learn	why people see colours differently.
I'm curious		how these illusions are done.

How can you	determine	how people learn best?
	figure out	if someone is colour blind?

The man told them	to remember the number carefully.
I instructed him	to pay close attention to the images on the screen.
He asked me	to concentrate on the movement of the hands.

We	will question	twenty people	about	the way they study.
I	've already asked	a number of pupils		colour blindness.
	can interview	my classmates		

I asked	some people	to write down their observations.
We instructed	the participants	to fill in a questionnaire.
	them	to arrange the colours in the correct order.

Lara	claims	she learns best	while chewing gum.
She	says	she can concentrate better	while listening to music.
		she can only focus	in the school library.

GRAMMAR

E GRAMMAR

10 Summary of the tenses (samenvatting werkwoordstijden) >> GS 1–7, page 135

He always **walks** to football practice. I **learn** best in the school library.	*Present simple*: gebruik je bij feiten, gewoonten, regelmatige gebeurtenissen en tijdschema's. GS 1.
It **is raining** heavily right now. At the moment we **are studying** for the test. They **are cooking** dinner tomorrow.	*Present continuous*: gebruik je als iets nu aan de gang is of bij afspraken in de nabije toekomst waarvan de tijd en/of plaats al vaststaat. GS 2.
The weather **was** terrible yesterday. He **asked** me to pay close attention.	*Past simple*: gebruik je om te zeggen dat iets in het verleden is gebeurd en nu is afgelopen. GS 3.
I **was watching** TV series all night. It **was raining** all last week.	*Past continuous*: gebruik je om te zeggen dat iets in het verleden een tijdje aan de gang was. GS 4.
Rupert **is going to** ask her on a date. The weatherman says it**'s going to** freeze in Wales.	*To be going to*: gebruik je als iemand iets in de toekomst (niet) van plan is of als je een voorspelling doet waarvoor je WEL bewijs hebt. GS 7.
I **will come** to your party. I promise. I **won't buy** any more shirts this month.	*Will*: gebruik je om iets aan te bieden, bij beloftes, aankondigingen en besluiten of als je een voorspelling doet waarvoor je GEEN bewijs hebt. GS 7.
Farah **has known** him for five years. I'm tired; I **haven't slept** well.	*Present perfect*: gebruik je wanneer iets in het verleden is begonnen en je nu het resultaat merkt of het nu nog bezig is; bij ervaringen tot nu toe. GS 5.
When he arrived at the party Sarah **had** already **left**.	*Past perfect:* gebruik je om aan te geven dat iets eerder gebeurd is dan iets anders. GS 6

F WATCHING

Selling it right

Meet Simon, director for a marketing company in Amsterdam. The company works with big clients from all over the world, from the United States to Japan. To make the best advertisements possible, Simon has to find out exactly what a customer wants. Watch the clip to find out how he does it.

G LISTENING

Back Forward Stop Refresh Home Search Favorites History Mail Print

http://www.mindblowing.co.uk/workshops/

Mind-blowing tricks

Workshop Mindreading
Youth club

What is Mindreading?
The workshop *Mindreading* presents a combination of illusion and scientific knowledge of body and mind. The term *Mindreading* refers to the capacity of people to understand each other's behaviour.

Reading minds
Our trainers will teach you the techniques that professional mind readers use to 'read' minds. You will learn how to predict people's answers by looking at their reactions. At the end of the workshop you will be able to apply the techniques in your everyday life!

For whom?
This workshop is perfect for anyone who is interested in how the mind works. Even sceptic people are invited to give it a try! You can participate individually as well as in groups.

H READING

Grocery shopping and ordering whoppers

Imagine someone grabs something out of your shopping basket and puts it in his own basket. You ask him why he is doing this. He simply answers 'It was easier to grab the items from your basket than from the shelf.' How would you react to this _1_? It is likely you would be annoyed, a bit angry or even furious.

The situation above is a famous example of a 'breaching experiment'. The breaching experiment was developed by professor Harold Garfinkel to test social norms. Social norms are unwritten rules such as giving up your seat in the bus to an old lady or shaking hands when meeting someone. Most of the time we aren't even aware of them. Garfinkel organised experiments to test the strength of these norms. He and his students observed how people react when these norms are _2_. In the case of the shopping basket it's quite obvious: shoppers shouldn't pick items out of other people's baskets; it is considered rude.

These social experiments can teach us interesting things about ourselves because people react differently to unusual events. If people break the social norms only a little bit, people may laugh about it or show confusion. **_3_**, if there is a more serious breach or break from social norms, people who witness it can become angry. In general, breaching experiments are a good way to learn about the social world that everybody takes for granted.

Breaching experiments are easy to conduct because they are characteristically low budget and do not require much time or planning. Popular examples of breaching experiments have been: standing backwards in a lift, negotiating the price of groceries at the supermarket and starting a conversation with a stranger in a public toilet.

A guest in your own home

Garfinkel demonstrated 'breaching' by instructing his students to act as guests in their own house. Students were excessively polite to their parents and even asked permission to use the bathroom. The students noticed that their parents were very **_4_** their behaviour. The parents generally demanded to know why their children were behaving this way. Many students reported they had difficulty with the assignment as well because it felt strange acting as a guest in their own house.

Boiling Points

Boiling Points was a show in which victims walked into set-ups in public places and were put in annoying situations by a team of actors (for instance, a stranger would be very rude to them). If they managed to keep their temper for a set period of time, they would win a cash prize.

Ordering Whoppers

Another famous breaching experiment involves hamburgers. A student cheerfully asked a McDonald's clerk for a Whopper, the hamburger made by McDonald's' rival Burger King. The clerk behind the register explained that they are in McDonald's, but the student again asked for a Whopper. At this point the clerk looked around to see if one of his colleagues had also heard this **_5_** order. Maybe the customer was joking? It was a successful breach.

Breaching on TV

Most of us probably wouldn't like to be the 'victim' of a breaching experiment. _6_, a lot of people do like to watch other people in this situation. *Boiling Points*, *Punk'd* and *Primetime: What would you do?* are examples of television programmes that show just that.

Of course, it's probably even more fun to carry out your own breaching experiment and see the results first-hand...

Adapted from: wiredcosmos.com

drastically	*op ingrijpende wijze*
etiquette norms	*omgangsvormen*

STONE

11 Making predictions

I	really think	that	brain-training games will become more popular.
We	expect		these exercises will soon be in everyone's daily routine.
They	predict		scientists will create robots with human intelligence.

We're certain	that	all people will live well into their hundreds	someday.
I'm sure		scientists will come up with a remedy for the fear of heights	in the future.
It's likely		computers will be able to store your memories	by 2050.

If	you get enough sleep,	it will be easier to study.
	you use brain-training apps,	you might perform better at school.
	you exercise regularly,	you will feel more energised.

Studies suggest that	in ten years' time	no one will use social media websites anymore.
They believe that	in 50 years' time	all teachers will use virtual reality in class.
I'm convinced that	by 2050	jetlag will be a thing of the past.

Brain scans	will	teach us interesting things about ourselves.
They	might	soon replace job interviews.
		be able to reveal everything you know.

In the distant future,	people will be able to	speak dozens of languages.
In the next century,	we will be able to	dream only happy dreams.

GRAMMAR

J GRAMMAR

11 'If' sentences >> GS 13, page 146

Je kunt *if-zinnen* voor drie dingen gebruiken.

If you **press** this switch, the light **goes on**. *if present simple present simple*		Je kunt *if-zinnen* gebruiken voor feiten.
Water **boils** if you **heat** it to 100°C. *present simple if present simple*		
If it **doesn't** rain, we'**ll go** to the park. *if present simple will + het hele werkwoord*		Je kunt *if*-zinnen ook gebruiken als je (bijna) zeker weet dat iets gaat gebeuren.
I'**ll send** him a card if you **give** me his address. *will + het hele werkwoord if present simple*		
If I **had** more money, I **would buy** a computer. *if past simple would + het hele werkwoord*		Je kunt *if*-zinnen ook gebruiken als je (bijna) zeker weet dat iets **niet** gaat gebeuren.
John **would go** on holiday if he **weren't** ill. *would + het hele werkwoord if past simple*		

K WATCHING

Moving legs

Have you always avoided insects because they're creepy? Think again: insects are useful! Researchers in Chile are doing experiments on cockroach legs. They're trying to move the insect's legs with their minds.

Task

>> TASKCARD

Senses survey
Je gaat een onderzoek doen naar hoe je zintuigen beïnvloed kunnen worden.

Taalportfolio
- A2 Ik kan schrijven over alledaagse aspecten van mijn omgeving in zinnen die met elkaar verbonden zijn.
- A2 Ik kan een korte, ingestudeerde presentatie geven over een onderwerp uit mijn dagelijks leven.
- B1 Ik kan een kort, eenvoudig verslag schrijven volgens een vast format.

ERK

The smell report

Topic
We wanted to find out if smells influence the way we think about objects.

How we tested it
50 people participated in this test. 25 people gave their opinion about a pair of jeans in a room with a pleasant smell; the other 25 gave their opinion about the same jeans but in a room with no smell.
Next, we asked them to answer a number of questions about the pair of jeans they had just seen. The questions were simple:

- Do you like these jeans?
- Would you consider buying them?

Results
The results were quite surprising. More than 20% of the people from the room with a pleasant smell said they would buy the jeans, while only 5% wanted to buy the jeans from the room with no smell.

Conclusion
We can conclude that smells do indeed affect the way we think about objects. More research is needed to study this.

Vocabulary

A LISTENING

I **barely** have time to do my homework let alone clean my room!	*nauwelijks*
Which **category** should I pick? Sport or general knowledge?	*categorie*
You are **clearly** ready for the survival challenge. Let's go!	*overduidelijk*
My brother's music is so loud I can't **concentrate** on my book.	*concentreren*
I'm confident that my dad can **fix** anything that breaks down.	*maken*
He was on his way to an interview when he got a **flat tyre**.	*lekke band*
Carly was shocked when she read the **headline**.	*krantenkop*
Finlay decided to **make up** an excuse why she couldn't go to the party.	*verzinnen*
Which languages do you think are the most important to **master**?	*beheersen*
Children should always be **obedient** to their parents or guardians.	*gehoorzaam*
Understanding **physics** can be a challenge sometimes.	*natuurkunde*
Just **the other day** I was telling you about that exhibition I want to go to.	*onlangs*
Trial and error is the key to suceeding in life.	*vallen en opstaan*

B THEME WORDS

I didn't think I will **be flabbergasted** when I get my exam results.	*stomverbaasd zijn*
Her **behaviour** was no longer acceptable and she was asked to leave.	*gedrag*
I tried to **conceal** the gift, because I wanted to surprise him.	*verbergen*
As an identical twin, there is always some **confusion** as to who is who.	*verwarring*
Frank his **disguise** for the paintball game was very good.	*vermomming*
My mobile phone is a welcome **distraction** when it comes to studying.	*afleiding*
Mr Gregory really helped me to **grasp** those scientific concepts.	*begrijpen*
If you use your **imagination**, you can be more creative than you think.	*verbeelding, fantasie*
His **intuition** told him he should leave the building as quickly as possible.	*intuïtie*
Recently we went to a show where there was an outstanding **magician**.	*goochelaar*
Children can try to **manipulate** parents to get what they want.	*manipuleren*
Just remember this act isn't real, it's just an **optical illusion**.	*gezichtsbedrog*
Gemma studied **psychology** at the University of Lancaster.	*psychologie*
I can't wait to see how Ron will **react** to our big surprise party.	*reageren*
My **senses** tell me that something is not right here.	*zintuigen*
Magicians are otherwise known as masters of **trickery**.	*bedrog*

C READING

It was a bit **awkward** when I asked Steven to go to the cinema with me.	*ongemakkelijk*
I think it shouldn't **bother** you what other people think.	*dwars zitten*
She has a natural **charm** that usually means she gets her way.	*charme*
Your tea has gone cold. Let me make you a **fresh** cup.	*nieuw, fris*
You must always **have** your member card **on you** at this gym.	*bij je hebben*
Surprisingly enough, this villain is actually quite **likeable**.	*sympathiek*
My dad sometimes **does magic** at parties. It's so embarassing!	*goochelen*
My heart is telling me one thing and my **mind** another.	*verstand*

Oliver was a very **mischievous** child who got up to all kinds of tricks.	*ondeugend*
I wasn't selected for the TV show. **Nevertheless**, I will try again next year.	*toch*
Bailey's dad has a really **old-fashioned** mobile phone. It's hilarious!	*ouderwets*
Jill's Personal Assistant was given a **pile** of job applications to review.	*stapel*
It took me a while to **process** the fact that I had just seen the Queen.	*verwerken*
Gareth is a **rising** star, you just watch! He's going to be famous.	*opkomend*
It's comical how upset you get if I don't **shuffle** the cards before we play.	*schudden*
Are you going to **sign up** for the ladies' football training at the stadium?	*(je) inschrijven*
Mum was grumpy because she had a **stack** of marking to do that night.	*stapel*
Kitty watched him **unwrap** her gift in great anticipation.	*uitpakken*
Is the watch a gift? I can certainly **wrap** it for you.	*inpakken*

D SPEAKING & WRITING

A number of passers-by were asked to take part in the survey.	*een aantal*
The **aim** of the experiment is to see how plants feed.	*doel*
The librarian will **arrange** various books in a particular order.	*rangschikken*
It has actually been proven that all dogs are **colour blind**.	*kleurenblind*
Jim is **curious** about the end of his book. He's thoroughly enjoying it.	*nieuwsgierig*
Gum is made from a tree that grows in Central America.	*kauwgom*
It looks like the magician cuts him in half, but that's just an **illusion**.	*illusie*
Stacy, can you **instruct** Kevin to clean the cafetaria when he gets in?	*opdragen*
I think you look very pale, but it's just an **observation**.	*waarneming*
Each **participant** should make sure they have registered at the desk.	*deelnemer*
The employees will **question** the manager about the rumours of closure.	*ondervragen*
If you could quickly fill in this **questionnaire**, I would be grateful.	*vragenlijst*

G LISTENING

Reading, writing and **arithmetic** are the three important skills to learn.	*rekenen*
If you want to come over, please give me a call **beforehand**.	*van tevoren*
Sometimes a **brain scan** is required to understand what is happening.	*hersenscan*
Keira had more than enough **capacity** to complete the assessment.	*vermogen*
What a **coincidence** that I should bump into you here in town!	*toeval*
Could you repeat the last **digit** of your phone number?	*cijfer*
That boy is really good with animals. I think he has a **gift**.	*gave*
Emily's **knowledge** of English literature is quite extensive.	*kennis*
Logan wished he could **memorise** the periodic table for his exam.	*onthouden*
It's **merely** five questions at the end of the phone call. That's all.	*slechts, alleen maar*
Your dog will always be loyal to you **no matter** what happens.	*ongeacht*
Everyone who wants to **participate** in the contest has to sign up.	*deelnemen*
Nina designed a mobile app to ask **random** times tables to children.	*willekeurig*
Harry's doctor had to **refer** him to a physiotherapist after his injury.	*verwijzen*
Do you know how to **reverse** the songs in my playlist?	*omdraaien*
I can't believe I forgot to **subtract** in this maths problem!	*aftrekken*
The cake is very tasty, and **what's more**, he made it himself!	*bovendien*

H READING

You need to **aim** the arrow at the big, red target.	*richten*
Janice is thrilled to have completed the huge **assignment**.	*opdracht*
The **clerk** apologised for our wait and offered us a free drink.	*bediende*
University students usually **conduct** research on a specific topic.	*uitvoeren*
I'm going to **demand** a refund for this faulty laptop!	*eisen*
Some people have great **difficulty** learning a foreign language.	*moeite*
Dancing **excessively** will make you extremely tired and achy.	*buitensporig*
Hannah was **furious** with her best friend for spreading her secret.	*woedend*
Can you **identify** which of these sentences are correct and incorrect?	*vaststellen*
Brian appears **ignorant** when you first meet him, but actually he's not.	*onwetend*
The film we watched last night was really bad. You can tell it is **low budget**.	*goedkoop*
Our neighbours have to **negotiate** a price for their house with the buyers.	*onderhandelen*
Divers like to **observe** marine life and take many photos.	*observeren*
It's **obvious** you love tennis, so why don't you learn to play?	*duidelijk*
Daniel had to get **permission** from his parents to go on the trip.	*toestemming*
Dogs **require** a lot of time and attention.	*vereisen*
I found the customer services representative **rude** and unhelpful.	*onbeschoft*
This evening there is a **set** menu, so you don't have much choice.	*vastgesteld*
There is so much in life we **take for granted**.	*vanzelfsprekend vinden*
Kirsty has quite a **temper** if she doesn't get what she wants.	*humeur*

I SPEAKING & WRITING

In the **distant** future I would love to write a best-selling novel.	*ver*
There are **dozens** of student jobs in the fast food industry.	*tientallen*
I was afraid to climb to the top of the tower due to my **fear of heights**.	*hoogtevrees*
Wouldn't it be amazing if we could find a **remedy** for cancer?	*geneesmiddel*
Michael has to **replace** the screen on his phone after he dropped it.	*vervangen*
This exam needs me to **store** too much information!	*opslaan*

PROVERBS & SAYINGS

Be in two minds (about something).	*Op twee gedachten hinken.*
Great minds think alike.	*Slimmeriken denken hetzelfde.*
In one's mind's eye.	*Tot de verbeelding spreken.*
My mind is playing tricks on me.	*Mijn gedachten brengen me in verwarring.*
To have a mind like a steel trap.	*Helder van geest zijn.*

Grammar overview

Summary of the tenses (*samenvatting werkwoordstijden*)

present simple	feiten, gewoonten	He always **walks** to football practice.
	toekomst: tijdschema's	The new *Spider-Man* film **starts** at eight.
present continuous	nu aan de gang	It **is raining** heavily right now.
	toekomst: afspraken met vaststaande tijd/plaats	They **are cooking** dinner tomorrow.
past simple	gebeurd en afgelopen vaak staat in zin wanneer het gebeurde	The weather **was** terrible yesterday.
past continuous	in het verleden een tijdje aan de gang	I **was watching** TV series all night.
to be going to	toekomstplannen	We **are going to** paint tomorrow.
	voorspelling MET bewijs	Look, it**'s going to** clear up soon.
will	aanbieding, belofte, aankondiging, besluit	I **will come** to your party. I promise.
	voorspelling ZONDER bewijs	Alisha **will** win the competition.
present perfect	in verleden begonnen, nu nog bezig	Farah **has known** him for five years.
	in verleden gebeurd, nu resultaat	I'm tired; I **haven't slept** well.
	ervaringen	We **have seen** this film three times already.
	verklikwoorden	*ever, never, already, yet, before, recently, lately*
past perfect	iets is eerder gebeurd dan iets anders	When we entered the cinema, the film **had** already **started**.
	indirecte rede	Alexis said that she **had**n't **read** the book.
	verklikwoorden:	*after, before, when, as soon as*

'If' sentences

feiten	*if + present simple*	*present simple*
	If you press this switch,	the light goes on.
bijna zeker dat iets gaat gebeuren	*if + present simple*	*will + het hele werkwoord*
	If it doesn't rain,	we will go to the park.
bijna zeker dat iets niet gaat gebeuren	*if + past simple*	*would + het hele werkwoord*
	If I had more money,	I would buy a computer.

TABLE OF CONTENTS

ERK

Reading/listening: A2 B1
Speaking/writing: A2 B1

5 English around the world

A
LISTENING

Quiz An English quiz

1 Where do more than 90% of people speak English as a first language?
A Barbados
B Canada
C India

2 '*High school*' is an American term that originated in the USA.
A true
B false

3 To who or what does an Australian refer when he uses the expression 'ankle biter'?
A a dangerous spider
B a small child

4 What do you get when you order a '*beaver tail*' in Canada?
A fried pastry in the shape of a beaver's tail.
B a real beaver's tail, because it is a delicacy in Canada

originated in	*komt oorspronkelijk uit ...*

B
THEME WORDS

THEME WORDS

to communicate
customs
inhabitant
native language
society
explorer
to influence
roots
to trade
ancestor
bilingual
constitution
cosmopolitan
gibberish
melting pot
to reign

C
READING

JAMAICA'S THREE LANGUAGES

1 'Bredrin, wa gwaan?' 'Bwai, ya done know seh mi deya gwaan easy.' This is a typical start of a conversation between two Jamaicans meeting each other. What are they actually saying? It's pretty simple, really: 'What 's up, man?' 'I'm here just taking it easy.'

2 As this example demonstrates, Jamaicans have a language all their own, a language partially based on, but very different from English. Although English is the official language of Jamaica and has been spoken nationally for more than 300 years, most Jamaicans speak Jamaican Patois. They speak Jamaican Patois mostly in casual situations and use Jamaican English (which sounds a lot like 'regular' English) for work. Jamaican Patois is seen as a totally different language amongst Jamaicans.

3 A British colony
Jamaica was a British colony from the 1650s (when the English captured it from Spain) until 1962, when it became independent. Since then English has been the most dominant language on the island. Jamaican Patois developed when slaves from West Africa were exposed to the forms of English their masters spoke. Jamaican Patois is, for the most part, a mixture of English and West African languages, but it also has many borrowed words from Portuguese and Spanish.

4 Rastafari
The two major languages, Jamaican Patois and Jamaican English, are not the only languages in Jamaica. They actually speak three languages in this country: there also exists a 'created English dialect' called Lyaric.

It is spoken by members of the Rastafari movement who consider English a language imposed upon them by the British colonizers. That's why they created a new dialect.

5 Common 'Rasta' words
Lyaric, the language of the Rastafarians has enriched everyday speech in Jamaica.

- Irie: means everything is 'alright'.
- Jammin: to be having a good time, or to play music with friends.
- Gweh: 'Go away.'

6 Bob Marley and reggae music
In the last forty years Rastafari has been linked to reggae music, especially following the worldwide success of Bob Marley. He spoke out against the inequality experienced by the black community and the negativity they were facing. Marley also helped spread awareness of the Rastafari movement and he also included many words from the Lyaric dialect in his lyrics.

7 Nowadays of course, Jamaica is still the best place to enjoy reggae music, but it is also a very unique place when it comes to language.

Adapted from: reallifeglobal.com

borrowed words	*leenwoorden*
imposed upon them	*die ze opgelegd kregen*

STONE

12 Talking about facts and convictions

It's a well-known fact	that	ice hockey is the most popular sport in Canada.
We all know		English is the official language in Jamaica.
Everyone knows		pub quizzes are a typically British tradition.

Anyone will tell you	fish and chips is	a common take-away food	in the UK.
Most people know	Indian curry is	a much-loved dish	over here.

I'm certain	that	they speak three languages in this country.
We're quite sure		India has the world's largest film industry.
He's absolutely positive		in most of Canada it's freezing cold in winter.

You can be sure that	sweet sixteen parties are	an important American tradition.
It's safe to say that	going to the prom is	a special occasion for lots of teens.

I'm convinced	English still is the most influential language	in this country.
I believe	cricket is more popular than football	in large parts of the world.

It is a custom	in the United States	to leave the tip on the table when you're done.
It's quite common	in this country	to bring a small gift when you're invited for dinner.

Jamaica	is definitely	the best place to enjoy reggae music.
This Caribbean island	is known as	a diverse country with interesting cultures.
	is certainly	

GRAMMAR

E GRAMMAR

12 Comparatives and superlatives (trappen van vergelijking) >> GS 17, page 149

Brady is smart. Chloe is smart**er**. But I am the smart**est** of them all!	Om dingen of mensen te beschrijven, gebruik je bijvoeglijke naamwoorden. Je kunt er vergelijkingen mee maken door ze in de vergrotende en overtreffende trap te zetten. Bij de vergrotende trap voeg je -**er** toe. Bij de overtreffende trap voeg je -**est** toe.
larg**e** – large**r** – large**st** nic**e** – nice**r** – nice**st** bi**g** – big**ger** – big**gest** ho**t** – hot**ter** – hot**test** happ**y** – happ**ier** – happ**iest** eas**y** – eas**ier** – eas**iest**	**Let op!** De spelling verandert wanneer het bijvoeglijk naamwoord: • eindigt op een -e. Dan voeg je alleen -r of -st toe. • eindigt op één klinker + één medeklinker. Dan verdubbelt de medeklinker. • eindigt op een medeklinker + y. Dan voeg je -ier of -iest toe.
Cricket is **popular** in the UK. Cricket is **more** popular than football. Cricket is the **most** popular sport in this country.	Bij bijvoeglijke naamwoorden van **drie lettergrepen en langer** gebruik je in de vergrotende trap **more** en in de overtreffende trap **most**. Dit geldt ook voor een aantal bijvoeglijke naamwoorden van twee lettergrepen, zoals *famous* en *boring*.
good/well – better – best bad/ill – worse – worst little – less – least much/many – more – most	Sommige bijvoeglijke naamwoorden hebben een onregelmatige vorm.

F WATCHING

English connection

Amsterdam is a big, multicultural city. People from dozens of cultures from all over the world visit it, and they are brought together by one language: English. Rebecca works there as a tour guide, and makes her living telling people about Dutch culture and history.

G LISTENING

Misunderstandings

H READING

IRISH AROUND THE WORLD

Ireland is famous for its music, folk dance, rugged coast and green hills and many other things. But did you know it is also a country of emigrants? And that, because of this, Irish culture was able to spread throughout the world?

The population of Ireland is about 6.4 million, but it is estimated that 50 to 80 million people around the world have Irish forebears. People of Irish descent are found mainly in English-speaking countries, especially Great Britain, the United States, Canada and Australia. The United States has the most people of Irish descent, while in Australia those of Irish descent are a higher percentage of the population than in any other country.

Irish influence abroad

The Irish brought some of their customs with them to these countries, and especially in the United States they have made their presence felt. Probably the most significant and well-known Irish custom that has been brought to American culture is St Patrick's Day, the festival of the patron saint of Ireland. St Patrick's Day is a holiday that celebrates all things Irish and it is an important part of Irish culture. Though St Patrick was an important figure in Irish history, the customs involving parades and large celebrations were created in the United States. On this day many people choose to wear green-coloured clothing and items as a tribute to Ireland. In many American cities they even dye their rivers green!

Irish folk music

Ireland also has a rich musical history. Irish Folk music played a seminal role in the development of America's folk and country music. Elements of traditional Irish ballads introduced during the 17th and 18th centuries can be found in many American folk songs. Today, Irish music is extremely popular, not only among Irish Americans, but among many Americans in general. Many learn to play such instruments as the pipes, flute, fiddle or harp.

Irish cuisine

It's impossible to talk about Irish food without mentioning the potato. The Irish introduced their potato-based dishes to the countries they emigrated to. Many Irish Americans still cook some of the dishes that make up the distinctive Irish cuisine. There is also a good market for the many shops in America that sell such Irish favourites as rashers (bacon), bangers (sausages), and black and white pudding. Sometimes typically Irish dishes are served on holidays. Boxty bread (a potato bread marked with a cross) and colcannon (a mixture of cabbage and mashed potatoes with a lucky coin placed inside) are still eaten by some on Halloween, for instance.

Irish symbols

Wearing the colour green is said to bring good luck, especially when worn on St Patrick's Day. Other Irish symbols associated with St Patricks' Day are pots of gold, harps and clovers.

Returning to Ireland

Nowadays, Ireland still is a country with a lot of emigrants. Many young Irish people emigrate to other, often English-speaking, countries. Most of the time they do it to further their careers or because education is better elsewhere. However, not as many young people leave the country as in the past, because Ireland's economy has changed for the better. Ireland used to be a poor country, but luckily times have changed and this has influenced the number of emigrants. Although the number is still considerable, it is lower than in the past. Hoping to bring down the number even further, the Irish government also has a special programme that encourages Irish emigrants to come back to their beloved 'Emerald Isle'.

Adapted from: everyculture.com

patron saint	*beschermheilige*
clovers	*klavertjes*
pipes	*doedelzak*
fiddle	*viool*

STONES

13 Making comparisons

Ireland / This country / It — used to be / was once — known for its textile industry, / famous for its storytellers, / a poor country, — but it no longer is. / but times have changed.

Canada / Scotland — has more — coastline / lakes — than — most other countries. / you might think.

Compared to / In comparison with — Australia, / our country, — Ireland has a lot of people working abroad. / India has many different religions.

England / Our country — has become — a more multicultural society / more densely populated — than it was in the past. / over the last few decades.

14 Asking for and giving clarification

What — do you mean by — 'cheers'? / that expression?

What — is Saint Patrick's Day?

I haven't got — the slightest idea. / a clue.

Saint Patrick's Day / It — is a holiday that celebrates all things Irish. / is an important part of Irish culture.

'Cheers' / It — is — a common expression that means 'thank you' or 'goodbye.' / used very frequently in the UK.

I'm sorry, but I don't — understand what you're talking about. / know the first thing about — this subject. / British history.

GRAMMAR

J GRAMMAR

13 Complex and compound sentences (*samengestelde en complexe zinnen*)
>> GS 14, page 147

Lawrence looks great in his new coat.	**Enkelvoudige zin**: **één onderwerp** en één persoonsvorm.
I've got a job, **so** I can buy my own clothes. Ireland was a poor country, **but** it no longer is. You can go to the park **or** you can go to the beach.	**Samengestelde zin**: twee enkelvoudige zinnen verbonden met een van de volgende **voegwoorden:** *and, but, for, nor, or, so, yet*.
They left **because** they had to catch the bus. Amy likes football, **although** she's not good at it. **After** I've finished my work, I will help you.	**Complexe zin**: een hoofdzin met een of meer bijzinnen. Je gebruikt hiervoor **andere** voegwoorden, bijvoorbeeld *because, since, after, although* of *when*.

14 Relative clauses (*betrekkelijke bijzinnen*) >> GS 15, page 148

The men **who** put out the fire are heroes. I want the dress **which** the girl over there is wearing. This is the dog **that** followed me home.	Als je extra informatie over iets of iemand wilt geven, gebruik je een bijzin met een betrekkelijk voornaamwoord (**who** bij personen; **which** bij dingen; **that** bij personen, dieren, dingen).
Cedric, **who** is my best friend, is older than I am. This watch, **which** is new, works under water. That girl, **who** has blond hair, is my sister.	Als je de bijzin kunt weglaten zonder dat de betekenis van de zin verandert, gebruik je *who* of *which*. Zo'n bijzin staat altijd tussen komma's.
This is the guy (who) I met on holiday. The charity (that) I run raised a thousand pounds.	Is de bijzin nodig om te begrijpen over wie/wat de zin gaat, dan kun je *who, which, that* vaak weglaten.

K WATCHING

The Orient Express!

Travel across Europe in style on the Orient Express, an old-fashioned train that runs between London and Venice. With luxurious restaurants, bars and fancy decor, the Orient Express is the best way to experience the luxury of travelling by train.

Task

>> TASKCARD

My videolog
Je gaat een vlog opnemen voor een uitwisseling.

Taalportfolio
A2 Ik kan in eenvoudige beschrijvende taal vergelijkingen maken tussen en korte uitspraken doen over dingen en bezittingen.
A2 Ik kan alledaagse aspecten beschrijven van mijn omgeving.

ERK

Back | Forward | Stop | Refresh | Home | Search | Favorites | History | Mail | Print

Home | Profile | Account

My videolog

'Hi Stacy, this is a vlog I made for our exchange project. I'm looking forward to having you over from Canada next month.
Just to give you an idea of what our country is like I recorded this video. I'll show you some things that are typically Dutch. I live in Alkmaar which is famous for its cheese and cheese markets. There are also quite a lot of mills where I live, but there used to be many more! Nowadays there are many more modern windmills (wind turbines) than traditional wind mills, unfortunately...
I play football at the local club. You probably already knew that this sport is really popular in the Netherlands. I guess Canadian kids don't play as much football as Dutch kids. Ice hockey is probably more your thing. Maybe you can tell me something about that.
If you got the idea that the Dutch are really down-to-earth people, well that's not true! Just have a look at me in my orange outfit supporting the Dutch team during a match they played against England...'

Vocabulary

A LISTENING

The **beaver** formed a dam which caused the trail to flood.	*bever*
My two sisters always yell when they **disagree**.	*het niet eens zijn*
You will know if your **exhaust pipe** is broken because it makes a lot of noise.	*uitlaatpijp*
I can tell by the **expression** on your face that you like him a lot.	*uitdrukking*
The artist was **formerly** known as a different name than he is now.	*vroeger*
My mum loves **fried** food, but she says it makes the house smell bad.	*gefrituurd*
Fumes from gasoline are very bad for your health.	*dampen*
Let's **go over** our homework together, so we can help each other.	*doornemen*
They need to **hurry** to catch the train; it's almost nine!	*zich haasten*
Martin Luther King was one of the most **influential** men of our time.	*invloedrijk*
Once you taste this banana bread you will **instantly** love it!	*meteen*
Kathleen **intensely** stared at the kettle, wishing for the water to boil.	*intensief*
Bob has got an appointment next week to have a **molar** removed at the dentist.	*kies*
I always take the **motorway** to get home since it is the fastest route.	*snelweg*
The football stadium was far too **noisy** with all the supporters cheering loudly.	*luidruchtig*
Car pools aim to **reduce** the amount of cars on the road and pollution levels.	*verminderen*
Someday that woman is going to **rule** a country. You'll see!	*regeren*
I can't **stress** how important it is to make sure your pin codes are kept secret.	*benadrukken*
Gran thinks **togetherness** in the family is the best thing ever.	*saamhorigheid*
Wow, that was a **tough** interview. I hope I made a good impression.	*moeilijk*
The restaurant chain hasn't been doing so well and its future is **uncertain**.	*onzeker*
I heard you passed your driving test yesterday. **Well done**!	*goed gedaan*

B THEME WORDS

He discovered that his distant **ancestor** was of royal blood.	*voorvader*
My brother lives abroad, so we mostly **communicate** by email.	*communiceren*
The American **constitution** is taken extremely seriously by all citizens.	*grondwet*
Meg has been travelling the world. She's a real **cosmopolitan**.	*wereldburger*
It's important to get to the airport on time because it can be busy at **customs**.	*douane*
From a young age, Ulrika always wanted to become an **explorer**.	*ontdekkingsreiziger*
Amy, please stop talking **gibberish**! I haven't got a clue what you're saying.	*wartaal*
You can **influence** the outcome of the talent show by texting your vote.	*invloed uitoefenen op*
Every **inhabitant** in England will have a National Insurance Number.	*inwoner*
London is considered a **melting pot** due to the many nationalities and cultures.	*smeltkroes*
Though her **native language** is Spanish, she speaks fluent Dutch.	*moedertaal*
When the old King dies, his daughter will **reign** the country.	*regeren*
Even though I live in Australia, my **roots** will always be in England.	*wortels*
The increasing amount of immigrants will have an impact on British **society**.	*maatschappij*
As members of European Union, countries are able to **trade** much easier.	*handelen*

C READING

The police were able to **capture** the thieves and return the goods to the shop.	*gevangennemen*
Our work's dinner was a **casual** affair, nobody had to dress up for it.	*informeel*
Some people **demonstrate** their views on political issues in organised marches.	*laten zien*
Adding some fresh ingredients can really **enrich** your meal.	*verrijken*
You shouldn't **expose** newborn babies **to** strong sunlight.	*blootstellen aan*
The band will have to **face** a lot of angry fans now that they cancelled their tour.	*te maken krijgen met*
Angela is against **inequality** in pay between men and women.	*ongelijkheid*
Susan played a **major** role in our project. We couldn't have done it without her!	*belangrijk*
Jim is **partially** blind in both of his eyes. He has a guide dog to help him.	*gedeeltelijk*
I don't want to **speak out against** my friends, but I think they are wrong.	*uitspreken tegen*
Children usually start to develop **speech** when they are two years old.	*spraak*

D SPEAKING & WRITING

Karen loves dancing and wants to **be known as** a good performer.	*bekend staan als*
It is quite **common** in the Netherlands not to have to wear a uniform at school.	*gewoon*
Robert didn't get the job due to his **conviction** from a few years ago.	*veroordeling*
I am **definitely** going to join a sports club this year; I just don't know what yet.	*zeker*
Mara has been outside in the snow all day and now she is **freezing cold**!	*ijskoud*
Sean is **positive** he put his car keys in his coat pocket, but now they're gone.	*zeker*
The first-year students are always nervous about their very first **prom**.	*gala (AmE)*
If you are really sick, you should **remain** at home until you feel better.	*blijven*
Luke loves **take-away food** because it means he doesn't have to cook.	*afhaalmaaltijden*

G LISTENING

Hank asked me to open the **bonnet** so that he could observe the damage.	*motorkap*
Pop the backpacks in the **boot**, please. We will have more room that way.	*kofferbak*
The **coastguard** watch the sea for ships that are in danger.	*kustwacht*
Look at all this **crap** everywhere! When was the last time you tidied up?	*rotzooi*
The survival course will **cripple** you, it's so exhausting!	*verlammen*
Testing make-up on animals is **cruel** and should be forbidden.	*wreed*
Some English words **derive from** German, for example 'hamster'.	*zijn afgeleid van*
The owner wanted to **display** the new collection in the shop window..	*weergeven*
Stan has been offered the job as a **fire fighter** and will start training soon.	*brandweerman*
Sonia is a strong swimmer and visits the local pool **frequently**.	*vaak*
A compass can be helpful if you go on a hike, in case you **get lost**.	*verdwalen*
Without **hesitation** the eagle swooped down and grabbed its prey.	*aarzeling*
If you should come across a **life-threatening** emergency, dial 999.	*levensbedreigend*
I think there has been a **misunderstanding**. I am not Mrs Harris!	*misverstand*
The principal placed his new schedule on the school's **notice board**.	*mededelingenbord*
Getting your ears pierced doesn't hurt at all. It's really hardly **noticeable**.	*merkbaar*
Your English **pronunciation** is getting better by the day! Keep practising!	*uitspraak*
I'm afraid there is a **slight** problem with your order. We are out of ice cream.	*klein*
The old lady dropped her shopping bag and her oranges got **squashed**.	*geplet*
The **trainee** chef did an excellent job on his first evening.	*leerling*

H READING

I'm not sure if I want **to be associated with** him anymore.	*verbonden zijn aan*
The park near our school is a **beloved** area for students and visitors alike.	*geliefd*
I'm one of the few people who actually like **cabbage** for dinner.	*kool*
I recently found out that my best friend Sophie is from Irish **descent**.	*afkomst*
Scientists at the university are monitoring the creature's **development**.	*ontwikkeling*
Mum claims she doesn't **dye** her hair, but I know she really does.	*kleuren, verven*
Many British people **emigrate** to mainland Europe for work or family reasons.	*emigreren*
As your teacher I would like to **encourage** you to participate in discussions.	*aanmoedigen*
Derek is interested in films **in general**, not a particular genre.	*in het algemeen*
She works **mainly** in the legal field, with an occasional job in education.	*voornamelijk*
It's a good idea to **mark** the most important pages of the book.	*markeren*
School dinner ladies always make delicious **mashed potatoes**.	*aardappelpuree*
Ben didn't seem to notice my **presence**. He was very distracted.	*aanwezigheid*
A **significant** number of customers complained about the product.	*aanzienlijk*

I SPEAKING & WRITING

Karen! **Cheers** for all the help you have given me today! I appreciate it.	*bedankt*
Hey Kathryn, it was great fun today. See you later, **cheers**!	*doeg, tot ziens*
The Netherlands is a very **densely populated** country.	*dichtbevolkt*
You got a fantastic score **in comparison with** the rest of the class.	*in vergelijking met*
The **textile industry** used to be booming business in England.	*textielindustrie*

PROVERBS & SAYINGS

A tree with strong roots laughs at storms. (Malaysia)	*In weer en wind positief blijven.*
All the things that are white are not milk. (India)	*Het is niet al goud wat er blinkt.*
The wise build bridges and the foolish build dams. (Nigeria)	*De wijzen zijn bruggenbouwers, de dommen zonderen zich af.*
What the goat does, the kid follows. (Jamaica)	*De jongeren leren van de ouderen.*
You can't catch skunks with mice. (Canada)	*Je moet vuur met vuur bestrijden.*

Grammar overview

Comparatives and superlatives (*trappen van vergelijking*)

	vergrotende trap	**overtreffende trap**
smart	smart**er**	smart**est**
larg**e**	larg**er**	larg**est**
big	big**ger**	big**gest**
happ**y**	happ**ier**	happ**iest**
beautiful	**more** beautiful	**most** beautiful

good/well	better	best
bad/ill	worse	worst
little	less	least
much/many	more	most

Complex and compound sentences (*samengestelde en complexe zinnen*)

enkelvoudige zin:	één **onderwerp** en één persoonsvorm
	Lawrence looks great in his new coat.
samengestelde zin:	twee enkelvoudige zinnen verbonden met *and*, *but*, *for*, *nor*, *or*, *so* of *yet*
	I heard the children playing, **but** I didn't see them.
complexe zin:	enkelvoudige zin met een of meer bijzinnen, verbonden met *because*, *since*, *after*, *although* of *when*
	After I've finished my work, I will help you.

Relative clauses (*samengestelde zinnen met voornaamwoorden*)

who	personen	The men **who** put out the fire are heroes.
which	dingen	I want the dress **which** the girl over there is wearing.
that	personen, dieren, dingen	This is the dog **that** followed me home.
noodzakelijke informatie	This is the guy (**who**) I met on holiday.	
extra informatie	This watch, **which** is new, works under water.	

Herhaling & Verrijking

Theme 4 Can you believe it?

	Activity Book ex.
Herhaling	
Vocabulary	
Vocabulaire	*1, 2*
Grammar	
10 Summary of the tenses (*samenvatting werkwoordstijden*)	*3*
11 'If' sentences	*4*
Stones	
10 Finding out how things work	*5*
11 Making predictions	*6*
Verrijking	
The power of the placebo	*1, 2*

Theme 5 English around the world

	Activity Book ex.
Herhaling	
Vocabulary	
Vocabulaire	*7, 8*
Grammar	
12 Comparatives and superlatives (*trappen van vergelijking*)	*9*
13 Complex and compound sentences (*samengestelde en complexe zinnen*)	*10*
14 Relative clauses (*betrekkelijke bijzinnen*)	*11*
Stones	
12 Talking about facts and convictions	*12*
13 Making comparisons	*13*
14 Asking for and giving clarification	*14*
Verrijking	leren
Life in Singapore	*3, 4*

THE POWER OF THE PLACEBO

Before new medicines are put on the market, clinical trials are organised to see whether these new drugs are effective by comparing them with substances that have no medical ingredients, so-called placebos. Research shows that over the last 25 years the difference between real drugs and these fake ones has become less clear.

There are many tests that show placebos are often just as effective as the real drug. In a recent experiment at Harvard Medical School, migraine sufferers were given either the drug Maxalt or a placebo. The participants received their drugs in envelopes with one of three labels: 'Maxalt', 'Placebo' or 'Maxalt or placebo'. 'When we gave them the placebo and the envelope said Maxalt, it had a positive effect on their migraine,' said a researcher. 'When we gave them Maxalt and told them it was a placebo, the effect was no different, meaning that by just changing the word on the envelopes we could make the placebo as effective as the medication.'

The phenomenon of patients feeling better simply because they believe a treatment will help them is known as the *placebo effect*. Scans of patients taking a placebo show that their brains switch on areas related to controlling stress and pain.

When new drugs are tested in the USA, the Food and Drug Administration (FDA) demands that the placebo effect is taken into account. Researchers do this by conducting trials in which some participants take the drug and some take a placebo – participants don't know which they are taking. Before a new drug can be put on the market, the FDA demands that it is shown to be significantly more effective than the placebo. It seems, though, that the placebo response has become stronger over the past few years. This trend is a huge concern for the pharmaceutical industry because despite millions spent on drug research and development, medicines aren't being approved.

Different explanations have been suggested for this rise in the placebo effect, like the friendly approach of the research staff for example: putting an arm around a patient, or even just shaking hands, could make someone feel better and this might influence the effect of the placebo.

However, so far there is no clear explanation for the rise of the placebo effect. Whatever the reason, it's clear that more research is needed.

Adapted from.bbc.com

LIFE IN SINGAPORE

VERRIJKING THEME 5

Singapore is an intriguing blend of western modernity and Asian culture. Within a total area of roughly 700 square kilometres, you'll find gleaming skyscrapers, Chinese shops, Malay mosques, Hindu temples, and endless chains of air-conditioned shopping malls. Singapore has a population of around 4.7 million, of which 1 million people are in Singapore on long- or short-term passes; they are often referred to as 'foreign talent' or expats. Two of these expats are Jonathan's parents, who moved from Australia to Singapore when he was only one year old.

Language

Singapore was a British colony for a long time; it gained independence in 1963. That's why nowadays most people still speak English, but Singapore has four official languages; English, Mandarin, Malay, and Tamil. For example, government signs are posted in all four languages. However, on the streets you'll soon be exposed to a constant stream of Singapore's unique brand of English: Singlish. Jonathan: 'Singlish came to me easily, probably because I was so young when I came here; I can switch it on and off very easily – I do that without even thinking about it. At school all my classmates know how to speak English properly.'

Strict

Singapore is known for its cleanliness and low crime rate. The country has such a strong reputation for being safe that the authorities had to put out a warning statement that 'low crime does not mean no crime'. But as with most good things, the high regard the country gets for its cleanliness and safety comes with a price. Singapore is sometimes called 'The Fine City', but the title has a double meaning that you don't want to be on the wrong end of.

The label refers to the immaculate, or fine, state that Singapore is but also to the many different fines that the country imposes.

Jonathan: 'People always look at me in amazement when I tell them that chewing gum is banned in Singapore. Most of the time they don't believe me when I tell them that importation of chewing gum into the country, even if it is not for trading, is illegal.' Improper disposal of gum, for example dropping it on the street, and carrying large quantities of it with you could cost you up to $1000.

If you drop other small items of rubbish onto the streets, like cigarette butts or candy wrappers, you will be fined $300 – that is, if you are a first offender. However, those who throw bigger items like drink cans or bottles have to appear before the court. The punishment usually involves a Corrective Work Order (CWO), where the offenders clean up a specified area while wearing a bright luminous green vest.

Leisure time

Jonathan: 'There's a lot on in Singapore. Universal Studios is pretty awesome (as long as it's not too busy), and so is the Luge and Adventure Cove Waterpark, but it's rather expensive so you don't really want to do that every single weekend. This is where the list of things for teenagers to do in Singapore on the internet always comes in handy.'

Because of the low crime rate, it is also safe to go out at night. You would have to be very unlucky to have something happen to you. This means you can safely get the bus or train home late at night, without really worrying about anything. Also public transport gets you basically anywhere, which is very convenient.

Social life

Jonathan: 'Because there are so many expats in Singapore many of my friends are from different countries. This also has a downside: you make a good friend, then the next thing you know the parents get another job back home or in another country. However, with social media it's pretty easy to keep in contact with everybody. Plus, there are new people arriving in Singapore all the time, so there's no shortage of potential friends to choose from.'

Weather

The weather here can get quite intense. It's either hot and humid, or raining cats and dogs. Because the weather can change in a second, it's not a good idea to plan anything weather-related a week in advance. Your plans could be ruined in a matter of minutes. Jonathan: 'Most people adjust well to the heat after some time. Can you believe that a lot of people even wear cardigans and jumpers? It's for inside buildings, because the air-conditioning is on everywhere you go and it's often freezing compared to the heat outside.'

Transport

A huge positive to Singapore is its small size. You can get anywhere in the country in a relatively short time (depending on traffic), and there is cheap public transport everywhere. It costs a maximum $2.80 to get from one side of the country to the other.

Adapted from: expatliving.sg / goabroad.com

immaculate	*brandschoon*
fine	*boete*

TABLE OF CONTENTS

Reading Matters

1 POEM

My big fat cousin's wedding

My favorite cousin named Marge
is almost as big as a barge.
So one would assume,
not knowing the groom,
the guy would most likely be large.

But he was a small man named Tim
'As thin as a broom' describes him.
While Marge would guffaw,
Tim would watch her with awe
and just smile for he was so prim!

When the preacher addressed him and said,
'You may now kiss the bride,' Tim turned red,
for their lips could not meet.
With high heels on her feet,
Marge stood towering over his head.

She leaned down while Tim stood on his toes,
but for being in such a strange pose,
Marge then came toppling down
crushing Tim neath her gown
while the whole church erupted in 'Ohhhhh's.'

All was well, and thereafter, we ate;
then we planned next to dance until late.
But none could foresee
the small tragedy
that had us all leaving by eight!

Marge had tossed off her heels for a glide
on the dance floor, but when they both tried
to dance, Tim got snagged
by that dang gown and dragged
as his bride was beginning to slide...

Now shoeless, poor Marge could not stop.
Toward a table with candles on top,
they slid, and the groom
then set fire to the room
by landing with a belly flop.

Poor Tim by the candles got lit,
and we were all having a fit,
for the fire got spread fast
till the Best Man at last
got us all wet extinguishing it!

Andrea Dietrich

barge	*schuit*
guffaw	*luidkeels lachen*
awe	*ontzag*
extinguishing	*blussen*

2 POEM

I often contradict myself

I often contradict myself.
Oh no, I never do.
I argue with me day and night.
That simply isn't true.

Oh yes it is. Oh no it's not.
I do this all day long.
Oh no I don't. Oh yes I do.
That's right. No way! It's wrong.

I'm really quite agreeable.
I argue night and day.
I love to be around myself.
I wish I'd go away.

So if you see me arguing,
it's certain that you won't.
I like to contradict myself.
I promise you I don't.

Kenn Nesbitt

Bottled up

Charlie closed his locker and held his head low as he hurried to biology class. It was last period. If he could make it through that door, he just might survive another day of high school.
Hefton appeared out of nowhere with his two big buddies at his sides. 'Hey, Charlie, where have you been all day? I've been looking for you.'
Charlie tried to sidestep them.
Hefton stretched out his long quarterback arm, hooked Charlie's neck, and slammed him against his beefy chest. 'I've been wanting to give you something.' He jabbed Charlie in the gut.
Charlie gasped.
'Ain't you got anything to say to me?' He chuckled and looked back at his two stooges, goading them to laugh along.
Charlie struggled to catch his breath. Then he saw her – across the hallway, through the door, sitting at her desk: the new girl in school. Her eyes full of concern – or maybe it was pity.

***

That night, as Charlie drifted off to sleep, he thought about the new girl, and how he didn't even know her name, and how it wouldn't really matter unless he could learn to stand up to Hefton.
His dreams were stranger than usual tonight – especially the one where he was walking along a deserted beach and found a bottle with a cork in it. He ran to pick it up. It might contain a love note to him from some beautiful mystery girl. Charlie held the bottle up to the sun. No note, but something was moving inside– a small crab, he thought. No – it was a tiny man, dressed in a Texas Rangers baseball jersey and cap.
The little man was pointing to the cork above his head. 'Get me the heck out of here.'
Charlie uncorked the bottle and...nothing happened – except that the little man had disappeared.
'Looking for me?' said a booming voice at Charlie's back.
Charlie spun around.

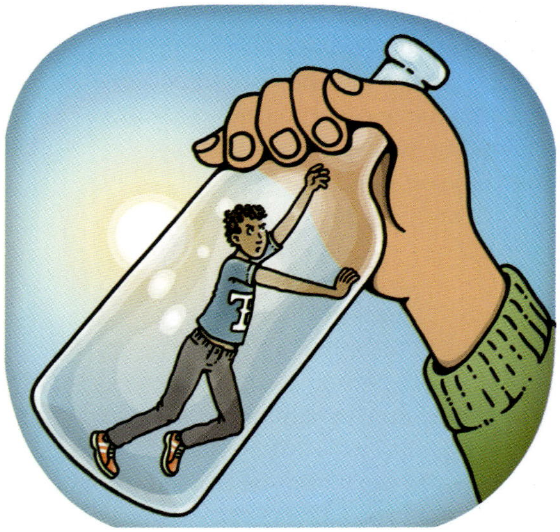

The baseball player was seven feet tall.
Charlie stumbled backward and fell in the sand.
'You're so tall. You must be a pitcher.'
'Oh, you mean this?' he said, pointing to his jersey. 'No, I'm just a fan. They don't let genies try out for the team – believe me, I tried.'
'You're a *genie?*'
'Sure. Who else lives in bottles but genies? That's our thing.'
'What about granting wishes? That's your thing too.'
'Sure, sure. So what do you got?'
'Huh?'
'What's your wish, kemosabe? What's your pleasure? How can I make your day?'
'I get three wishes, right?'
'Three?!' He stepped back and put his hands on his hips. 'Kinda greedy, aren't we?'
'Well, I thought that was how it worked.'
'Not with me, Buddy. That's too much work.'
'But don't you guys have to follow some kind of genie rules?'
The genie looked around, making sure they were still alone, and then leaned in to Charlie. 'I've gone rogue.'
'That's not fair. For the first time in my life I've found my own genie, and –'
' – listen to me, Boy. You'll take your one wish and be happy with it or I'll just turn you into

dust and go back into my bottle.'
'You could do that – turn me into dust?'
The genie laughed. 'No, of course not.' His face turned serious. 'Unless I really wanted to.'
'Well, if I can't have the traditional three wishes, how about a two-part wish?'
'I knew you were gonna be trouble.'
'Aw, come on, genie.'
'Let's hear it.'

***

'Wake up, Charlie, you're going to be late for school.' Charlie's mom banged on the door until he began to stir. He had forgotten all about his dreams.
Running into the school, he headed straight for his locker. The hallway was nearly empty. Hefton came around the corner. There was no escape.
'What are you doing out here, Loser? Don't you know it's time for class?' He punched Charlie in the stomach hard enough to take his breath away.
Charlie heard a voice. 'Hit him.' He looked around. Where was it coming from?
'Hit him hard – now,' said the voice. Charlie recognized it: the genie. 'Punch him in the face. Do it!'
Before Charlie could stop himself, his fist flew at Hefton's face.
His mind could not fully process what was happening. In slow motion, he saw his fist crush Hefton's chin, causing the bully's head to twist violently to the side.
Hefton quickly regained his composure. 'You think you can hurt me, you little sissy?'
Charlie knew he was a dead man.
'Go for the groin,' said the genie.
Charlie felt his foot go airborne – a Tomahawk missile racing <u>inexorably</u> to its target.
'Bull's eye,' said the genie, laughing.
Hefton bent over, grabbing his crotch, clearly in excruciating pain.
'Knock him down. Kick his stomach. Laugh at him.'
Charlie followed every command to the letter.
'What are you doing?!'
He turned. It was the new girl, running toward him.
'Kick him in the head, Charlie,' said the genie. 'Kill him!'
'Please, stop,' said the girl, sprinting directly at Charlie.
He felt his leg move backward.
The genie screamed in excitement. 'This kick will send ol' Hefton to the hospital, Charlie. Go for it!'
'Stop, Charlie!' said the girl.
Charlie hesitated, surprised that the girl knew his name.
'Do it, Charlie!' screamed the genie. 'Do it now! He doesn't deserve to live. Kill him!'
Charlie didn't want to listen to the genie anymore. He wanted to listen to the girl – the new girl who actually knew his name. But his body was out of his control. His leg continued to move forward. His foot would connect with Hefton's head at any moment and there was nothing he could do to stop – .
Something hit Charlie – hard, and he went flying backward. His head hit the floor.

***

'Charlie?'
His head was lying on a soft pillow. No – it was the new girl's lap! She was gently rubbing his forehead.
'I'm sorry, Charlie. I hope I didn't hurt you too bad.'
'You didn't hurt me.' He grinned. 'Why do you think you hurt me?'
'I tackled you – because you were about to kick that kid's head off. I could see it in your eyes: the rage.
And I can't say I blame you. I saw how he picked on you every day. But I couldn't let you do it.'
'I don't know what got into me.'
'We've never actually met. My name is Jeanie.'
He sat up and shook her hand. 'You're kidding me. *Jeanie?*'
'What?'
'Nothing, sorry.' Charlie stood up.
She got up. 'So, are you okay?'
'I will be...if you'll go out with me to a movie tomorrow night.' He smiled.

3 SHORT STORY

'Sorry, I've got plans.'
He frowned.
'I can't miss a Rangers game.'
'You're a Texas Rangers fan?'
'I'm a *huge* fan.'
'Crazy.'
'What? You have something against the Rangers?'
'No, not at all. But I've never been much of a sports fan.'
'Really? Come to the game with me. I'll teach you to love baseball. Maybe I'll even buy you a hot dog.'
'I do love hot dogs.'
'Great,' she said. 'Then it's a date.'
'There's no tackling in baseball, right?'
She giggled. 'I won't tackle you anymore.'
'I kinda liked it.'
Jeanie pushed him hard and he nearly fell down.
They both started laughing.

***

Charlie and Jeanie went to that Texas Rangers game, and many others. He fell in love with the game almost as quickly as he fell in love with her.
Charlie's dearest wishes came true – because of his Jeanie.

Robert Burton Robinson

stooges	*handlangers*
cork	*kurk*
kemosabe	*vriend (slang)*
I've gone rogue	*ik houd me niet meer aan de regels*
inexorably	*onverbiddelijk*

4 SHORT STORY

The case of the lower case letter

She breezed into my office one cold September morning. I'd been enjoying a hot cup of Starbuck's finest and surfing the web for local news. The famous lexical semanticist Professor Edgar Nettleston had been found dead, a gunshot wound to the head. The police verdict was suicide.

She held out an elegant hand as she floated towards me and I glimpsed a wedding band with a stone the size of a peanut M&M.

'I'm Edith Nettleston.'

'Sorry about the old man.'

'I'm not. He loved me, but he loved words more. I'll be brief. My husband was working on a paper that will rock the very foundation of lexical semantics. It's worth a fortune in lecture tours, but nobody can find it. I believe his suicide note is a clue to its whereabouts.'

She removed a scrap of paper from her blouse.

'edith. i'm not going to whine, i've had a good life. i've found wealth and happiness as a teacher, a seller of knowledge. but i find myself depressed beyond hope... and so i'm choosing the hour and manner of my own demise. i have treated you badly. i demanded you dyed your brown curls blonde. i thought i could buy you when i should have won your love. i called you a witch. i'd complain: where's the woman i married? i said you ate too much. if i wanted change, i could have used a carrot rather than a stick. you probably wanted to wring my neck. forgive me. farewell.'

'It's all written in lower case. My husband was a stickler for correct grammar. I refuse to believe it doesn't mean something.'

'Mrs. Nettleston, I think I can help you. There's a couple of odd things about this letter. Firstly, as you say, it's written entirely in lower case. Mr. Nettleston was a world-renowned lexical semanticist, not a teenager texting his BFFs.'

'Secondly, it has a more than usual number of homophones, words where there is another word with the same sound but different spelling and meaning. When dealing with a lexical semanticist, that's surely no accident.'

'If we read those homophones in order, we have: whine, seller, hour, manner. And translating to their homophones: Wine cellar our manor.'

Several hours later, we arrived at the Nettlestons' country house and immediately headed for the basement. A flip of a light switch revealed tunnels filled with rows of dark bottles.

'Where is it? It would take years to search this place.'

'Not so fast, Mrs. Nettleston. First I have to ask you something: your wedding ring diamond, how large is it?

'It's eight carats. Edgar wouldn't stop talking about it.'

'That's what I feared.' I pulled out my trusty revolver. 'How you must have hated him and his lexical semantics! You figured you'd kill him and keep the money from the paper yourself. You forced him to write that suicide note, thinking you knew where it was. But he was suspicious and he'd already hidden it. And he had another surprise for you: the rest of the note, it doesn't reveal where the paper is, it reveals his killer. The final homophones: dyed buy won witch where's ate carrot wring. That is: died by one which wears eight carat ring.'

As the cops left with Mrs. Nettleston I took a quick trip round the maze of tunnels. It didn't take me long to find it. Most of the wine lay unpacked on racks but in one corner two cases sat stacked, one on top of each other. Carefully, I opened the lower one.

Jack Delany

lexical semantist	*expert in woorden en zinnen*
lower case	*kleine letters*

Never always sometimes

Best friends Dave and Julia were determined to never be clichés, so they wrote their own Never List of everything they would never, ever do in high school.

'Hey, you goof. Sorry I'm late.'
Dave looked up just as Julia was sitting down. She was wearing her usual: shorts, a plaid blue shirt over a tank top, the pair of flip-flops she loved so much that they were now made up of more duct tape than the original rubbery material. Her light brown hair was in a loose ponytail, two perfect strands looped around her ears. If the lights ever went out in her presence, Dave was pretty sure the brightness of her eyes would be more useful than a flashlight.
'S'okay. How was hanging out with your mom this weekend?'
'Greatest thing ever. Don't get me wrong, the dads are awesome. But my mom is the coolest person alive.' (...)

'Tell me more about your mom. What makes her so cool?'
'Everything,' Julia said. She lives the kind of life that I didn't even understand was an option. She once biked from Canada to Chile. On a bicycle. For, like, months. Other adults work from nine to five and then go home to watch TV. She bikes a whole continent.'
'Huh,' Dave said impressed. 'That's pretty cool. How come she's never come by before?'
'She's too busy being awesome,' Julia said. She glanced around for a little while, swirling the drink in her hand. Dave followed her gaze to a little boy riding his tricycle down the harbor, his parents walking calmly behind, beaming with pride. 'So, high school tomorrow. Big day.' (...)

She scrunched her mouth to one side of her face, then looked straight at him, which always made Dave feel like he was either lucky or about to turn into a puddle. A lucky puddle, that's what he'd felt like ever since he'd met Julia. 'We're still gonna be us?'
'What do you mean?'
'I mean... we're kind of different from most people, right?'
'We don't do what everyone else does. We're more likely to bike a continent than watch TV all afternoon.'
'I guess so.' (...)

She kicked at the backpack by his feet. 'You have any paper in there? I have an idea.

The Nevers
or
Dave and Julia's Guide to an Original High School Experience

– Never be recognized by your lunch spot. Keep moving.

– Never run for prom king/queen, student body president, or any other position that would have its own page in the yearbook.

– Definitely never host a 'BEER' party while parent(s) is/are out of town.

– Never dye your hair a color found in a rainbow.

– Never pine silently after someone for the entirety of high school.

– Never date your best friend.

Four years later, on the last year of high school...

'Look what I just found.'
'Is it Marrony's mole from sophomore year?'
'Our Never list.'
Julia turned around to face him. A couple of football players passed between them talking about a party happening on Friday. She was quiet, studying Dave with a raised eyebrow.
'You wouldn't lie to me, would you, O'Flannery? I could never forgive you.'
'Gutierrez. My last name is Gutierrez.'
'Don't change the subject. Did you really find it?' She mentioned for him to hand the paper over, which he did, making sure their fingers would brush. The linoleum hallways were starting to empty out, people were settling into their lunch spots. 'I was actually thinking about this the other day. I even wrote my mom about it,' Julia said, reading over the list. A smile shaped her lips, which were on the thin side, though Dave couldn't imagine wishing for them to be different. 'We did a pretty good job of sticking to this.' (...)

Before Julia said anything, Dave knew what she'd been thinking about. He knew her well enough to read her silences, and there's been only one thing on her mind since he'd found the list. He smiled as she spoke.
'What if we did the list?'

Adi Alsaid

swirling	*ronddraaiend*
tricycle	*driewieler*

The adoration of Jenna Fox

Seventeen-year-old Jenna Fox has just awoken from a year-long coma – so she's been told – and she is still recovering from the terrible accident that caused it. But what happened before that? She's been given home movies showing her entire life, which brings back a few memories. But are the memories really hers? And why won't anyone in her family talk about the accident? Jenna is becoming more curious. But she is also afraid of what she might find out if she ever gets up the courage to ask her questions.

What happened to Jenna Fox? And who is she, really?

I used to be someone.
Someone named Jenna Fox.
That's what they tell me. But I am more than a name. More than they tell me. More than the facts and statistics they fill me with. More than the video clips they make me watch.
More. But I'm not sure what.
'Jenna, come sit over here. You don't want to miss this. 'The woman I am supposed to call Mother pats the cushion next to her. 'Come,' she says again.
I do.
'This is a historic moment,' she says. She puts her arm around me and squeezes. I lift the corner of my mouth. Then the other: a smile. Because I know I am supposed to. It is what she wants.
'It's a first,' she says. 'We've never had a woman president of Nigerian descent before.'
'A first,' I say. I watch the monitor. I watch Mother's face. I've only just learned how to smile. I don't know how to match her other expressions. I should.
'Mom, come sit with us,' she calls out toward the kitchen.
'It's about to start.'
I know she won't come. She doesn't like me. I don't know how I know. Her face is as plain and expressionless to me as everyone else's. It's not her face. It is something else.
'I 'm doing a few dishes. I'll watch from the monitor in here,' she calls back.
I stand. 'I can leave, Lily,' I offer.
She comes and stands in the arched doorway. She looks at Mother. They exchange an expression I try to understand. Mother's face drops into her hands. 'She is your nana, Jenna. You've always called her Nana.'
'That's all right. She can call me Lily,' she says and sits down on the other side of Mother.

...

The accident was over a year ago. I've been awake for two weeks. Over a year has vanished. I've gone from sixteen to seventeen. A second woman has been elected president. A twelfth planet has been named in the solar system. The last wild polar bear has died. Headline news that couldn't stir me. I slept through it all.
I cried on waking. That's what they tell me.
I don't remember the first day. Later I heard Lily whisper to Mother in the kitchen that my cries frightened her. 'It sounds like an animal,' she said.
I still cry on waking. I'm not sure why. I feel nothing. Nothing I can name, anyway. It's like breathing – something that happens over which I have no control. Father was here for my waking. He called it a beginning. He said it was good. I think he may have thought that anything I did was good. The first few days were difficult. My mind and body thrashed out of control. My mind settled first. They kept my arms strapped. By the second day my arms had settled, too. The house seemed busy. They checked me, probed, checked again and again, Father scanning my symptoms into the Netbook several times a day, someone relaying back treatment. But there was no treatment that I could see. Each day I improved. That was it. One day I couldn't walk. The next day I could. One day my right eyelid drooped. The next day it didn't. One day my tongue lay like a lump of meat in my mouth, the next day it was articulating words that hadn't been spoken in

over a year.
On the fifth day, when I walked out onto the veranda without stumbling, Mother cried and said, 'It's a miracle. An absolute miracle.'
'Her gait is still not natural. Can't you see that?' Lily said.
Mother didn't answer.
On the eighth day Father had to return to work in Boston. He and mother whispered, but I still heard. *Risky...have to get back...you'll be fine.* Before he left he cupped my face in both of his hands. 'Little by little, Angel,' he said. 'Be patient. Everything will come back. Over time all the connections will be made.' I think my gait is normal now. My memory is not. I don't remember my mother, father, or Lily. I don't remember that I once lived in Boston. I don't remember the accident.
I don't remember Jenna Fox.
Father says it will come in time. 'Time heals,' he says.
I don't tell him that I don't know what time is.

(...)

I open my eyes and examine my computer. I wonder what's on it. Schoolwork? Letters to friends? I feel a surge, like a jolt of energy has shot through me. History. *My history*. It should be in *my* room. I try to lift it from the table, but it is secured with a metal bracket. I work to pull it loose. One rivet pops out, but the rest stay secure. I pound at the bracket with the heel of my hand, throwing the full force of my weight behind it, but my hand slips and slices into the sharp edge. Pain rips up my hand and I fall back, but just as quickly the pain is gone. I hug my hand to my stomach, afraid to look. I know the slash is deep. If Mother had a meltdown over the tiny cut on my knee, I can't imagine what she will do when she sees this one. A trickle of blood oozes through my fingers. I will have to retrieve my computer later. I step out of the closet, lock it, and hurry to my room, trying to slip silently upstairs. I go to my bathroom and lock the door behind me.
How bad could it be? It was only a little piece of metal. I hold my hand over the sink to spare the floor, but thankfully the blood has already stopped flowing. A three-inch gash runs from the fleshy part of my thumb to my wrist. I am surprised that it no longer hurts. Will I need stitches? I pull the flesh apart to see how deep the wound goes.
It is deep.
What. How.
Oh my God.
I can't. Think.
Deep.
The stairs rock. Sway.
I clutch my gashed hand to my stomach. The other gropes at the stair rail.
Only a small smear of blood stains my shirt. So little. And it is barely red. Is it red at all?
My feet stumble on the stairs, and I fall down three at a time.
'Jenna?' A distant call from the kitchen.
More stairs. And no pain. My hand doesn't hurt.
The hallway rocks and the doorway sways.
Mother and Lily are framed in light at the kitchen table.
They stop their conversation. Stare at me. Mother focuses on my shirt. The bloodstain. She begins to rise, but a single word from me stops her.
'When?'
'Jenna – '
'When were you going to tell me!' I yell. I shove my hand out in front of me. *'What is this?'*
Mother's hand comes to her chin, half covering her mouth.
'Jenna, let me explain – '
Lily rises. 'You should sit down,' she says. She steps behind her own chair and offers it.
I sit down because I don't know what else to do. I look up at Claire. 'What's wrong with my hand?' I lay it on the table and spread the gash apart with my fingers. The skin lies on a thick layer of blue. Blue gel. Beneath that is the silvery white glimmer of synthetic bone and ligaments. Plastic? Metal composite?

Mary E. Pearson

probed	*onderzochten*
gait	*manier van lopen*
surge	*golf*
jolt	*schok*
oozes	*sijpelt*

REFERENCE

Yellow Pages

Grammar Survey

Exam Help

1 Words

Sleutelwoorden (*keywords*)

Er wordt bij lezen en luisteren vaak naar *keywords* gevraagd om te kijken of je de hoofdzaken uit een tekst kunt halen. Je moet dus weten welke woorden belangrijk zijn en welke niet. Met *keywords* kun je heel goed een samenvatting maken van een tekst.

Woorden raden

Onbekende woorden hoef je niet direct op te zoeken. Je kunt ze vaak raden als je de hele zin goed leest. Soms kun je ze afleiden uit een andere taal.

- Bedenk wat voor soort woord het woord is (werkwoord, zelfstandig naamwoord, bijvoeglijk naamwoord, enzovoort).
- Kijk welke informatie er in de zin en de omringende tekst staat.
- Bepaal wat de meest logische betekenis van het woord is.
- Controleer of het woord past in de zin.

Woordenboek gebruiken

> **Present** [preznt] **I** *bn.* tegenwoordig, aanwezig, present; **II** zn. **1** tegenwoordige tijd; at (*for the*) ~ op (voor) 't ogenblik; **2** geschenk, cadeau; **III** *ww.* voorstellen, presenteren

Zoek woorden pas op als het echt nodig is.

- Bepaal de woordsoort: werkwoord (ww = *verb*), zelfstandig naamwoord (zn = *noun*), enzovoort. Deze afkortingen staan meestal achter het woord in het woordenboek.
- Zoek de juiste betekenis. Een woord, zoals *present* in het voorbeeld, kan meerdere betekenissen hebben. Kijk goed of de betekenis past in de zin uit je tekst.
- Let op samengestelde woorden (bijvoorbeeld *price tag* of *flea market*) en uitdrukkingen. Je moet hier de betekenis van het helewoord of de hele uitdrukking vinden, en niet de woorden apart opzoeken. Zoek uitdrukkingen op in het woordenboek onder het belangrijkste woord. Een uitdrukking als *pull someone's leg* zoek je op onder het belangrijkste woord: *leg*.

2 Reading

Voorbereiden

Voordat je een tekst gaat lezen, is het handig om je af te vragen wat je al over het onderwerp weet. Dan kun je vaak voorspellen waar de tekst over gaat en wordt het lezen van de tekst makkelijker. Lees ook de vragen in het *Activity Book* van tevoren goed door, zodat je weet waar je op moet letten tijdens het lezen.

Oriënterend lezen (= skimmen)

Bij oriënterend lezen stel je het onderwerp van een tekst vast. Als je weet wat het onderwerp van een tekst is, begrijp je de tekst beter wanneer je hem helemaal leest.

Bij oriënterend lezen:

- lees je de titel
- lees je de inleiding (de eerste alinea)
- lees je tussenkopjes
- kijk je naar de bronvermelding onder de tekst. Die vertelt je vaak wat voor soort tekst het is: een tijdschrift- of internetartikel, verhaal, gedicht, advertentie, brief, enzovoort
- kijk je naar de foto's en afbeeldingen
- kijk je naar lijstjes, rijtjes of schema's in de tekst
- kijk je naar anders gedrukte woorden (bijvoorbeeld **vet**, *cursief*, enzovoort)

Globaal lezen

Bij globaal lezen lees je oppervlakkig en achterhaal je alleen de belangrijkste informatie. Je hoeft niet ieder woord te begrijpen.
Bij globaal lezen:

- lees je de titel en tussenkopjes
- lees je de inleiding en het slot
- lees je de eerste en laatste zin van elke alinea

Ga je een interview lezen? Lees dan eerst alleen de interviewvragen zonder de antwoorden. Je komt dan te weten welke informatie je kunt vinden in de tekst.

Zoekend lezen (= scannen)

Met zoekend lezen kun je gericht informatie zoeken, bijvoorbeeld hoe duur de kaartjes voor een film zijn of hoe laat je favoriete tv-programma begint. Je leest dus niet de hele tekst!

Bij zoekend lezen:

- lees je de titels en tussenkopjes
- zoek je naar kernwoorden die te maken hebben met wat je zoekt
- kijk je naar anders gedrukte woorden (bijvoorbeeld **vet**, *cursief*, enzovoort)
- stop je met lezen als je het gevonden hebt

Intensief lezen

Bij intensief lezen probeer je alle informatie in de tekst te begrijpen. Dit doe je bijvoorbeeld bij vragen over de inhoud van de tekst.
Bij intensief lezen:

- lees je de hele tekst
- let je op de inleiding en de tussenkopjes
- zoek je de belangrijkste zinnen en woorden uit de alinea's
- zoek je de betekenis van belangrijke, moeilijke woorden op

Tekstdoel

De schrijver van een tekst wil bij de lezer iets bereiken. Hij wil bijvoorbeeld iets aan de lezer uitleggen of hij wil dat de lezer iets doet. De tekst die hij schrijft, heeft dus een doel.

De schrijver wil	Doel	Voorbeelden van tekstsoorten
dat je iets te weten komt	informeren	krantenbericht, folder, verslag van een sportwedstrijd
zeggen hoe je iets moet doen	instrueren	recept, gebruiksaanwijzing
dat je iets wel of niet gaat doen	overhalen/ activeren	uitnodiging, advertentie
zijn mening geven	overtuigen	reactie op website, recensie van een cd of film
je vermaken	amuseren	fictief verhaal, strip, songtekst

Als je weet met wat voor soort tekst je te maken hebt, begrijp je sneller wat het doel van de schrijver is.

Structuur in teksten

De meeste teksten bestaan uit een inleiding, middenstuk en slot. Deze opbouw geeft de tekst structuur.

De inleiding is het eerste deel van de tekst. Hierin wordt duidelijk wat het onderwerp van de tekst is. De inleiding is meestal een aandachtstrekker, een verhaaltje of voorbeeld dat de lezer nieuwsgierig maakt naar de rest van de tekst.

Het middenstuk is opgebouwd uit alinea's. In iedere alinea wordt één deelonderwerp behandeld. Dat deelonderwerp wordt meestal in één zin weergegeven: de kernzin. Deze zin staat meestal aan het begin van de alinea, maar soms ook in het midden of aan het eind. De rest van de alinea bestaat uit argumenten, uitleg of voorbeelden bij de kernzin.

Het slot is het laatste deel van de tekst. Hierin wordt de belangrijkste informatie uit de tekst kort herhaald. Bij nieuwsberichten ontbreekt het slot vaak. In deze artikelen staat het belangrijkste in de eerste alinea's. Latere alinea's geven alleen extra informatie.

Moeilijke woorden

Soms loop je tijdens het lezen tegen moeilijke woorden aan, maar je hoeft niet alle Engelse woorden te kennen om een tekst te kunnen begrijpen.
Soms kun je raden wat een woord betekent doordat je:

- een (bijna) Nederlands woord herkent
- een woord uit een andere taal herkent
- een deel van het woord herkent
- de betekenis kunt afleiden uit de context (de zin waarin het woord staat en/of de zinnen eromheen)

Pas als je met deze manieren niet verder komt, gebruik je een (online/papieren) woordenboek.

Gatenteksten

In een gatentekst zijn een of meer woorden of tekstgedeeltes weggelaten. Je moet een woord of zinsdeel kiezen dat op die plek past. Je kunt daarbij altijd kiezen uit meerdere mogelijkheden.

Bij gatenteksten:
- lees je de tekst voor en na het invullijntje
- lees je de antwoorden waar je uit moet kiezen nog niet
- bedenk je eerst zelf welk (Nederlands) woord op de open plek zou kunnen staan
- vergelijk je jouw antwoord met de antwoordmogelijkheden en kies je het goede antwoord

Meer informatie over gatenteksten kun je vinden in de *Exam Help* op bladzijde 000 van je Textbook.

3 Listening/Watching

Voorbereiden
Je vraagt jezelf af wat je al over het onderwerp van het fragment weet en je leest de vragen in het *Activity Book* goed door.

Globaal luisteren/kijken
Je probeert alleen de belangrijkste informatie te achterhalen. Je hoeft niet elk woord te begrijpen.

Gericht luisteren/kijken
Je zoekt naar specifieke informatie en luistert woord voor woord tot je deze specifieke informatie hoort.

Intensief luisteren/kijken
Je luistert/bekijkt het hele fragment van begin tot eind. Je probeert alle informatie te begrijpen.

Intonatie
Je let op de toon van de sprekers om erachter te komen hoe de sprekers zich voelen.

Achtergrond
Je kunt ook letten op achtergrondgeluiden of -beelden. Die helpen je om meer te weten te komen over de situatie.

Moeilijke woorden
Je hoeft niet alle Engelse woorden te kennen om een luisterfragment/clip te kunnen begrijpen. Soms loop je tijdens het luisteren/kijken tegen moeilijke woorden aan, die belangrijk zijn voor het begrip. Doe dan het volgende: kijk of je een Nederlands woord of een woord uit een andere taal erin herkent; kijk of je een deel van het woord herkent; en kijk of je de betekenis kunt afleiden uit de context.

4 Speaking

Een gesprek voeren
- Zorg ervoor dat je elk gesprek op een gepaste manier begint en afsluit.
- Probeer te voorkomen dat het gesprek vastloopt. Maak hierbij gebruik van de volgende strategieën.

Als je de ander niet begrijpt, kun je:

1 zeggen dat je iets niet begrijpt	I'm sorry, but I don't understand. Could you say that again? I don't know what that means.
2 om uitleg vragen	What does that mean? What does it look like? Can you describe it? Can you give me an example?

Als je zelf een woord niet weet, kun je:

1 uitleggen hoe iets eruitziet	It looks like a mouse, but it's bigger. (rat)
2 uitleggen waarvoor je iets kunt gebruiken	You can put tea or coffee in it to keep it hot. (thermosfles)

Een presentatie geven

A Voorbereiding
- Vraag aan je docent hoelang je spreekbeurt/presentatie mag duren en welke materialen je mag gebruiken (beamer, enzovoort).
- Verzamel informatie (zie *Yellow Pages* 10).
- Haal die punten eruit die jij belangrijk vindt voor je spreekbeurt of je presentatie.
- Zet deze punten op een *prompt card*, een spiekbriefje met steekwoorden.

- Zet je punten in een logische volgorde. Een presentatie bestaat meestal uit drie delen.
  Inleiding: in het kort waarover je het gaat hebben en waarom.
  Kern: je eigenlijke verhaal waarin je de punten bespreekt die je hebt uitgekozen.
  Conclusie: afsluiting van je presentatie met een korte samenvatting of je eigen mening. Vraag je klasgenoten of ze vragen hebben.
- Gebruik afbeeldingen tijdens je presentatie.
- Oefen je presentatie hardop en let ook op de tijd.

B Uitvoering
- Kijk je publiek aan.
- Spreek rustig, natuurlijk en niet te zacht.
- Gebruik zo veel mogelijk je eigen woorden.

Je *prompt card* gebruik je alleen als geheugensteuntje.

5 Writing

Tips bij het schrijven
- Gebruik zo veel mogelijk woorden en uitdrukkingen die je kent.
- Gebruik een (online) woordenboek of internet als je een woord nog niet kent.

Het schrijven van een brief of e-mail

Voorafgaand aan het schrijven

Wat ga je schrijven?
- Een persoonlijke brief of e-mail, bijvoorbeeld aan een vriend of een familielid?
- Een zakelijke brief of e-mail, bijvoorbeeld als je informatie wilt opvragen?

Tijdens het schrijven
- Houd je aan de opdracht.
- Gebruik de *Stones*, *Grammar*, *Vocabulary* en eventueel een woordenboek.
- Gebruik de voorbeelden.

Na het schrijven
- Controleer of je alle punten uit de opdracht hebt verwerkt.
- Gebruik de *spellingchecker* op de computer.
- Controleer alle onderdelen van je brief (datum, adres, aanhef, enzovoort).
- Bewaar alle schrijfopdrachten in je portfolio.

Een voorbeeld e-mail

De e-mail hieronder is een voorbeeld van een persoonlijke e-mail.

A *To: mandy99p@live.co.uk*
Subject: sunglasses?

B Hi Mandy,

C How are you? I'm fi ne, but I wish I was still in London with you. We had a great time and it was nice to see you after such a long time!

You know what, I forgot my sunglasses! Have you found them? If you have, please send them back to me. Of course I'll pay for the postage. It would be nice to meet again soon. My next holidays will be in October, so maybe you can come and see me then.

I hope you're also enjoying your last days of freedom... holidays are always too short.

I hope you'll write back soon. I'm looking forward to seeing you again!

D Love,

E Lisa

A Vul het **e-mailadres** in. Vul bij *Subject* altijd het onderwerp van je e-mail in.

B Open een persoonlijke e-mail met *Dear, Hello* of *Hi*. Gebruik voor een formele e-mail dezelfde **aanhef** als voor een formele brief.

C Sommige mensen ontvangen honderden e-mails per dag; houd je boodschap kort.

D Sluit een persoonlijke e-mail af met *Take Care, Love,* enzovoort. Gebruik voor een formele e-mail de afsluiting *Yours faithfully*.

E Sluit af met je voornaam. Een formele e-mail sluit je af met je voor- en achternaam.

Een voorbeeldbrief
De brief hieronder is een voorbeeld van een zakelijke brief.

A Poortstraat 4
3572 HH Utrecht
The Netherlands

B The National Trust
PO Box 574
Manvers, Rotherham, S63 3FH
United Kingdom

C 15 February 2016

D Dear Sir / Madam,

E My name is Bas and I live in Utrecht, in the Netherlands. For one of my school subjects I need to write an essay and give a talk about the National Trust.
I was hoping you could answer some questions.

I have chosen the National Trust, because I think it's a great organisation and I am interested in nature. I have already read the information on your website, but could you explain in short what the organisation does? Are the people who work there all volunteers?

I would appreciate it if you could answer these questions.

I hope to hear from you soon.

F Yours faithfully,

G Bas Dekker

H Bas Dekker

A Hier staat **jouw adres**. Schrijf het land er alleen bij als je de brief naar het buitenland stuurt.

B Hier schrijf je de **naam** en het **adres** van degene **waar je naar schrijft**. Dat hoeft niet als je schrijft naar iemand die je kent.

C Je kunt de datum op verschillende manieren schrijven: February 15, 2016 of 15th February 2016 of February 15th, 2016.

D Als je niet precies weet naar wie je schrijft, gebruik je in de **aanhef** *Sir / Madam*. In andere gevallen kun je ook *Dear* gebruiken, wat 'geachte' of 'beste' betekent. Neem in dat geval alleen de achternaam van de geadresseerde op: *Dear Mr McDonald*.

E Let erop dat je je brief in **alinea's** (stukjes) verdeelt. Sla na elke alinea een regel over.

F Gebruik in de **afsluiting** *Yours faithfully* ('hoogachtend') of *Kind regards* ('met vriendelijke groeten'). Als je de persoon goed kent, kun je ook *Best wishes* gebruiken. Ken je de persoon heel goed, dan kun je ook *Take care* of *Love* gebruiken.

G Hier zet je je **handtekening**.

H Hier schrijf je je eigen **voor-** en **achternaam**. In een brief aan een vriend(in) schrijf je alleen je voornaam.

Handige zinnen voor het schrijven van een (zakelijke) brief of e-mail

Openen van een brief

- I'm writing to you to inquire about ... — *Ik schrijf u om te informeren naar ...*
- Thank you very much for your letter, ... (*datum*) — *Hartelijk dank voor uw brief van ... (datum)*
- In reply to your letter of ... (*datum*) — *In antwoord op uw brief van ... (datum)*

Informeren, vragen of iets mogelijk is

- Would it be possible to ... — *Zou het mogelijk zijn dat u ...*
- I would be very pleased if ... — *Ik zou heel blij zijn als ...*
- If you ... — *Indien u ...*

Informeren of men akkoord is

- Could you please let me know whether you agree with ... — *Kunt u me laten weten of u akkoord kunt gaan met ...*

Klagen over iets

- Unfortunately I still have not received your answer. — *Helaas heb ik nog steeds geen antwoord van u ontvangen.*
- Unfortunately you did not ... — *Helaas heeft u niet ...*
- I am not very pleased with ... — *Ik ben niet erg blij met ...*

Verwijzen naar een bijlage

- I am enclosing a copy of ... — *Als bijlage stuur ik u ...*

Vragen om (spoedig) antwoord

- I look forward to hearing from you. — *Ik zie uw antwoord met belangstelling tegemoet.*

Bedanken

- Thank you very much. — *Hartelijk dank.*
- Thanking you in advance. — *Bij voorbaat dank.*

Afsluiten

- We look forward to hearing from you soon. — *We zien ernaar uit snel van u te horen.*
- We look forward to seeing you. — *We zien ernaar uit u te zien.*
- Yours sincerely/faithfully (formeel) — *Hoogachtend*
- Kind regards (formeel/informeel) — *Met vriendelijke groeten*
- Best wishes (informeel) — *Met de beste wensen*

Een voorbeeld-cv (curriculum vitae)

Bij een sollicitatiebrief stuur je altijd een curriculum vitae (cv) mee. Hieronder volgt een voorbeeld van een cv.

A	Name:	Jorrit de Boer
	Sex:	male
	Date of birth:	15 March 2000
	Place of birth:	Groningen
	Address:	Winschoterdiep 70A, 9723 AB Groningen, the Netherlands
B	Certificates and diploma:	vocational degree in IT vmbo-t
C	Education:	Alfa-college Groningen: business administration
D	Work experience:	apprenticeship at Photonis Saturday job at PRIMARK department store in Groningen
E	Skills:	web design typing driving
F	Interests and hobbies:	travelling ice hockey

A Hier staan je persoonlijke gegevens inclusief je geboortedatum en adres.

B Hier zet je je diploma's die je hebt behaald. Het diploma dat je het laatst hebt behaald, zet je bovenaan.

C Hier zet je de opleidingen en trainingen die je hebt gevolgd. De opleiding die je het laatst hebt gevolgd (of die je nu volgt), zet je weer bovenaan.

D Hier zet je je werkervaring (inclusief stages). Het werk dat je het laatst hebt gedaan (of nu doet), zet je bovenaan.

E Hier noem je verdere bekwaamheden die van belang kunnen zijn voor de baan waarnaar je solliciteert.

F Hier zet je je belangrijkste interesses en hobby's.

6 Leesdossier

Lezen is leuk, ook in het Engels! In *Reading Matters* vind je verschillende leesteksten. Het zijn andere teksten dan die je in de thema's tegenkomt. Het gaat hier namelijk om fictie: verhalen over gebeurtenissen die niet echt gebeurd zijn, maar zich afspelen in de fantasie van de schrijver en/of de lezer. Je zult merken dat je de ene tekst beter begrijpt dan de andere, en dat het ene verhaal of gedicht beter bij je past dan het andere.
Om goed te kunnen onthouden wat je allemaal gelezen hebt in het Engels, maak je een verslag. Een verzameling van zulke verslagen heet een **leesdossier**. De vragen en opdrachten hieronder zijn bedoeld om je te helpen bij het samenstellen van je leesdossier.

Het maken van een verslag

Beantwoord om een goed verslag te maken de onderstaande vragen. Natuurlijk kan het voorkomen dat je bij een bepaald verhaal of gedicht niet alle vragen even goed kunt beantwoorden. Schrijf je antwoorden altijd zo op dat je ze als een doorlopende tekst kunt lezen; dan heb je het beste verslag.

Het gedicht, verhaal of boek

- Wat is de titel en wie heeft het geschreven?

Het genre

- Wat voor soort verhaal of gedicht is het volgens jou?
  Is het bijvoorbeeld een liefdesverhaal, een verhaal over geweld, een avonturenboek, of sciencefiction? Leg uit waarom.
- Is het verhaal of gedicht realistisch? Leg uit waarom.

De personages

- Wie zijn de belangrijkste personen? Beschrijf twee of drie van hen in ongeveer 50 woorden.

De setting

- Waar en wanneer speelt het verhaal of gedicht zich af?
- Zijn de tijd en de plaats belangrijk?
- Is de achtergrond belangrijk? (Denk bijvoorbeeld aan leefomstandigheden, familie, ras, enzovoort.)

Een samenvatting van de gebeurtenissen

- Kijk nog eens naar het begin en naar het einde. Beschrijf in ongeveer 100 woorden wat daartussenin gebeurt.

De titel

- Vind je dat de titel goed gekozen is? Waarom? Zou je zelf een andere titel hebben gekozen? Waarom?

Je eigen mening

- Heb je het gedicht, verhaal of boek met plezier gelezen? Wat vond je er leuk aan? Wat vond je minder leuk?
- Heb je weleens een ander verhaal of gedicht gelezen dat je hiermee kunt vergelijken?
- Waarom zou je iemand aanraden of afraden dit verhaal of gedicht te lezen?

Je kunt je verslag afsluiten met een van de keuzeopdrachten uit het *Activity Book*. Hierbij kun je je eigen fantasie gebruiken om een aanvulling op je verslag te maken. Je kunt er ook mee laten zien dat je het verhaal goed begrepen hebt.

Literaire termen

action	actie, handeling (wat de personages in een verhaal doen)
author	auteur, schrijver
autobiography	autobiografie, een literair werk dat de levensloop van de auteur beschrijft; de auteur zelf is de hoofdpersoon
character	karakter, persoon in een literair werk
chick lit	chicklit (afkorting van *chick literature*), verhalen speciaal geschreven voor (en meestal: door) vrouwen
children's literature	kinderboeken, literatuur voor kinderen (tot ongeveer 12 jaar)
chronological order	chronologische volgorde, op volgorde van tijd

chronology	de volgorde (in de tijd) waarin een verhaal verteld wordt
cliffhanger	spannend moment waarop (een deel van) het verhaal eindigt
comedy	komedie of blijspel, humoristisch verhaal of verhaal met een goede afloop
coming-of-age story	een verhaal over volwassen worden
crime fiction	misdaadliteratuur
detective novel	misdaadliteratuur, verhaal met een speurder (een detective) in de hoofdrol
dialogue	dialoog; wat twee personen tegen elkaar zeggen in een verhaal of toneelstuk
diary	dagboek
drama	drama, toneel(kunst), dus geen poëzie of proza
fable	fabel, verhaal met een boodschap, vaak met dieren als karakters
fairy tale	sprookje
fantasy	fantasie- / fantastische literatuur, onwerkelijke verhalen
fiction	fictie, verzonnen verhaal
flashback	terugblik
flash-forward	vooruitblik
genre	verzameling van dezelfde soort teksten of verhalen, zoals (auto)biografie, detective, sciencefiction.
hero	held, hoofdpersoon van het verhaal
humour	humorliteratuur, grappige verhalen
limerick	humoristisch gedicht bestaande uit vijf regels met rijmschema a a b b a.
literature	literatuur, erkende geschreven kunst in poëzie, proza of toneel
main character	hoofdpersoon in een literair werk
minor character	persoon met een kleinere rol dan de hoofdpersoon
moral	moraal, les in een literair werk
mystery	geheim, mysterie, raadsel
narrator	verteller
non-fiction	non-fictie: niet-verzonnen verhaal, op waarheid gebaseerd
novel	roman
perspective	perspectief, vanuit welk oogpunt een persoon of een handeling wordt bezien
plot	plot, waar het verhaal om draait
poem	gedicht
poetry	dichtkunst, poëzie (dus geen proza of toneel)
prose	proza, verhalende tekst zonder rijm (geen dichtkunst of toneel)
repetition	herhaling
rhyme	rijm, twee of meer woorden (of lettergrepen) die hetzelfde klinken
scene	scène, deel van groter (literair) werk, bijvoorbeeld akte uit toneelstuk
science fiction	sci-fi of SF: verhaal over – meestal – personen en gebeurtenissen in de toekomst
setting	tijd en plaats van een literair werk (letterlijk: omgeving)
short story	kort verhaal
stanza	couplet, deel van een gedicht
theme	thema, waar een verhaal in grote lijnen over gaat (bijvoorbeeld 'liefde')
thriller	spannend verhaal
title	titel
tragedy	tragedie of treurspel, een verhaal met een slechte afloop
twist	een onverwacht einde aan een verhaal
young adult literature	jeugdliteratuur, voor jongeren van 12 tot ongeveer 18 jaar

7 Hoe leer ik voor een proefwerk?

- Leer de woorden uit de *Vocabulary*.
- Bestudeer de *Grammar*.
- Neem de *Stones* nog een keer goed door.
- Maak de *Test Yourself*, kijk deze goed na en verbeter de fouten.
- Neem de volgens jou belangrijkste opdrachten in het *Activity Book* nog een keer door.
- Oefen in *Stepping Stones online*.

8 Hoe leer ik de woorden?

We onthouden maar ongeveer tien procent van wat we lezen. Als we woorden leren, zullen we dus wat trucs moeten toepassen om ze te onthouden.

Enkele tips
- Spreek woorden hardop uit.
- Leer niet alles tegelijk, maar elke dag een stukje (bijvoorbeeld tien woorden).
- Gebruik het rode plastic dat in het *Textbook* zit om jezelf te overhoren.
- Schrijf de woorden die je steeds fout doet op en herhaal ze.
- Overhoor jezelf of vraag iemand anders je te overhoren.
- Oefen ook in *Stepping Stones online*.

9 Hoe leer ik de Stones?

- Zoek woorden uit de *Stone* die je niet kent op in de *Vocabulary*.
- Als er bij een opdracht staat *Use Stone 17*, zoek die *Stone* dan op. Gebruik de voorbeeldzinnen als je de opdracht maakt. Op deze manier leer je de *Stone* al een beetje.
- Bij het leren van de *Stones* moet je niet alleen de *Stones* zelf bekijken, maar ook de opdrachten die bij de *Stones* horen.
- Schrijf de *Stones* over. Zo maak je minder schrijffouten en onthoud je de *Stones* beter.
- Probeer ook zelf zinnen te maken die in de *Stone* zouden kunnen passen.

10 Informatie verzamelen

Voor het maken van een werkstuk of een presentatie heb je informatie nodig. Die kun je als volgt verzamelen.

Werkwijze

A Voorbereiding
1. **Brainstorm**: Maak een *woordspin* met in het midden het onderwerp van je werkstuk of presentatie. Schrijf alles op wat je over dit onderwerp te binnen schiet.
2. Kies uit je *woordspin* de dingen die je goed kunt gebruiken voor je presentatie of werkstuk en waarover je meer wilt weten.
3. Bedenk hoe je aan meer informatie kunt komen:
   - uit boeken, encyclopedieën, kranten of tijdschriften
   - uit radio- en televisieprogramma's of dvd's
   - van internet
4. Maak een **planning**. Neem daarin op:
   - wanneer je alle informatie moet hebben
   - wanneer en waar je alle informatie gaat verzamelen (bibliotheek of mediatheek)

B Uitvoering
- Verzamel de informatie volgens je planning.
- Schrijf bij alle informatie de volgende dingen op.
  De bron: waar heb je de informatie vandaan gehaald (welk boek, welke krant of site)?
  De datum: wanneer is de informatie verschenen?
- Bewaar de informatie op een overzichtelijke manier (in een map, op een usb-stick).

Neem informatie nooit letterlijk over.
Gebruik altijd je eigen woorden!

C Controleer jezelf
- Heb je alle informatie gevonden die je nodig hebt?
- Klopte je planning?

11 Samenwerken

Bij sommige opdrachten werk je samen in een groepje. Dat betekent dat jullie samen verantwoordelijk zijn voor het eindresultaat. Bij samenwerken moet je goede afspraken maken, zodat iedereen precies weet wat hij of zij moet doen. Tijdens het werken aan de opdracht moet je met elkaar overleggen. Soms staat er in de opdracht wat er moet gebeuren, soms moeten jullie dat samen bedenken.

Werkwijze

A Voorbereiding

1 Verdeel de taken:
- Verdeel de taken en schrijf op wat iedereen moet doen.
- Als je 'ja' zegt tegen een taak, dan ben jij verantwoordelijk voor die taak.

2 Maak een planning:
- Bedenk hoeveel tijd elke taak kost.
- Maak een planning voor de hele opdracht.
- Plan een tussentijds overleg om te kijken of alles goed verloopt.

B Uitvoering

3 Zorg voor een goede samenwerking:
- Luister naar elkaar.
- Laat iedereen zijn of haar mening geven.
- Houd je aan de afspraken.

4 Overleg met elkaar:
- Wissel ideeën en resultaten met elkaar uit.
- Gebruik de planning om te kijken of iedereen zich houdt aan de afspraken.
- Geef opbouwende feedback.

C Controleer jezelf
- Heb jij je taak gedaan?
- Is elk lid van de groep tevreden over de samenwerking?
- Wat zou je de volgende keer anders doen?

12 Werken met het ERK en het taalportfolio

Europees Referentiekader

Een 8 voor Engels in Nederland betekent misschien iets heel anders dan een 8 voor Engels in Spanje. Daarom is er in Europa een systeem gemaakt dat geldt voor alle landen en dat voor iedereen hetzelfde is. Dit systeem heet het Europees Referentiekader (ERK).
Het ERK heeft zes niveaus: A1, A2, B1, B2, C1 en C2. Daarbij is A1 voor beginners en C2 voor mensen die de taal heel goed beheersen. Deze zes niveaus zijn er voor lezen, luisteren, spreken, gesprekken voeren en schrijven. Met dit systeem kun je laten zien waar je goed in bent en waar je nog niet zo goed in bent.

Europees Taalportfolio

Om te laten zien wat je allemaal al kunt en wat je bijgeleerd hebt, is er een Europees Taalportfolio. Je kunt je eigen Taalportfolio maken op www.europeestaalportfolio.nl.

Hoe vul je je taalportfolio in?

In ieder hoofdstuk vind je aan het eind bij de Task een verwijzing naar het Europees Referentiekader. In de blauwe *Taskcard* zie je waar je aan werkt. Dat is omschreven in *ik-kan-formuleringen*, bijvoorbeeld:
Gesprekken voeren, niveau A1: Ik kan mezelf en anderen voorstellen.

Wanneer je klaar bent met de Task, kun je je taalportfolio invullen op www.europeestaalportfolio.nl.

Let op!

Als je aan een *ik-kan-formulering* hebt gewerkt, betekent het niet dat je het niveau direct al helemaal beheerst. Vaak moet je de vaardigheid die bij deze *ik-kan-formulering* hoort een aantal keer oefenen, voordat je die helemaal beheerst.

13 Tussendoelen/tussentoetsen

Stepping Stones 5e editie is niet alleen ERK-proof maar ook tussendoel-/tussentoets-proef. Ga naar *Stepping Stones online* voor gedetailleerdere informatie hierover.

A Verbs

1 Present simple (*tegenwoordige tijd*)

I	like	rock music.	Je gebruikt de *present simple* (tegenwoordige tijd) bij feiten, gewoonten en regelmatige gebeurtenissen. In de *present simple* komt er bij *he*, *she* en *it* een -s achter het werkwoord. Bijvoorbeeld: *Susan = she*, dus *Susan loves chocolate*.
You	love	comics.	
He/Jack	like**s**	his family.	
She/Susan	love**s**	PE.	
It	dislike**s**	candy.	
We	like	gossip.	
You	dislike	rap music.	
They/Susan and Jack	hate	rain.	
I	study	a lot.	Als een werkwoord eindigt op een medeklinker + y, dan krijgt het werkwoord -ies bij *he*, *she* en *it*.
She/Lisa	stud**ies**	a lot.	
I	buy	a book.	Maar als er een klinker (a, e, i, o, u) voor de -y staat, komt er bij *he*, *she*, en *it* gewoon een -s achter het werkwoord.
She/Karen	buy**s**	a book.	
I	play	hockey.	
He/Matt	play**s**	hockey.	
I	watch	TV every day.	Als een werkwoord eindigt op een s-klank, dan krijgt het werkwoord -es bij *he*, *she* en *it*.
He/Tom	watch**es**	TV every day.	

Present simple of *to be*

I	**am**	**'m**	Megan Roberts.	Het werkwoord *to be* betekent *zijn*. In het Nederlands is *zijn* een onregelmatig werkwoord en verandert het dus van vorm bij elke persoon (ik ben, jij bent, hij is, wij zijn). *To be* is ook een onregelmatig werkwoord en verandert dus ook van vorm. De vormen van *to be* hebben ook een verkorte vorm. Deze verkorte vormen worden vaak in spreektaal gebruikt, maar je mag ze ook schrijven.
You	**are**	**'re**	crazy about Max.	
He/she	**is**	**'s**	into pop music.	
It	**is**	**'s**	interested in birds.	
We	**are**	**'re**	crazy about dancing.	
You	**are**	**'re**	really into sports.	
They	**are**	**'re**	big fans of Justin Bieber.	

Present simple of *to have (got)*

I	**have (got)**	**'ve got**	one sister.	*Have* and *have got* betekenen allebei *hebben*. Na *he*, *she* en *it*, of woorden die daarnaar verwijzen zoals Matt (= he), gebruik je *has* of *has got*.
You	**have (got)**	**'ve got**	a nice family.	
He/Matt	**has (got)**	**'s got**	three sisters.	
She/Karen	**has (got)**	**'s got**	a fake tattoo.	
It	**has (got)**	**'s got**	yellow feathers.	
We	**have (got)**	**'ve got**	two dogs.	
You	**have (got)**	**'ve got**	an interesting hobby.	Je gebruikt meestal de verkorte vormen van *have got* en *has got*.
They	**have (got)**	**'ve got**	a difficult surname.	

2 Present continuous (*tegenwoordige tijd in duurvorm*)

I'**m reading** a book.
Look! It'**s raining**!
He'**s watching** that stupid show again.
They'**re** always **complaining** about the weather.

Je gebruikt de *present continuous* (duurvorm) om te zeggen dat iets **nu** bezig is. Er staan in de zin vaak woorden die aangeven dat het **nu** bezig is. Voorbeelden van deze woorden zijn: *now, at the moment, look!, listen!, hurry up,* enzovoort. Je kunt de duurvorm ook gebruiken om **irritatie** aan te geven. Er staan in de zin dan vaak woorden als *always, again, still, constantly*, enzovoort.

I	**am studying**	for a big test.	De *present continuous* maak je met een vorm van *to be* (*am, are, is*) en een werkwoord + ing.
You	**are playing**	a game.	
He	**is writing**	an email.	
We	**are watching**	a film.	
They	**are drinking**	tea.	
I	**'m playing**	a game.	Vaak gebruik je de verkorte vormen van *am, is, are* (*'m, 's, 're*).
He	**'s chatting**	with his friend.	

to chat to stop	I'm cha**tting** with a friend. He is pu**tting** sugar in his tea.	**Let op!** Soms verandert de spelling van een werkwoord als je er *-ing* achter zet. Bij werkwoorden van één lettergreep met een korte klinker (a, e, i, o, u), zoals *stop, sit, run* en *chat*, wordt de medeklinker verdubbeld om de korte klinkerklank te behouden.
to have to give	I'm ha**ving** lunch. He's gi**ving** us homework.	Bij een werkwoord dat eindigt op een -e, valt die -e weg.

Present simple* versus *present continuous

I usually **have** breakfast in the kitchen.
They always **take** the bus to school.

Je gebruikt de *present simple* (tegenwoordige tijd) bij feiten, gewoonten en regelmatige gebeurtenissen.

I'**m chatting** with my uncle in America right now.
It'**s raining** at the moment.

Je gebruikt de *present continuous* (duurvorm) om te zeggen dat iets **nu** aan de gang is of dat iemand iets **nu** aan het doen is.

Katy's brother **organises** school parties.
(*Het organiseren van schoolfeesten is zijn taak.*)

Katy's brother **is organising** a field trip for his team.
(*Hij is nu iets anders aan het organiseren, bijvoorbeeld in zijn vrije tijd.*)

Let op! De verschillende tijden drukken beide dus iets anders uit, zoals te zien is in de eerste en tweede voorbeeldzin.

3 Past simple (*verleden tijd*)

I **travelled** to Spain last year.
She **talked** a lot when she was younger.
We **watched** a very funny film yesterday.

Je gebruikt de verleden tijd (*past simple*) om te zeggen dat iets in het verleden is gebeurd en nu is afgelopen. Vaak staat er in de zin een verledentijdsbepaling zoals *yesterday*, *last week*, *a month ago* of *in 2012*.

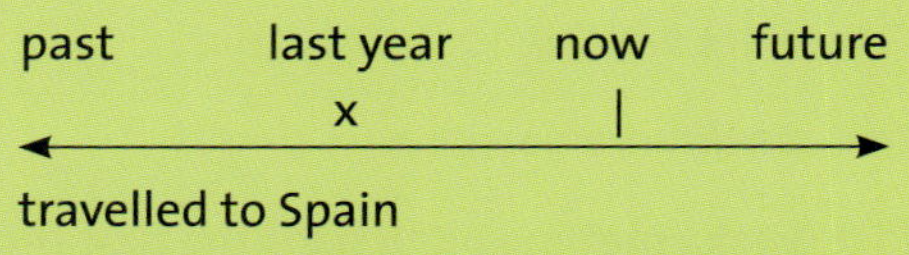

I	**stayed**	at home.
You	**loved**	knitting.
He	**talked**	fast.
She	**walked**	a marathon.
We	**cleaned**	the house.
You	**asked**	a question.
They	**played**	a game.

Bij regelmatige werkwoorden maak je de verleden tijd door -ed achter het het hele werkwoord te zetten.

Laura	tr**ied**	to call him this morning. (*try*)
We	stud**ied**	very hard for the test. (*study*)
It	sto**pped**	working two days ago. (*stop*)
We	gra**bbed**	a burger on our way home last night. (*grab*)

Bij sommige werkwoorden verandert de spelling.
Als het werkwoord eindigt op een medeklinker + y, dan verandert de -y in -ied.

Bij een aantal werkwoorden van één lettergreep met een korte klinker (a, e, i, o, u), zoals *stop* en *grab*, wordt de medeklinker verdubbeld.

They	**had**	a dog. (*have*)
She	**did**	her homework. (*do*)
They	**went**	to the dentist. (*go*)
We	**bought**	a car. (*buy*)

Er zijn ook onregelmatige werkwoorden. Deze krijgen in de verleden tijd geen -ed. Zij hebben een eigen onregelmatige vorm. Kijk voor de lijst onregelmatige werkwoorden in *Grammar* Survey 25 op bladzijde 153 van je *Textbook*.

Past simple of *to be*

I	**was**	at a party last week.
You	**were**	late for class.
He	**was**	with his friends yesterday.
She	**was**	at home.
It	**was**	very cold last night.
We	**were**	on holiday last month.
You	**were**	a very good goalie.
They	**were**	very funny.

To be heeft twee vormen in de *past simple* (verleden tijd): *was* en *were*.

4 Past continuous (*verleden tijd in duurvorm*)

Angela **was watching** TV.
*Angela **was** tv **aan het kijken**.*

Adam **was doing** his chores.
*Adam **was** zijn klusjes **aan het doen**.*

Je gebruikt de *past continuous* om aan te geven dat iets op een bepaald moment een tijdje aan de gang was. In het Nederlands zeg je dan vaak: 'was/waren aan het ...' of 'zat/zaten te ...'

Janet **was listening** to a rap song.
They **were waiting** for us to arrive.

Je maakt de *past continuous* met *was/were* + het hele werkwoord + ing.

Past continuous versus *past simple*

Last week I **met** my penpal for the first time!
The fireman **rescued** a cat from a tree yesterday.
Last month we **went** to the zoo.
My parents **ate** sushi in a nice restaurant last night.

Of je de *past continuous* of de *past simple* gebruikt, hangt af van wat je wilt vertellen. Als je wilt zeggen dat iets in het verleden is gebeurd en nu is afgelopen, gebruik je de *past simple*. Vaak staat er in de zin een verledentijdsbepaling zoals *yesterday, last week, a month ago* of *in 2012*.

I **was playing** football with my team.
Jessie **was walking** the dog.
We **were doing** some work in the garden.
My friends **were studying** for a big test.

Als je wilt zeggen dat iets in het verleden een tijdje aan de gang was, gebruik je de *past continuous*.

I **was waiting** for my friends when it **started** to snow.
Cody **was doing** his chores when I **ran into** him.
She **saw** him when she **was running** laps.
We **were having** lunch when the phone **rang**.
They **were doing** their homework when I **called**.

Je gebruikt ze samen in een zin om aan te geven dat iets gebeurde (*past simple*) terwijl er al iets aan de gang was (*past continuous*). In de zin staat het woord *when* (toen).

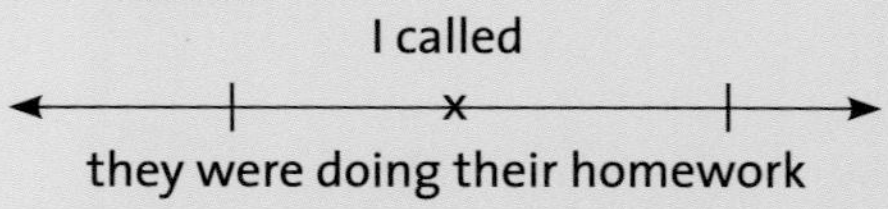

We **were watching** a film, while they **were playing** video games.
Henry **was doing** the dishes, while his mother **was talking** on the phone.

Wanneer er twee dingen tegelijk aan de gang zijn in het verleden, gebruik je twee keer de *past continuous*. In de zin staat het woord *while* (terwijl).

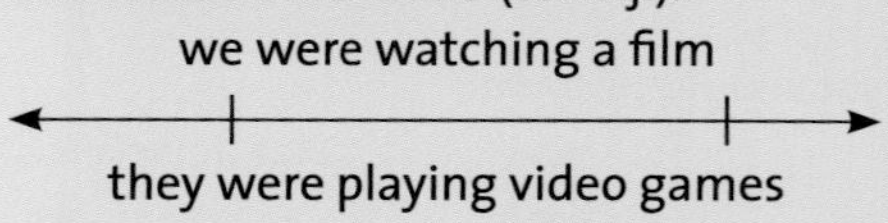

5 Present perfect (*voltooid tegenwoordige tijd*)

We **have played** soccer since 2002.
Yasmin **has won** the second prize!

	past simple	voltooid deelwoord
to play	played	**played**
to know	knew	**known**
to be	was/were	**been**

Je maakt de *present perfect* met *have/ has* + voltooid deelwoord. Bij regelmatige werkwoorden maak je het voltooid deelwoord door -ed aan het hele werkwoord toe te voegen. Bij onregelmatige werkwoorden heeft het voltooid deelwoord een eigen vorm. Zie *Grammar Survey* 25 op bladzijde 153 van je *Textbook* voor een lijst onregelmatige werkwoorden.

Ethan **has known** Sam for three years.
Ethan kent Sam al drie jaar.

My aunt and uncle **have lived** in Montreal since August.
Mijn oom en tante wonen sinds augustus in Montreal.

Je gebruikt de *present perfect* om te zeggen dat iets in het verleden is begonnen en nu nog aan de gang is. Vaak staat een van de volgende verklikwoorden dan in de zin: *since* (sinds), *for* (al), *always* (altijd al), *ever* (weleens), *never* (nog nooit), *how long?* (hoelang al?), *often* (vaak), *sometimes* (soms).

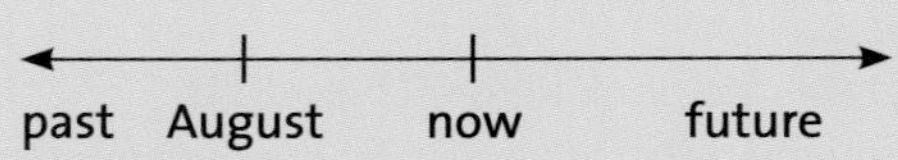

Let op! In het Nederlands gebruiken we voor dit soort zinnen **niet** altijd een voltooid deelwoord.

I**'ve** never **been** to Paris in my life.
Ik ben nog nooit in mijn leven naar Parijs geweest.

She**'s** already **visited** Julie in hospital three times.
Zij heeft Julie al drie keer bezocht in het ziekenhuis.

Je gebruikt de *present perfect* ook om te praten over ervaringen (in iemands leven) tot nu toe. Vaak staat een van de volgende verklikwoorden dan in de zin: *ever* (weleens), *never* (nog nooit), *already* (al) of *yet* (al), *before* (voorheen), *recently* (recentelijk), *lately* (de laatste tijd).

Karim feels nauseous. He**'s eaten** too many fries.
Karim voelt zich misselijk. Hij heeft te veel patat gegeten.

We**'ve washed** the car and now it's clean again.
We hebben de auto gewassen en nu is hij weer schoon.

Je gebruikt de *present perfect* ook om te zeggen dat iets in het verleden is gebeurd en dat je daar nu het resultaat van merkt. Er staat dan **niet** in de zin wanneer het is gebeurd. Het resultaat is belangrijker dan wanneer het gebeurde.

In dit soort zinnen gebruiken we in het Nederlands ook altijd het voltooid deelwoord.

1 Brian ... (*to live*) here since last year.
Ja: Brian has lived here since last year.

2 Martin ... (*to see*) this film twice already.
Ja: Martin has seen this film twice already.

3 I can't walk. I ... (*to break*) my leg.
Ja: I can't walk. I have broken my leg.

Als je niet zeker weet welke tijd je moet gebruiken, kun je de volgende vragen stellen:

1 Is het op dit moment nog aan de gang?
Ja: *present perfect*. Nee: ga naar vraag 2.

2 Gaat het over ervaringen tot nu toe?
Ja: *present perfect*. Nee: ga naar vraag 3.

3 Is het resultaat van de actie nu merkbaar?
Ja: *present perfect*. Nee: *past simple*.

6 Past perfect (*voltooid verleden tijd*)

When we entered the cinema, the film **had** already **started**.
As soon as everyone **had left** he went to bed.
Before I went to school I **had eaten** a sandwich.

Je gebruikt de *past perfect* om aan te geven dat iets eerder is gebeurd dan iets anders. Je maakt de *past perfect* met *had* + voltooid deelwoord.

I **had read** the book before I bought it.
The boy ran away after he **had broken** the window.
We had a celebration after we **had won** the match.

De *past perfect* staat vaak samen met de *past simple* in een zin. De *past perfect* geeft dan aan wat het langst geleden is.

As soon as I **had finished** my homework I went out.
Before he moved to London he **had lived** in York.
When he arrived at the party Jo **had** already **left**.

Vaak staat in een zin met een *past perfect* een van de volgende woorden: *after*, *before*, *when* of *as soon as*.

Alexis said that she **had**n't **read** the book.
Lucas mentioned that he **had bought** a new game.

Je gebruikt de *past perfect* ook bij de *indirecte rede*. Je geeft dan aan wat iemand anders eerder al heeft gezegd.

7 Future (*toekomende tijd*)

They**'re going to** fly to New York this summer.
It **will rain** tomorrow.
We**'re taking** the six o'clock train.
The zoo **opens** at 8am.

Er zijn verschillende manieren om aan te geven dat iets in de toekomst gaat gebeuren.

Future: present simple

The plane to Malaga **leaves** at four.
Their flight **arrives** at a quarter to ten.
Spring break **starts** next Monday.
The swimming pool **closes** at ten on Thursdays.
The tours **start** at eight.

Je gebruikt de *present simple* om te praten over vaststaande gebeurtenissen in de toekomst die onderdeel zijn van een dienstregeling, rooster of ander schema. Het gaat dan bijvoorbeeld om aankomst- en vertrektijden en begin- en eindtijden.

Voor verdere uitleg over de *present simple*, zie *Grammar Survey 1* op bladzijde 135 van je *Textbook*.

The train **departs** in five minutes.
The store **opens** at ten and **closes** at six.
What time does your class **finish**?
My favourite film **starts** in five minutes.
The plane **arrives** in half an hour.
What time does the party **end**?

Als er een van de onderstaande werkwoorden in de zin staat, gebruik je vaak de *present simple*.

arrive	end
start	begin
close	depart
finish	leave
open	

Future: present continuous

I'**m playing** a hockey match on Wednesday.
We'**re flying** to Paris next week.
Jules **is taking** Daisy out on Friday.
I'**m meeting** Sarah for lunch next week.

Je gebruikt de *present continuous* om te praten over afspraken in de nabije toekomst waarvan de tijd en/of plaats al vaststaat. Denk bijvoorbeeld aan een vliegreis waar je al een ticket voor hebt gekocht of een afspraak die je met iemand hebt gemaakt, bijvoorbeeld om naar de film te gaan.

Je maakt de *present continuous* met *am/is/are (not)* + het hele werkwoord + ing.

Voor verdere uitleg over de *present continuous*, zie *Grammar Survey 2* op bladzijde 136 van je *Textbook*.

Future: to be going to

I **'m going to call** him later this week.
Ik ga hem later deze week bellen.

Ana **is going to visit** friends and family in England.
Ana gaat vrienden en familie bezoeken in Engeland.

We **'re going to buy** a lot of cheap souvenirs in London.
Wij gaan een heleboel goedkope souvenirs kopen in Londen.

Je gebruikt *to be (am, are, is) + going to* + het het hele werkwoord als je wilt aangegeven dat iemand in de toekomst iets (niet) van **plan** is. In het Nederlands gebruik je vaak het werkwoord 'gaan'.

Look! He'**s going to** fall off his skateboard!
It **isn't going to** rain today. The sky is blue.
Look at the score! They'**re going to** win!

Je gebruikt *to be + (not) going to* + het hele werkwoord ook als je een voorspelling doet waarvoor je WEL bewijs hebt. Je ziet het bijna letterlijk aankomen.

Future: to be going to* versus *present continuous

We **are going to move** to England someday.
(Je zou graag ooit naar Engeland willen verhuizen.)
They **are moving** to London tomorrow.
(Je hebt al ingepakt en de verhuiswagen komt morgen.)

We **are going to** take the four o'clock train.
(Je moet de treinkaartjes nog kopen.)
We **are taking** the four o'clock train.
(Je hebt de treinkaartjes al gekocht.)

Let op! Je gebruikt *to be (not) going to* in plaats van de *present continuous*:
- wanneer het gaat om een plan, om iets wat nog NIET vaststaat
- voor dingen waarover je zelf geen controle hebt, zoals het weer

Future: will

Your favourite programme **will** start in an hour.
I **will** do my chores tomorrow. I promise.
We **will not** buy our child a dog.

Je gebruikt *will (not)* + het hele werkwoord om iets aan te bieden, bij beloftes, aankondigingen en besluiten.

I think we **will** win the lottery.
You **will** probably win the car in bingo.
Jack **will** become an astronaut.

Je gebruikt *will (not)* + het hele werkwoord ook als je een voorspelling doet waarvoor je GEEN bewijs hebt. Je denkt dat iets gaat gebeuren, maar je hebt geen bewijs dat het ook echt gaat gebeuren.

8 Used to

I **used to** play basketball; but now I'm into soccer.
Ik speelde vroeger altijd basketbal, maar nu ben ik gek op voetbal.

We **used to** play video games every day.
Wij speelden vroeger iedere dag computerspellen.

Thom **used to** live with his parents, but now he lives on his own.
Thom woonde vroeger bij zijn ouders, maar nu woont hij op zichzelf.

Je gebruikt *used to* + het hele werkwoord om te zeggen:
- dat iets in het verleden regelmatig gebeurde (een gewoonte was), maar nu niet meer
- dat iets in het verleden zo was, maar nu niet meer zo is

In het Nederlands zeggen we 'vroeger (altijd)'.

B Sentences

9 Questions (*vragen*)

A bear	**is**	wild.	Vraagzinnen met *to be* (*am, are, is, was, were*) en hulpwerkwoorden (*can, could, will, should, may, might, must, should, ought to*) maak je door de persoonsvorm en het onderwerp om te draaien. De rest van de zin blijft hetzelfde.
Is	a bear	wild?	
It	**was**	in a cage.	
Was	it	in a cage?	
Aria	**is studying**	for an important test.	
Is	Aria **studying**	for an important test?	
Janet	**was listening**	to a rap song.	
Was	Janet **listening**	to a rap song?	
Monkeys	**can**	climb trees.	
Can	monkeys	climb trees?	
He	**should**	tidy his room.	
Should	he	tidy his room?	
Jack	**will**	become an astronaut.	
Will	Jack	become an astronaut?	

Could you open that window, please?
Could you give me a glass of water, please?

Als je iets beleefd wilt vragen, gebruik je *could* in plaats van *can*.

Shall I ask Jennah to join us?
Shall we call on grandma tomorrow?

Let op! Bij *I* en *we* gebruik je *shall* in plaats van *will*.

She	**has got**	brown eyes.	Vraagzinnen met *have got* (hebben) maak je op dezelfde manier. **Let op!** Het woordje *got* verandert **niet** van plaats.
Has	she **got**	brown eyes?	
Matt and Jill	**have got**	enough pocket money.	
Have	Matt and Jill **got**	enough pocket money?	

Have you ever **talked** to your idol?

Let op! Je maakt vragen met de *present perfect* door *have/has* vooraan in de zin te zetten.

	Lions live in the wild.	Bij bijna alle andere werkwoorden gebruik je een vorm van *to do*. Bij vragen met *I*, *you*, *we* en *they*, of woorden die daarnaar verwijzen, begint de vraag met *do* in de tegenwoordige tijd. De rest van de zin blijft hetzelfde. In de verleden tijd, begint de vraag met *did*. De rest van de zin blijft weer hetzelfde.
Do	lions live in the wild?	
Did	My grandfather liked classical music.	
	your grandfather like classical music?	

GRAMMAR SURVEY

	It **lives** in the wild.	**Let op!** In de tegenwoordige tijd gebruik je bij *he, she* en *it*, of woorden die daarnaar verwijzen, *does* en verander je het werkwoord in het **het hele werkwoord**. Dit geldt ook voor vragen met *have* en *has*.
Does	it **live** in the wild?	
Did	Helen **liked** chocolate.	
	Helen **like** chocolate?	
Do		
	You **have** curly hair.	
Did	you **have** curly hair?	In de verleden tijd gebruik je bij *he, she* en *it*, of woorden die daarnaar verwijzen, *did* + het hele werkwoord.
	He **had** a nice job.	
	he **have** a nice job?	

10 Negations (*ontkenningen*)

I	**am not**	a big fan of rap music.	Als je wilt zeggen dat iets **niet** zo is, maak je een ontkenning. In het Engels gebruik je hiervoor het woordje *not*. Als er in een zin een vorm van *to be* (*am, are, is, was, were*) staat, dan maak je een ontkenning door *not* achter de vorm van *to be* te zetten.
You	**are not**	funny!	
He/she	**is not**	into pop music.	
It	**is not**	my book.	
We	**are not**	crazy about sports.	
You	**are not**	really into films.	
They	**are not**	very tall.	
I	**'m not**	really into sports.	Ontkenningen met *to be* hebben een verkorte vorm. **Let op!** *I'm not* heeft maar één verkorte vorm.
You	**'re not / aren't**	very tall.	
He/she	**'s not / isn't**	interested in football.	
It	**'s not / isn't**	tame.	
We	**'re not / aren't**	crazy about dancing.	
You	**'re not / aren't**	into knitting.	
They	**'re not / aren't**	big fans of PE.	
They	**are** drinking	tea and coffee.	Je maakt ontkenningen met de *present continuous* en de *past continuous* dus door *not* achter de vorm van *to be* te zetten.
They	**aren't** drinking	tea and coffee.	
We	**were** playing	computer games.	
We	**weren't** playing	computer games.	
Monkeys	can	climb trees.	
Monkeys	can**not** / **can't**	climb trees.	

The ambulance **will not** be there on time. The ambulance **won't** be there on time.	Ook ontkenningen met hulpwerkwoorden (*can, could, will, should, may, might, must, should, ought to*) maak je door *not* achter het hulpwerkwoord te zetten. Je kunt meestal ook verkorte vormen gebruiken.

Kim	has got	a new skateboard.	Ontkenningen met *have got* maak je door *not* achter *have* of *has* te zetten. Bij *I, you, we* en *they* gebruik je *haven't got* (*have not got*). Bij *he, she* en *it* gebruik je *hasn't got* (*has not got*).
Kim	has**n't** got	a new skateboard.	
We	have got	our own rooms.	
We	have**n't** got	our own rooms.	

Lions		live	in the wild.	Bij bijna alle andere werkwoorden zet je een vorm van *to do* + *not* ervoor.
Lions	**don't**	live	in the wild.	
He		**stayed**	at a hotel.	
He	**didn't**	**stay**	at a hotel.	
Eric		**likes**	hot chocolate.	**Let op!** In de tegenwoordige tijd gebruik je bij *he, she* en *it*, of woorden die daarnaar verwijzen, niet *do not* (*don't*), maar *does not* (afgekort: *doesn't*) en verander je het werkwoord in het **het hele werkwoord**.
Eric	**doesn't**	**like**	hot chocolate.	
He		**had**	a tiger for a pet.	In de verleden tijd gebruik je bij *he, she* en *it*, of woorden die daarnaar verwijzen, *didn't* + het hele werkwoord.
He	**didn't**	**have**	a tiger for a pet.	

They	**have**	a caravan.	Dit geldt ook voor ontkenningen met *have, has* en *had*.
They	**don't have**	a caravan.	
She	**had**	a pet.	
She	**didn't have**	a pet.	

I'm sad because I **haven't passed** the test.
Hailey **hasn't stolen** your phone!

Let op! Je maakt ontkenningen met de *present perfect* door *not* achter *have* of *has* te zetten.

11 Negative questions (*ontkennende vragen*)

Isn't it her dream to become a doctor?
Weren't you scared when you went bungee jumping?
Haven't they got any chocolate in this store?
Don't you ever listen to what I say?
Didn't the alarm go off when they broke in?
Didn't John tell you why he never showed up?

Je gebruikt ontkennende vragen om:
- te vragen om bevestiging
- ergernis uit te drukken
- ongeloof uit te drukken

	Julie	**was**	at her grandparents.	Wanneer er een vorm van *to be* (*am, is, are, was, were*), *have got/has got* of *can* in de zin staat, zet je deze vooraan in de zin, gevolgd door *not*.
Wasn't	Julie		at her grandparents?	
	Aram	**has got**	a best friend named Leon.	
Hasn't	Aram	**got**	a best friend named Leon?	
	You	**can** take	the bus to school tomorrow.	
Can't	you	take	the bus to school tomorrow?	

	Sally	likes	chocolate very much.	In alle andere gevallen maak je ontkennende vragen met *don't/doesn't* of *didn't*. Deze worden gevolgd door het *onderwerp* en het *hele werkwoord*. **Let op!** Ontkennende vragen met *have* maak je ook met *doesn't/don't* of *didn't*.
Doesn't	Sally	**like**	chocolate very much?	
	Her parents	**have**	a campervan.	
Don't	her parents	**have**	a campervan?	
	He	visit**ed**	the Himalayas.	
Didn't	he	**visit**	the Himalayas?	

12 Word order (*woordvolgorde*)

Mary walks to school every day.
We read the newspaper in the morning.
The teacher is explaining grammar.
Do they love each other?

In het Engels hebben zinnen grotendeels een vaste volgorde. Je begint met het onderwerp (wie?), dan komen alle werkwoorden (doet?), het lijdend voorwerp (wat?), de plaats (waar?), en tijd (wanneer?). Bij vragen komt het hulpwerkwoord vooraan in de zin.

Wie – doet – wat – waar – wanneer?

He	bought	a	leather	jacket.
ow	*pv*	*lv*		
pers. vnw.	*ww*	*lw*	*bn*	*zn*

Did	they	move?
hww	*ow*	*ww*

They	didn't	move.
ow	*hww*	*ww*

Er zijn twee manieren om de delen van een zin te benoemen; je kunt de woordsoort benoemen, of je kunt de functie van een woord in de zin benoemen. Zo zegt een 'werkwoord' wat voor soort woord het is, maar vertelt de 'persoonsvorm' wat voor rol dat woord in de zin heeft.

They	always	go	to the sports centre	on Mondays.
	bw frequentie	*ww*	*plaatsbepaling*	*tijdsbepaling*
He	is	usually	at his dad's place	on Sundays.
	ww	*bw frequentie*	*plaatsbepaling*	*tijdsbepaling*

Often, never, sometimes, always, frequently, rarely en *usually* zijn bijwoorden van frequentie. Ze zeggen hoe vaak iets gebeurt. Bijwoorden van frequentie staan **voor** het werkwoord.

Let op! Als het werkwoord een vorm is van *to be* (*am, are, is, was, were*), dan staat het bijwoord van frequentie **achter** het werkwoord.

13 'If' sentences (voorwaardelijke bijzinnen)

If you **press** this button, the doorbell **rings**.
The dough **rises** if you **add** yeast.
If you **leave** now, you**'ll be** in time.
I **would be** really sad if my experiment **didn't work**.

Je gebruikt *if-zinnen* om voorwaarden aan te geven en hun (mogelijke) gevolgen. De voorwaarde staat in de bijzin met *if* en het gevolg staat in de hoofdzin.

If you **melt** ice, it **becomes** water.
The light **goes** on if you **press** the switch.
Water **boils** if you **heat** it to 100°C.

Je gebruikt in de bijzin *if* + *present simple* en in de hoofdzin de *present simple* als het gevolg vaststaat; het is een feit.

If you **help** me, I**'ll give** you some chocolate.
If I **receive** an invitation, I **will go** to the party.
The party **will be** cancelled if it **rains**.

Je gebruikt in de bijzin *if* + *present simple* en in de hoofdzin *will* (*not*) + het hele werkwoord als het waarschijnlijk is dat er aan de voorwaarde voldaan wordt.

They **would be** really happy if they **won** the match. I **would buy** a castle if I **had** a million pounds. If Tom **knew** your phone number, he**'d call** you.	Je gebruikt in de bijzin *if* + *past simple* en in de hoofdzin *would* (*not*) + het hele werkwoord als het onwaarschijnlijk is dat er aan de voorwaarde voldaan wordt.

14 Complex and compound sentences (*samengestelde en complexe zinnen*)

Simple, complex and compound sentences *He* likes playing games in the afternoon. *We* have bought some tickets for next week. *The zoo* adopted two Sumatran tigers last month.	Je gebruikt enkelvoudige zinnen om één complete gedachte over te brengen. Enkelvoudige zinnen hebben altijd *één onderwerp* en *één persoonsvorm*.
I always take the train, **for** I haven't got a car. The oil spill ruins beaches **and** kills animals. I've got a job, **so** I can buy my own clothes. They want a new car **but** think it's too expensive. We heard a loud thunder, **yet** there wasn't any rain. The staff were not kind, **nor** were they attentive. An earthquake struck the area, **but** nobody was hurt.	Je maakt een samengestelde zin door twee enkelvoudige zinnen samen te voegen met behulp van een van de volgende voegwoorden *for*, *and*, *nor*, *but*, *or*, *yet* of *so*.
The protesters didn't leave **because** they were angry. We help injured animals, **although** it takes some time. I got a job **so** that I could buy you this present. They can't enter the area, **because** it's unsafe. **When** you have no spare time, you can't volunteer. **After** I've finished my work, I will help you. He's not someone **who** turns a blind eye to the poor. Aid workers can't get in, **which** makes matters worse. He's someone **who** will always help those in need. Did you hear about the typhoon **that** hit the US?	Een complexe zin is een hoofdzin samengevoegd met een of meer bijzinnen, verbonden met een **ander** voegwoord (*because*, *since*, *after*, *although*, *when*) of betrekkelijk voornaamwoord zoals *that*, *who* of *which*.
I am going to bed. I am tired. *Ik ga naar bed. Ik ben moe.* I am going to bed because **I am tired**. *Ik ga naar bed omdat ik moe ben.* This is the T-shirt. I bought it yesterday. *Dit is het T-shirt. Ik heb het gisteren gekocht.* This is the T-shirt **which I bought yesterday**. *Dit is het T-shirt dat ik gisteren gekocht heb.*	**Let op!** In het Engels verandert de woordvolgorde in de bijzin **niet**, maar in het Nederlands **wel**.

15 Relative clauses (*betrekkelijke bijzinnen*)

The thief **who** robbed an old lady was sent to jail. This is the car **which** was involved in an accident. There goes the girl **that** looks like Alice.	Als je extra informatie over iets of iemand wilt geven, gebruik je een betrekkelijke bijzin. Zo'n bijzin begint meestal met *who*, *which* of *that*. In het Nederlands gebruik je *die* of *dat*. Je gebruikt: • **who** bij personen • **which** bij dieren en dingen • **that** bij personen, dieren en dingen **That** heeft hier dezelfde betekenis als **who** of **which**, maar het is informeler.
Franklin, **who** is my nephew, is younger than I am. This bank, **which** is quite old, is hard to break into.	Soms geeft een bijzin alleen extra informatie: je kunt de bijzin weglaten zonder dat de betekenis van de zin echt verandert. Je gebruikt dan nooit *that*, maar altijd *who* of *which*. Zo'n bijzin staat altijd tussen komma's.
This is the suspect (**who**) the police arrested yesterday. Here is the hat (**that**) I bought in New York.	Soms is de bijzin nodig om te begrijpen over wie of wat de zin gaat. In zo'n bijzin kun je *who*, *which* of *that* vaak weglaten.
The village (**which**) I lived <u>in</u> has really changed. The owner (**who**) the police had talked <u>to</u>, was afraid.	Je kunt *who* en *which* samen met voorzetsels gebruiken. Meestal staat het voorzetsel dan achteraan in de bijzin.
The village <u>in</u> **which** I lived has really changed. The owner <u>to</u> **whom** the police had talked, was afraid.	Het voorzetsel kan ook vooraan in de bijzin staan. Dat is formeler. *Who* verandert met een voorzetsel erbij soms in *whom*.
The banker **whose** story was on the news was a fraud. Marvin, **whose** bike was stolen, had to walk home.	*Whose* geeft bezit aan. Je vertaalt het met: van wie, wiens of waarvan.

C Words

16 *One* and *ones*

A used car is much cheaper than a new **one**.
Do you prefer the black shoes or the red **ones**?

Je gebruikt *one* (enkelvoud) of *ones* (meervoud) wanneer je een zelfstandig naamwoord verderop in een zin wilt herhalen. Het zelfstandig naamwoord zelf is dan al eerder voorgekomen.

These are big problems and small **ones**.
I have to read a book. Which **one** should I pick?
Do you like thrillers? This **one** is a must-read.
Muffins? I like the **ones** with chocolate best.

Je gebruikt *one* (enkelvoud) of *ones* (meervoud) om een zelfstandig naamwoord te vervangen:
- na een bijvoeglijk naamwoord
- na *which*
- na *this*, *that*, *these* en *those*
- als zelfstandig naamwoord

17 Comparatives and superlatives (*trappen van vergelijking*)

Box A is **small**.
Box B is **smaller** than box A.
Box C is the **smallest** of all.

Chrystal is **smart**.
Toby is **smarter**.
But I am the **smartest** of them all.

Om dingen of mensen te beschrijven, gebruik je bijvoeglijke naamwoorden, zoals *small*, *old*, *strong*, *cold* en *fast*. Je kunt er vergelijkingen mee maken door ze in de vergrotende en overtreffende trap te zetten. Bij de vergrotende trap voeg je -er toe. Bij de overtreffende trap voeg je -est toe.

large – large**r** – large**st**
close – close**r** – close**st**

Let op! Soms moet je als je -er of -est achter bijvoeglijk naamwoorden wilt zetten ook de spelling iets veranderen. Bij bijvoeglijke naamwoorden die eindigen op een -e, krijg je -r en -st in plaats van -er en -est.

hot – hot**ter** – hot**test**
big – big**ger** – big**gest**

Bij bijvoeglijke naamwoorden van één lettergreep eindigend op één klinker (a, e, i, o, u) + één medeklinker, moet je de medeklinker verdubbelen. Dit is om de klank van de klinker kort te houden.

happy – happ**ier** – happ**iest**
silly – sill**ier** – sill**iest**

Bij bijvoeglijke naamwoorden die eindigen op een medeklinker + y, krijg je -ier en -iest in plaats van -er en -est.

My life is exciting.
My brother's life is **more** exciting.
My sister's life is the **most** exciting of all.

His stories are boring.
Your stories are **more** boring.
Her stories are the **most** boring stories I've ever heard.

Bij bijvoeglijke naamwoorden van **drie lettergrepen en langer**, gebruik je in de vergrotende trap *more* en in de overtreffende trap *most*. Dit geldt ook voor een aantal bijvoeglijke naamwoorden van twee lettergrepen, zoals *famous* en *boring*.

good/well – better – best
goed – beter – (het) best(e)

bad/ill – worse – worst
slecht – slechter – (het) slechtst(e)

much/many – more – most
veel – meer – (het) meeste

little – less – least
weinig – minder – (het)minst(e)

Sommige bijvoeglijke naamwoorden, bijvoorbeeld *good* en *bad*, hebben een eigen onregelmatige vergrotende en overtreffende trap. Ze krijgen dus **geen** -er en -est erachter of *more* en *most* ervoor!

D Spelling

18 -y wordt -ie

to **She**	stud**y** stud**ies** a lot.		Als een werkwoord eindigt op -y, krijgt dat werkwoord -ies bij *he*, *she* en *it* in de *present simple* (tegenwoordige tijd).
I Lisa I Marc	play play**s** buy buy**s**	in a team. in a team. a diving suit. a diving suit.	Maar als er voor de -y een klinker (a, e, i, o, u) staat, komt er bij *he*, *she* en *it* in de *present simple* gewoon een -s achter het werkwoord.
to Robert	**try** **tried**	 it on.	Als een werkwoord eindigt op een medeklinker + y, dan verandert de -y in -ied in de *past simple* (verleden tijd).
to We	pla**y** play**ed**	 tennis yesterday.	Maar als er voor de -y een klinker (a, e, i, o, u) staat, komt er in de *past simple* gewoon -ed achter het werkwoord.
one two	hobby hobbies		Een woord dat eindigt op -y, krijgt -ies in het meervoud.
one two	day day**s**		Maar als er voor de -y een klinker (a, e, i, o, u) staat, krijgt het woord gewoon een -s.
eas**y** happ**y**	eas**ier** happ**ier**	eas**iest** happ**iest**	Een woord dat eindigt op een medeklinker + y, krijgt -ier in de vergrotende trap en -iest in de overtreffende trap.

19 -es na sisklank

to He	watch watch**es**	 TV every evening.	Als een werkwoord eindigt op een sis-klank, dan krijgt het -es in plaats van -s bij *he*, *she* en *it* in de *present simple* (tegenwoordige tijd).
one two one three		box box**es** guess guess**es**	Een woord dat in de uitspraak eindigt op een sis-klank, krijgt in het meervoud -es in plaats van -s.

20 Stomme -e valt weg

to ha**ve** to gi**ve**		I'm ha**ving** a bath. He's gi**ving** her coffee.	Als een werkwoord eindigt op een -e die je niet hoort, dan valt die -e weg in de *present continuous* (duurvorm).
to I	lo**ve** love**d**	 that dress.	Als een werkwoord eindigt op een -e die je niet hoort, komt er in de *past simple* (verleden tijd) alleen een -d achter het werkwoord.
larg**e** simpl**e**	larg**er** simpl**er**	larg**est** simpl**est**	Als een woord eindigt op een -e die je niet hoort, dan valt de -e weg bij de vergrotende en overtreffende trap.

21 Verdubbeling van medeklinker

to She's to I'm		sto**p** sto**pp**ing for the traffic lights. si**t** si**tt**ing on the floor.	In de *present continuous* (duurvorm) wordt de laatste medeklinker van het werkwoord verdubbeld als er één korte klinker (a, e, i, o, u) voor staat.
to She		sto**p** sto**pped** the thief.	In de *past simple* (verleden tijd) wordt de laatste medeklinker van het werkwoord verdubbeld als er één korte klinker (a, e, i, o, u) voor staat.
bi**g** fa**t**	bi**gger** fa**tter**	bi**ggest** fa**ttest**	Bij de vergrotende en overtreffende trap wordt een medeklinker verdubbeld als er één korte klinker (a, e, i, o, u) voor staat.

22 -f wordt -ves

one loa**f** two loa**ves**	Veel woorden die eindigen op een -f krijgen in het meervoud -ves.
one hal**f** two hal**ves**	

23 -o wordt -oes

to	**go**		*Do* wordt *does* en *go* wordt *goes* bij *he*, *she* en *it* in de *present simple* (tegenwoordige tijd).
She	**goes**	to school every day.	
to	**do**		
She	**does**	her homework in the evening.	
one		potat**o**	Veel woorden die eindigen op een -o krijgen in het meervoud -oes.
a bag of		potat**oes**	

24 Pitfalls (*valkuilen*)

De volgende woorden worden vaak door elkaar gehaald. The car is going **too** fast. He said he would be there **too**. This present is from me **to** you.	*Too* betekent 'te' (voor bijvoeglijke naamwoorden) en 'ook' (aan het einde van een zin). *To* betekent 'naar', 'om te', 'aan', 'te' (voor een werkwoord).
I like chemistry better **than** biology. **Then** he scored the winning goal.	*Than* betekent 'dan' (in vergelijkingen). *Then* betekent 'toen', 'dan' (geeft een tijd aan).
Where is **your** bag? **You're** late. Do get up earlier.	*Your* betekent 'jouw/jullie/uw' (bezittelijk voornaamwoord). *You're* is een samentrekking van *you are*.
The cat was washing **its** paws. **It's** almost time for dinner.	*Its* betekent 'van hem/haar' (bezittelijk voornaamwoord). *It's* is een samentrekking van *it is* of *it has*.
They left **their** coats at home. Have you ever been **there**? **They're** my best friends.	*Their* betekent 'hun' (bezittelijk voornaamwoord). *There* betekent 'er', 'daar' (plaats). *They're* is een samentrekking van *they are*.
Where did you buy that dress? They **were** very nice to me. **We're** not really into sports.	*Where* betekent 'waar' (vraagwoord). *Were* betekent 'was', 'waren'. *We're* is een samentrekking van *we are*.

E Irregular verbs

25 Irregular verbs (*onregelmatige werkwoorden*)

De 1e vorm = *infinitive* (hele werkwoord)
De 2e vorm = *past simple* (verleden tijd)
De 3e vorm = *past participle* (voltooid deelwoord)

1e vorm – 2e vorm – 3e vorm	betekenis
to be – was/were – been	zijn; worden
to beat – beat – beaten	(ver)slaan
to become – became – become	worden
5 to begin – began – begun	beginnen
to bet – bet – bet	wedden
to bite – bit – bitten	bijten
to bleed – bled – bled	bloeden
to blow – blew – blown	blazen
10 to break – broke – broken	breken
to bring – brought – brought	brengen
to build – built – built	bouwen
to buy – bought – bought	kopen
to catch – caught – caught	vangen
15 to choose – chose – chosen	kiezen
to come – came – come	komen
to cost – cost – cost	kosten
to cut – cut – cut	snijden; knippen
to dig – dug – dug	graven
20 to do – did – done	doen
to draw – drew – drawn	tekenen; trekken
to drink – drank – drunk	drinken
to eat – ate – eaten	eten
to fall – fell – fallen	vallen
25 to feel – felt – felt	voelen
to fight – fought – fought	vechten
to find – found – found	vinden
to fly – flew – flown	vliegen
to forbid – forbade – forbidden	verbieden
30 to forget – forgot – forgotten	vergeten
to get – got – got	krijgen; worden
to give – gave – given	geven
to go – went – gone	gaan
to grow – grew – grown	groeien; worden
35 to have – had – had	hebben
to hear – heard – heard	horen
to hide – hid – hidden	(zich) verbergen
to hit – hit – hit	slaan; raken
to hurt – hurt – hurt	pijn doen
to keep – kept – kept	houden
40 to know – knew – known	weten
to learn – learnt – learnt	leren
to leave – left – left	(ver)laten
to let – let – let	laten
to lose – lost – lost	verliezen
45 to make – made – made	maken
to mean – meant – meant	menen
to meet – met – met	ontmoeten
to pay – paid – paid	betalen
to put – put – put	zetten; leggen
50 to read – read – read	lezen
to ring – rang – rung	(op) bellen
to run – ran – run	rennen
to say – said – said	zeggen
to see – saw – seen	zien
55 to sell – sold – sold	verkopen
to send – sent – sent	(ver)zenden; (ver) sturen
to sing – sang – sung	zingen
to sit – sat – sat	zitten
to speak – spoke – spoken	spreken
60 to spend – spent – spent	doorbrengen
to stand – stood – stood	staan
to steal – stole – stolen	stelen
to swim – swam – swum	zwemmen
to take – took – taken	nemen
65 to teach – taught – taught	onderwijzen
to tell – told – told	zeggen; vertellen
to think – thought – thought	denken
to throw – threw – thrown	gooien
to wake – woke – woken	wakker worden
to wear – wore – worn	dragen
70 to win – won – won	winnen
to write – wrote – written	schrijven

F Phrasal verbs

26 Phrasal verbs (*samengestelde werkwoorden*)

	be fond of	gek zijn op
	be good at	goed zijn in
	be interested in	geïnteresseerd zijn in
	be keen on	enthousiast zijn over
5	be proud of	trots zijn op
	bring along	meebrengen
	bring back	terugbrengen
	bring in	binnenbrengen, opleveren
	bring up	grootbrengen
10	carry out	uitvoeren
	cut back	bezuinigen
	cut down	terugbrengen in hoeveelheid, vellen
	cut off	afsnijden, onderbreken
	cut out	uitknippen
15	feel like	voelen als, zin hebben om
	get off	uitstappen
	get on	instappen
	get to	mogen
	get up	opstaan
20	give away	weggeven
	give back	teruggeven
	hand in	inleveren
	hand out	uitdelen
	hand over	overhandigen
25	hand round	rondgeven
	leave behind	achterlaten
	leave out	weglaten
	let in	binnenlaten
	lie down	gaan liggen
30	look at	kijken naar
	look for	zoeken naar
	look like	lijken op
	pick up	oppakken
	point out	wijzen op/naar
35	push around	rond duwen
	push over	omstoten
	put away	wegdoen
	put down	neerleggen
	put on	aandoen (kleding)
40	put through	doorverbinden, iemand iets aandoen
	put together	in elkaar zetten
	read out	voorlezen
	set back	terugzetten
	set down	neerleggen
45	shut off	afsluiten
	sit down	gaan zitten
	smell like	ruikt als
	sound like	klinkt als
	stand up	opstaan
50	take back	terugnemen
	take down	neerhalen, noteren
	take in	innemen, begrijpen
	take off	uitdoen (kleding)
	take on	aanvaarden, beginnen
55	take over	overnemen
	taste like	smaakt als
	think over	nadenken over
	think through	doordenken
	turn off, switch off	uitdoen (licht, en dergelijke)
60	turn on, switch on	aandoen (licht, en dergelijke)

Centraal Schriftelijk Examen (CSE)

1 Leesvaardigheid

Op het Centraal Schriftelijk Examen (CSE) krijg je te maken met verschillende soorten teksten, zoals folders, advertenties, krantenartikelen en brieven. Bij deze teksten worden verschillende soorten vragen gesteld. Hierbij kun je denken aan meerkeuzevragen, open vragen en vragen bij gatenteksten. De volgende algemene tips en stappenplannen kunnen je helpen bij het maken van het examen.

Algemene tips

- Zoek onbekende woorden uit de vraag en/of de antwoordmogelijkheden op in je woordenboek. Let er bij het gebruik van je woordenboek op dat je niet zomaar de eerste betekenis opschrijft die je ziet. Vaak staan er meerdere betekenissen achter een woord. Kies de betekenis die het beste in de tekst past.
- Belangrijk: het goede antwoord staat altijd in de tekst! Vaak op een iets andere manier dan in de vraag, maar dat moet je juist herkennen.

Meerkeuzevragen

Meerkeuzevragen zijn vragen waarbij je het antwoord moet kiezen uit drie tot vijf mogelijkheden. De mogelijke antwoorden kunnen je op een dwaalspoor brengen. Het volgende stappenplan kan je helpen om meerkeuzevragen te beantwoorden.

Stappenplan

- Bepaal, voordat je gaat lezen, wat voor soort tekst het is. Dat doe je door oriënterend te lezen (**skimmen**). Je kijkt naar de titel, de inleiding (eerste alinea), de tussenkopjes, de illustraties, de bronvermelding, de lijstjes/rijtjes/schema's en naar anders gedrukte woorden (bijvoorbeeld **vet**, *cursief*) om te ontdekken waar de tekst over gaat. Als je dat weet, is het makkelijker om de inhoud van de tekst te begrijpen. Gebruik de informatie om te bepalen wat voor soort tekst het is: een tijdschrift- of internetartikel, verhaal, gedicht, advertentie, brief, enzovoort.
- Lees eerst de vraag zodat je weet waar je naar moet zoeken. Lees de antwoordmogelijkheden nog niet.
- Ga nu in de tekst gericht op zoek naar de gevraagde informatie (**scannen**). Daarbij moet je ook letten op hoe de tekst eruitziet (foto's, illustraties, titel). Als je een eigen antwoord hebt gevonden, vergelijk dit dan met de keuzemogelijkheden en kies het goede antwoord.

Meerkeuzevragen bij korte(re) teksten

Over korte teksten worden in het Centraal Schriftelijk Examen Engels vaak een of twee vragen gesteld. Dat gebeurt meestal in het Nederlands. Je wordt gevraagd om specifieke informatie uit de tekst te halen. Om het antwoord op de vraag/vragen te vinden moet je scannen. Voorbeelden van korte teksten zijn folders, advertenties en korte krantenartikelen.

Meerkeuzevragen bij lange(re) teksten

Meerkeuzevragen bij langere teksten worden vaak in het Engels gesteld. Daarbij is het altijd belangrijk na te gaan of je begrijpt wat er gevraagd wordt en wat er in de antwoordmogelijkheden staat. Kijk voor veelgebruikte vragen in het examen ook bij *2 Veelgebruikte vragen en uitdrukkingen bij het CSE.*

True/False-vragen

True/False- (Waar/Niet waar-) vragen zijn vragen waarbij je van een bewering moet aangeven of deze juist is. Het volgende stappenplan kan je helpen om True/False-vragen te beantwoorden.

Stappenplan

- Lees de bewering.
- Onderstreep de kernwoorden in de bewering.
- Zoek het tekstgedeelte of de alinea dat/die verband houdt met de bewering.
- Vergelijk de bewering goed met de informatie in de tekst. Wat in de tekst staat, moet dezelfde betekenis hebben als in de bewering. Laat je daarbij niet teveel afleiden door losse woorden in de tekst.
- Kies je antwoord: *true* of *false*.
- Tip: de juiste bewering is meestal een samenvatting van een wat langer stukje tekst.

Open vragen

Open vragen zijn vragen waarop je het antwoord zelf moet vinden in de tekst. Je hebt dus geen keuze uit antwoordmogelijkheden. Het volgende stappenplan kan je helpen om open vragen te beantwoorden.

Stappenplan

- Een open vraag moet je altijd in het Nederlands beantwoorden, behalve als je iets (een Engels(e) woord of zin) **letterlijk** uit de tekst moet citeren.
- Lees de vraag eerst goed door.
- Bepaal dan in welk gedeelte van de tekst je het antwoord kunt vinden. **Trek geen eigen conclusie**, maar geef aan hoe de vraag **in de tekst** wordt beantwoord.
- Houd je antwoord zo kort mogelijk. Geef niet meer informatie dan gevraagd wordt, tenzij er staat 'motiveer je antwoord'.

Gatenteksten

In het examen komen ook vragen voor waarbij woorden of tekstgedeeltes zijn weggelaten. Je moet een woord of zinsdeel kiezen dat op die plek past. Je kunt daarbij altijd kiezen uit meerdere mogelijkheden. Het volgende stappenplan kan je helpen om invulvragen bij gatenteksten te beantwoorden.

Stappenplan
- Skim de tekst. Probeer erachter te komen wat het onderwerp van de tekst is.
- Lees het gedeelte van de tekst waar de open plek staat. Begin daarbij ruim **voor** de open plek en lees ook nog een stuk door **na** de open plek. Je krijgt dan een goed beeld van de betekenis van het weggelaten woord of tekstgedeelte.
- Bedenk voor jezelf welk (Nederlands) woord op de open plek zou kunnen staan. Vergelijk jouw antwoord met de antwoordmogelijkheden bij de vraag en kies het goede antwoord.
- Zoek zo nodig moeilijke woorden in de vraag op in je woordenboek.

2 Veelgebruikte vragen en uitdrukkingen bij het CSE

Vraagstellingen

What can be concluded from the first paragraph?	*Wat kun je concluderen uit de eerste alinea?*
What does the writer mean by ... ?	*Wat bedoelt de schrijver met ... ?*
What is the main point described in paragraph 2?	*Wat is het belangrijkste punt dat wordt beschreven in alinea 2?*
What view does the writer express?	*Welke mening drukt de schrijver uit?*
What does ... describe in paragraph 1?	*Wat beschrijft ... in alinea 1?*
What is true according to the last paragraph?	*Wat is waar volgens de laatste alinea?*
What does ... say about ... ?	*Wat zegt ... over ... ?*
What is the function of paragraph 3?	*Wat is de functie/bedoeling van alinea 3?*
What does the writer want to point out?	*Wat wil de schrijver duidelijk maken?*
What does this come down to, according to ... ?	*Waar komt dit, volgens ... , op neer?*
What is the purpose of this article?	*Wat het doel van dit artikel?*
How does the writer introduce the article?	*Hoe leidt de schrijver het artikel in?*
Which of the following is true?	*Welke van de volgende beweringen is waar?*
What becomes clear from lines 1-7?	*Wat wordt duidelijk uit de regels 1-7?*
Which of the following statements is **not true**, according to paragraph 4?	*Welke van de volgende beweringen is **niet waar**, volgens alinea 4?*

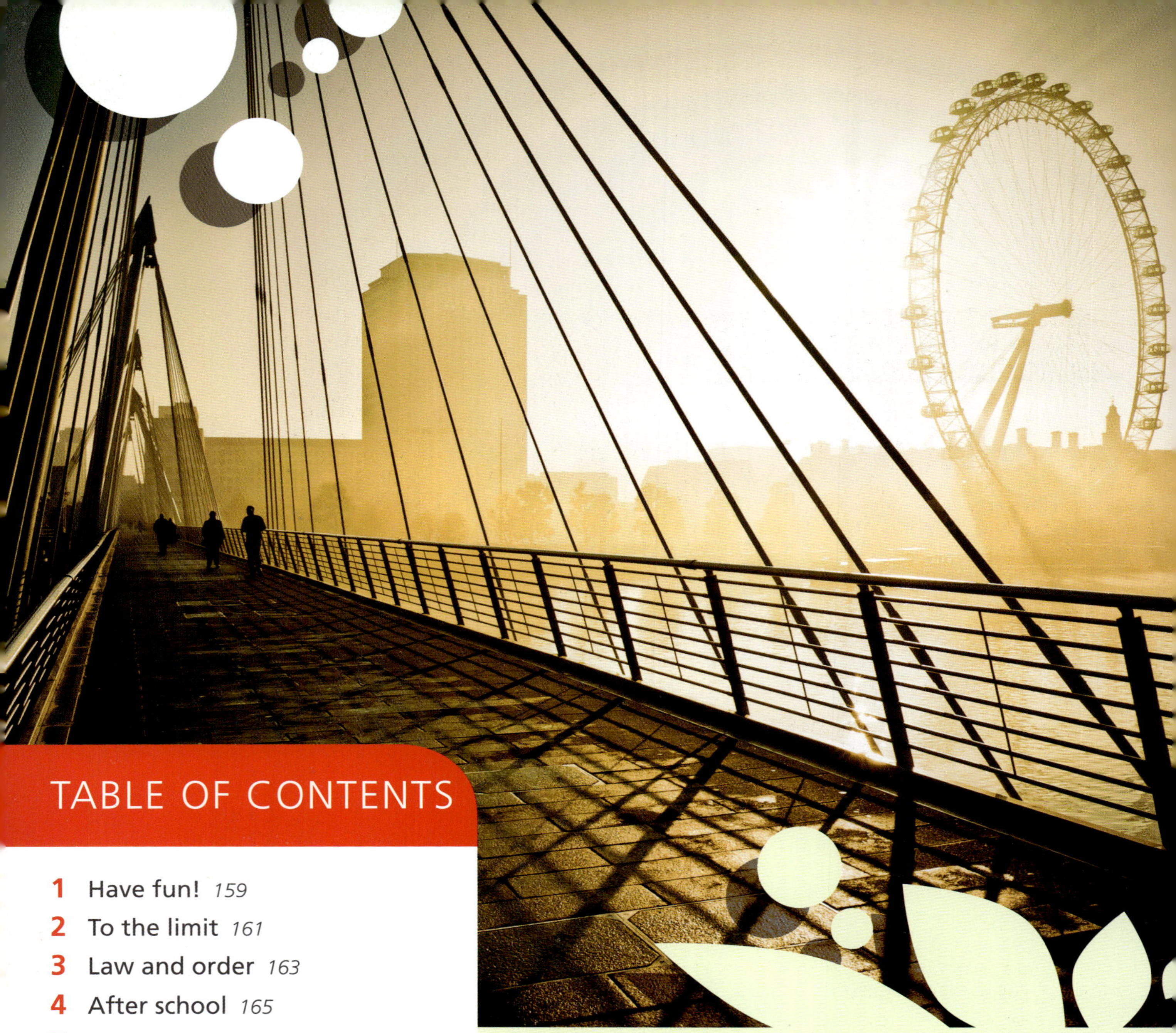

TABLE OF CONTENTS

Bridging the Gap
Year 3
Brug van klas 3 naar klas 4

1 Have fun!

A
WORDS

THEME WORDS

audience
bouncer
dress code
entrance fee
front row
gig
reduction
seat

to applaud
to dress up
to go Dutch
to have a blast

anniversary
diversity
edition
surroundings

to make a reservation
to manage
to provide
to succeed

excellent
flabbergasted
particularly
probably

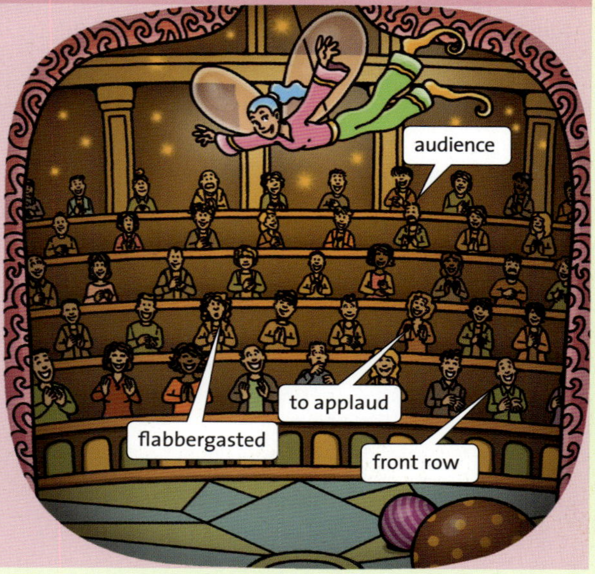

B
DIALOGUE

The teen festival

Holly: Thanks Mum for booking the tickets for *London 13up*. **Can I pick them up today?**
Mum: You can pick them up after 4pm tomorrow.
Jason: *London 13up*? What's that?
Holly: **I'm going to this festival next week**. It's especially for teens; it's the biggest teen festival in the world!
Jason: Oh, really? There are probably loads of parents too, afraid their child will get lost in the crowd, ha ha! And who is performing? Boogie Beebies and Andy's Dinosaur? Well, I'm sure you'll have a blast!
Mum: Jason! Just because you turned 18 last week doesn't mean you can make fun of everyone younger, you know.
Holly: I don't mind Mum! I'll be dancing and singing along to *Disclosure* in a few days... and he won't. Oh, I'm sure **it will be great fun!**
Jason: *Disclosure*? Are you serious? Let me see the line-up on the leaflet. Mum, **could I also go to the festival?** We don't want Holly to get lost in the crowd do we? I won't let her out of my sight, I promise....
Holly: Sorry Jason, **you're only allowed to attend the festival if you're between 13 and 17 years old**. You have to show your ID. Such a pity you're an adult now...

C
GRAMMAR

GRAMMAR

Modals

Modals zijn hulpwerkwoorden. Je kunt hulpwerkwoorden gebruiken om bijvoorbeeld toestemming, beleefdheid of verplichting uit te drukken.

can *could* (beleefder)	vragen of iets mag	**Can** we watch this film tonight? **Could** I borrow your pen?
can('t)	zeggen dat iets (niet) mag	You **can** borrow my pen. You **can't** watch this film tonight.
to be allowed to	vragen of/zeggen dat iets (niet) is toegestaan volgens de regels	**Are** we **allowed to** take pictures in here? You **are not allowed to** play loud music after ten pm.
must / mustn't	je vindt zelf dat iets (niet) moet	I **must** go to her and apologise.
have to	zekerheid, noodzaak, verplichting	I **have to** go now, or I'll miss my bus.
have to	iemand anders vindt dat iets moet	Mum says I **have to** do the dishes.
don't / doesn't have to	geen verplichting	You **don't have to** come with us.
should	advies of suggestie	Peter **should** study for the test.

D
READING

Fun events

Newmindspace is a non-profit organization founded by Kevin Bracken and Lori Kufner; two fun-loving artists who met in Toronto, Canada. Since a few years they have been organizing free, fun and all-ages events like parties on subway cars, public pillow fights, massive bubble battles, and much more.

One of their more well-known events is a street parade called *Castles in the Sky*. During this event the streets are taken over by hundreds of people dancing and singing to music made by several marching bands. People attending this event bring all kinds of noise-makers and wear crazy, colourful costumes. All in all, it's a massive celebration.

However, the biggest day of the year for Newmindspace is the *Bubble Battle*. This event has attracted thousands of people over the years to public spaces in New York City like Times Square. Here people of all ages come to meet each other and everybody can bring all kinds of bubble toys. The result? Millions of bubbles in the sky and loads of fun!

Both Lori and Kevin think people all around the world should communicate more and have more fun together. So far, they have organized over 85 outdoor events in New York City, Toronto, Montreal, San Francisco and Vancouver. Some of the events raise money for charity.

Adapted from: newmindspace.com

2 To the limit

THEME WORDS

adrenaline rush
bold
boost
first aid kit
limit
precaution
thrill seeker
torch

to hike
to overcome
to run a risk

exceptional
exhausted

anxiety
belongings
edge

to avoid
to encounter
to make sure
to take charge of

exhilarated
necessary
out of the ordinary
sensibly
unaccompanied

A
WORDS

The birthday party

B
DIALOGUE

Elly: Dad, I've got a great idea for my adventurous birthday party.
Father: Why don't you just want a traditional sweet 16 party at home?
Elly: Because I'm a thrill seeker, Dad! And so are all my friends. I'd like to go snowboarding at Cairngorm Mountains with them.
Father: Do you really want to run a risk of breaking bones or being caught in an avalanche on your 16th birthday?
Elly: Relax, dad! **You don't have to worry**.
Father: But there are often snowstorms in that area in March. You know **it's not wise to go into mountainous areas when there's a snowstorm**, don't you?
Elly: Of course I know, but we'll be taking a class with an experienced instructor. I promise I will **always act sensibly and follow the instructions of the instructor**.
Father: But do you remember Nigel? He had an accident in those mountains!
Elly: Because he didn't wear a helmet! Everybody knows you should **never go off piste without a helmet on**. Now, **wouldn't it be better if you stopped worrying about it?** We'll take all the necessary precautions and listen to the instructor, I promise.

C
GRAMMAR

GRAMMAR

Future (*toekomende tijd*)

present simple	vaststaande gebeurtenissen in de toekomst die onderdeel zijn van dienstregeling, rooster, ander schema	The bus **leaves** at six o'clock. The cinema **closes** at midnight.
present continuous	afspraken in de nabije toekomst waarvan tijd en/of plaats al vaststaat	I **am meeting** my brother at five o'clock.
will	iets aanbieden	We **will help** you clean up the house.
	beloftes	I **will call** Patrick tomorrow. I promise!
	aankondigingen	The auction **will start** in a few minutes.
	besluiten	They **won't sell** these chairs at the yard sale.
	voorspelling zonder bewijs	Alicia **will become** a famous singer.
going to	iemand is iets (niet) van plan	We**'re going to go** to the museum this afternoon.
	voorspelling met bewijs	Look at the sky. It **is going to rain** soon.

D
READING

The scavenger hunt

On Saturday 8 August some 180 bank employees assembled at a dock along the East River of Manhattan. They were divided into 20 teams. Standing on a platform overlooking the crowd was a man dressed in a red T-shirt printed with the words 'Game Master'. He handed each team captain a blue plastic bag containing some strange items including a pack of bubble gum, a poem and plastic cubes.

This was the beginning of *Midnight Madness*, an over-the-top scavenger hunt played by groups of financiers. The game requires every team to solve a series of complicated puzzles placed around New York City. Solving one puzzle points the employees to the location of the next puzzle, and so on.

Before the night was through, all participants had played laser mini golf, a game invented for this event, in an abandoned palace with multi-coloured lasers bouncing over the ruins. In one puzzle, players used an iPhone app to actually change the colour of the lights atop the tower at One Bryant Park, a major New York skyscraper.

The next *Midnight Madness* is on the 8th of December. The costs for this upcoming night of fun will probably be even higher than this year's $280,000, as they are going to add even more spectacular activities. The organisers have announced that from now on they will also accept teams from outside the world of banking, as long as the team is prepared to pay the extreme $50,000 admission fee....

Adapted from: qz.com

3 Law and order

A
WORDS

THEME WORDS

guilty
innocent
judge
lawyer
offence
robbery
suspect
victim

to fine
to investigate
to punish
to witness

advantage
characteristic
investigation

to damage
to examine
to get in touch with
to increase
to threaten

anonymous
rather than
suspicious
unlikely

B
DIALOGUE

Damaged bikes

Jayden: Hi Tom. Do you remember that **last week someone damaged the bicycles outside our school**?

Tom: Of course, I remember. They damaged my little brother's brand new bike. He was in tears when he found out. Is there any news?

Jayden: Yeah there is! **Police investigators used social media to help solve the crime**. They put some pictures from a surveillance camera online. It turned out there were two vandals; a man and a boy. **The man had dark hair and he was wearing old clothes. The boy was quite small and he was wearing red trainers.** Someone recognised them and **both suspects were tracked down by the police**. Of course they said they were innocent...

Tom: ...but the pictures proved they were guilty. So what will happen now?

Jayden : Well, damaging bikes is not a major criminal offence, so they will probably only be fined.

Tom: Or maybe they will be sentenced to community service.

Jayden: Yeah, they should make them work long hours in a bike store, repairing all the bikes they've damaged.

C GRAMMAR

GRAMMAR

If and when

if (als)	als je niet zeker weet of iets gaat gebeuren	**If** you see Francis, tell her we're leaving in an hour.
	om een voorwaarde aan te geven	You can still catch the train **if** you leave now.
when (wanneer)	wanneer je zeker weet dat iets gaat gebeuren	I'll visit you **when** I'm in England next month.

D READING

Why crime drama is good for your brain

Have you ever been told you watch too much television? Well, new research gives you the perfect excuse to lounge on the sofa and watch TV all night long – as long as you're watching a good TV crime drama.

Dr Amanda Allison from Durham University says these kind of programs provide an excellent workout for your brain. The best TV crime dramas build up suspense over a number of episodes. They challenge viewers to pay attention to complicated stories and to remember them from episode to episode. So, keeping the brain active means keeping it healthy.

When you challenge your brain, it becomes sharper. And when you watch complex TV drama, you challenge it even more. While watching, many regions in the brain are activated at the same time; for example the area in the left brain helps you understand the script of the show, and the area on the right side of the brain analyses all the different emotions of the characters. The memory area of the brain helps us remember who's who, how they relate to each other and what has happened in the previous episodes.

As mentioned before, the more suspense is built up during the series, the more active our brains get. However, if you get distracted, by, for example, your phone or social media, the brain becomes less active. So for the best brain workout, watch a crime show filled with suspense and give it your full attention.

Adapted from: www.telegraph.co.uk

4 After school

THEME WORDS

application form
colleague
devotion
enthusiast
job interview
part-time job
spare time
vacancy

to apply for
to be passionate about
to get fired
to spend time on

ambitious

movement
profession
satisfaction
workload

to accomplish
to distinguish
to inspire

broke
compared to
generally
hardly ever
thrifty

A
WORDS

Making money from a hobby

B
DIALOGUE

Reporter: Hello listeners. Welcome to today's show in which we talk to teenagers who combine their hobby with work. Here in the studio is Chris Isaacs, a freestyle skateboarding enthusiast. Chris, **when did you take up skateboarding?**

Chris: Well, **my love for it started when I was ten years old**. I was actually inspired by my brother, who participated in many competitions at the time. He bought me my first skateboard for my eleventh birthday and I've been spending nearly all my spare time on skateboarding ever since.

Reporter: And do you also spend all your money on it? Is it an expensive hobby?

Chris: It is if you are passionate about collecting skateboards like I am. **At the moment I'm saving money to buy a limited edition skateboard**. Luckily I've got a part-time job giving weekly skateboard workshops to young children. **I get paid £25 per workshop**, so **I earn about £100 a month**. But I have to add: it's not all about the money; it's a great job too!

C
GRAMMAR

GRAMMAR

Both, each, all, every, none

both (beide)	twee personen, dieren, dingen	zelfstandig naamwoord: meervoud	**Both** watches belong to Henry.
each (elke)	twee of meer personen, dieren, dingen	zelfstandig naamwoord: enkelvoud, nadruk op individuele dingen	He has a small tattoo on **each** arm.
every (elke)	drie of meer personen, dieren of dingen	nadruk op geheel	**Every** motorcyclist should wear a helmet.
all (alle)			They won **all** the challenges.
none (geen)			**None** of the trails are very dangerous.

D
READING

Just the job

Every week we ask someone about his or her job. This week we talked to Andy Walker, attraction manager at Thorpe Park.

What does an attraction manager do?
I look after the operation of the Park's rides and attractions, as well as the planning and operation of the entertainment in the park and our on-site accommodation, The Crash Pad.

How did you get your job?
Like all of my colleagues, I started with a seasonal job working on the rides. At the same time I was studying for a degree in Business Marketing, and when I graduated I applied and was accepted onto a special training programme at Merlin Entertainments Group. As part of this, I spent time working at a number of attractions and in a number of different functions. After building up all of this experience, I got my current job.

Why do you like your job?
Every day is completely different. I get involved in new ride projects, visit our competitors to develop new ideas, plan our special events and, most importantly, I have the pleasure of working with the best team and most thrilling rides in the country.

What's difficult about your job
Thorpe Park is constantly developing, which means there is always something different happening or being planned for the future. The development of both the rides and the entertainment teams is challenging for me, and not always easy.

Where to start
Merlin Entertainments Group is fantastic at talent management and career progression. Working for a global company opens up a whole range of opportunities to someone who is passionate and enthusiastic about the industry. Many of my colleagues have worked their way up to management positions.

Adapted from: First News, 2013

5 Down Under

A
WORDS

THEME WORDS

coastline
continent
coral reef
mountain range
outback
territory

to go backpacking

down-to-earth
laid-back
remote
vast
venomous

admission
custom
downside
hiking trail
sense of humour

to be aware
to insist
to involve
to spend time with

easy-going
rare
traditional

B
DIALOGUE

Where to go?

Mr Aran: So Rachel, Rob told us you could help us decide which holiday destination to choose; England or New Zealand? It's our first holiday outside the USA and we just can't make up our minds.

Rachel: I'm sure I can help Mr Aran. I've visited both countries. I loved England and especially London, but let me tell you... **New Zealand is the best country in the world!**

Mr Aran: Oh really? **Why do you think it's such a wonderful country to visit?**

Rachel: Well, how do exotic beaches, great mountain ranges, a laid-back lifestyle and easy-going people sound? You could say **New Zealand is wonderful because it has a lot to offer**.

Mr Aran: But England also has a lot to offer of course.

Rachel: You're right, but **people in England aren't as outdoorsy as people in New Zealand. New Zealanders like outdoor activities, like fishing and surfing.**

Mr Aran: Well, they should make you ambassador to New Zealand; I certainly think you've convinced us!

C
GRAMMAR

GRAMMAR

Past simple, present perfect, past continuous

past simple	iets is in het verleden gebeurd en is nu afgelopen vaak staat in de zin wanneer het gebeurde	I **worked** at a theme park last summer.
present perfect	iets is in het verleden begonnen en is nu nog bezig	Colleen **has lived** in Seattle since 2013.
	het resultaat is nog merkbaar	I **have broken** my leg, so I can't walk.
	een ervaring tot nu toe	Tami **has watched** that film ten times already.
	verklikwoorden	*ever, never, already, yet, before, recently, lately*
past continuous	iets was in het verleden een tijdje aan de gang	We **were talking** about the weather.

When the doorbell **rang**,	I **was studying**.
past simple	*past continuous*
iets gebeurde	terwijl iets anders al langere tijd aan de gang was

D
READING

Lauren's Australia blog

9-13 6:57 PM
Our first day in Australia! We started off the day early with a trip to a 'zoo.' A zoo here is something like an enclosed animal area, and it is often extremely interactive. We got to feed kangaroos – there were probably 30 of them hopping around asking for food! It was really awesome to interact with them and have them eat right out of your hand.

Then we met some koalas. They are actually the laziest animals in the world. They sleep 20 hours a day perched up in a tree. I got to take really close photos and even snuggle next to one for a photo. It didn't open its eyes or budge or anything.

9-15 8:30 PM
Today we were off to the Blue Mountains. They are blue because the leaves from the eucalyptus tree that grow on the mountains give off a blue reflection when they are blown off the tree. It really is spectacular. Then we headed down into the rainforest for a little hike. We walked pretty far down into the mountains, under a waterfall, and came back up via the steepest railway in the world. It was truly amazing! Our tour guide let us hop over the fence to get awesome photos underneath the waterfall... which is exactly what we did!

We took a ferry back to Sydney and had our first glimpse of the Opera House and the Harbour Bridge. As the sun set behind the ferry, the glow on the Sydney skyline was unforgettable.

6 Get involved

A
WORDS

THEME WORDS

climate change
community
litter
human rights
inequality
responsibility

to campaign
to contribute
to donate
to pollute

reusable
wealthy

ban
conversation
majority

to determine
to exaggerate
to intend to
to get involved

challenging
environmentally-friendly
in my opinion
vulnerable

B
DIALOGUE

Turning trash into homes

Liv: **Did you read about the Trash to Treasure contest?**

Tom: No, I didn't. **Could you tell what it was about?**

Liv: It's the contest Max participated in, remember? The theme of the contest was **What could you do to improve your neighbourhood?** Teenagers were asked to make an environmentally-friendly product from reusable materials.

Tom: Right, I remember. Max told me he wanted to make small houses for the homeless. To be honest, I thought his ideas sounded a bit too big for one 16-year-old.

Liv: Well, take a look at this picture. It turns out he has won the contest with his shelter for the homeless! It's made completely out of trash. He is now looking for funds to produce the shelters on a large scale.

Tom: Wow, these shelters look amazing! What about helping him? **Do you have any ideas on how to support his project?**

Liv: Maybe we can donate some money...

Tom: **I'd rather get involved myself instead of donating money.** Let's give him a call to ask how we can contribute to his project.

C
GRAMMAR

GRAMMAR

Prepositions (*voorzetsels*)

Voorzetsels van tijd geven aan wanneer iets gebeurt of gebeurd is.

voorzetsel	gebruik	voorbeelden
on	dagen, data	**on** Saturday, **on** May the 1st
in	maanden, jaartallen, seizoenen, dagdelen	**in** 1999, **in** the morning
at	tijdsaanduidingen	**at** 7 o'clock, **at** 8pm
	vaste uitdrukkingen	**at** the weekend, **at** Christmas, **at** the same time

Voorzetsels van beweging geven aan in welke richting iets of iemand zich beweegt.

Throw the rock **across** the river.	*over*	Don't jump **into** the river.	*in, naar binnen*
Walk **around** the stadium.	*om*	The car went **off** the road.	*van*
Drive **away from** the station.	*weg van*	Jump **over** this fence.	*over*
Don't fall **down** the stairs.	*naar beneden*	Run **through** the forest.	*door*
He began to walk away **from** her.	*van*	Go **to** school.	*naar*

D
READING

A good deed every day of the year

Every New Year, millions of people make resolutions only to see them fall by the wayside within a few months, weeks, or even days. However, 26-year-old Luke Cameron is not among them. Last year he vowed to do at least one good deed a day for 365 days and now, at the end of the year, his project is nearly completed.

Cameron decided that he would do a random act of kindness each day in honour of a friend he lost to cancer, who he says 'gave her whole life selflessly helping others' and who inspired him to 'give something back to those who need more than I do'.

Over the course of the year Cameron has done a range of 'good deeds'; giving clothes to charity, making cookies and cakes for his colleagues, giving hot food to the homeless, doing his father's ironing, and helping an elderly lady cross the street. He documented everything on his Good Deed Diary blog, which had thousands of followers in the past 12 months.

Next week, on New Year's Eve, Cameron will round off his year of kind acts. On December 31st he will go to Cheltenham and give out £365 to 73 random people by handing them each a £5 note. Because he is curious about people's responses, he is going to wear a hidden camera on his front to film this. 'After this last deed I will probably feel sad that my project is over, but I hope others will feel inspired to do the same in the coming year.'

Adapted from: independent.co.uk

Vocabulary

Go to Stepping Stones online to practise with the complete Vocabulary.

appropriate	*passende*
be supposed to	*geacht worden, horen te zijn*
besides that	*daarnaast*
cause	*veroorzaken*
challenge	*uitdagen*
comment	*opmerking*
conditions	*omstandigheden*
cooperate	*samenwerken*
crucial	*beslissend*
depend on	*afhangen van*
determination	*vastberadenheid*
disadvantage	*nadeel*
distract	*afleiden*
enjoyable	*plezierig*
enough	*genoeg*
forgiven and forgotten	*vergeven en vergeten*
fortnight	*twee weken*
imagine	*je voorstellen*
in common	*gemeen*
keep in mind	*onthouden*
likely	*waarschijnlijk*
look	*uitstraling*
meaningful	*zinvol*
nature	*aard, karakter*
neighbouring	*aangrenzend*
prohibited	*verboden*
report	*melden, schrijven*
respond	*antwoorden*
reveal	*onthullen*
several	*verscheidene*
spoil	*bederven*
suitable	*geschikt*
survival	*overleven*
team up with	*samenwerken met*
to have in common	*gemeen hebben*
tough luck	*dikke pech*
turn out fine	*goedkomen*
uncomfortable	*ongemakkelijk*
uncommon	*ongewoon*
violence	*geweld*

TABLE OF CONTENTS

Bridging the Gap mbo

Brug van klas 4 naar mbo

1 Administrative and clerical services

A
WORDS

THEME WORDS

access
balance sheet
bookkeeping
entry pass
entry-level job
executive
filing cabinet
industry
negotiations
policy
reception hall
schedule
storage

tax
temp
trial period
VAT

to be in charge of
to brief
to confirm
to postpone

efficient
inconvenient
transferred

B
DIALOGUE

Introductions

Mr Cameron: Hello Louise, I'm glad to see you. How are you?
Louise: Hello Mr Cameron. Fine, thanks.
Mr Cameron: Shall I give you a short tour of the company so you can get acquainted with the building and our administrative team?
Louise: Yes, please. I'm looking forward to meeting my new colleagues.
Mr Cameron: Ah, there's Tim Parker. Tim is in charge of the sales department, which is on the second floor. Tim, meet Louise, our new receptionist.
Tim: Pleased to meet you. Sorry, we'll talk later. I've got a meeting at nine.
Mr Cameron: So let's meet the team. This is Mr Bhamidipati, our accountant.
Louise: Mr ...? I'm sorry I didn't get your last name.
Raj: Never mind. You can call me by my first name, Raj.
Louise: Hi Raj. I'm Louise, the new receptionist.
Raj: Pleased to meet you. So, you're the latest addition to our team.
Louise: Yes, I am. I actually worked as a temp here for a fortnight, but that was during the holidays.
Raj: Ah well, it looks like you've already passed your trial period then!

C READING

Whoa! An administrative assistant does ALL that?

One minute you're making sure the director is prepared for his meeting and offering your opinion on what he should say, the next you're sorting through mail and handling phone calls. You're definitely not limited to one type of task and there's no doubt that without you the office would come to a screeching halt. So, who are you? The administrative assistant.

If you asked a group of people what their 'dream job' would be, how many do you think would say being an administrative assistant? Probably not many. Yet this job can be both exciting and rewarding.

As a modern administrative assistant, you're very much involved with what is happening in the company. You're basically the person who makes sure that everything is running smoothly and efficiently. Because administrative assistants usually interact with executives, managers, and other professionals, their days will vary depending on the schedules of those other members of the company.

At a lot of smaller companies, the role of the administrative assistant is more like that of an office manager or an executive assistant. Although the job will vary depending on the industry and size of the company, there are some tasks that almost all administrative assistants will need to know how to do. Some of those typical duties include bookkeeping, scheduling appointments, coordinating meetings, taking notes, answering emails, transferring or setting up calls and entering data.

So those are the typical duties of an administrative assistant. Now let's start exploring why this job might appeal to some people – and why others may choose a different career.

Cons

Salary. Even though your salary will probably increase as you gain more experience, starting

salaries for administrative assistants aren't very high.

Dealing with difficult people. This job requires a lot of interaction with other people and there are going to be times when you have to deal with disgruntled employees, clients, or managers.

Not all tasks are exciting. Not all tasks that come with this job are that thrilling. You'll be doing a lot of data entry and other work that can be considered 'tedious'.

Pros

You play a pretty large part in the effectiveness of a company. A lot of businesses would be completely lost without the organisation and work done by the administrative assistant who works there.

Every day is different. Whatever is needed by the company on that day is what you'll be doing.

You can work in any field. Almost every company needs administrative assistants. That means you have the chance to work in almost any environment or industry that interests you.

Adapted from: blog.aftercollege.com

disgruntled	*ontevreden*

2 Welfare

THEME WORDS

A WORDS

- appointment
- bandage
- consultation hours
- dentistry
- disabilities
- disorder
- filling
- GP
- health care
- home care
- nappies
- pulse
- prescription
- social security number
- social workers
- surgeon
- treatment
- upbringing
- walker
- wheelchair

- to administer a drip
- to recover
- to tackle
- to treat

The internship

B DIALOGUE

Mrs Hunt: Hi Selma, please come in. We're here to discuss your internship at Chesterfield Royal Hospital. So how do you feel about it?

Selma: I'm looking forward to it, although I'm also a bit nervous.

Mrs Hunt: I can imagine that, but you don't have to be. You've got plenty of classroom experience, so you're well prepared.

Selma: I guess that's true.

Mrs Hunt: So, shall we discuss what's expected of you during the internship? First, you will shadow other nurses to learn about their job. You can ask them questions and observe their work. Don't just focus on the practical tasks they perform but also pay attention to how they communicate with their patients.
After a month you will also support doctors and nurses in diagnostic procedures and technical treatments. You may be instructed to clean and treat wounds, apply bandages and administer drips.

Selma: I think I can manage that.

Mrs Hunt: I'm glad to hear that. If things go well, they will give you more responsibilities, such as drawing blood under supervision or perhaps even seeing patients yourself.

Selma: That would be awesome! I can't wait to get started.

C
READING

Working as a dental nurse

Would you like to work in dentistry? Check out this interview with Sophie Houghton, a dental nurse at Braden Dental Care, to see what it's like.

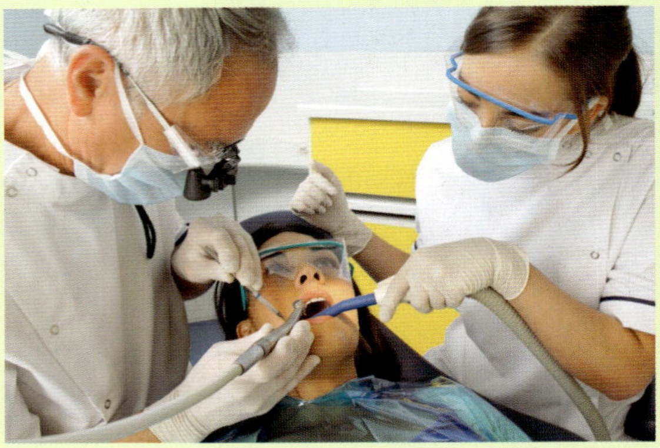

What does your job entail?

I'm a dental nurse at Braden Dental Care. I assist with all dental procedures, help write up dental records on the computer and I'm also responsible for cleaning and sterilising all equipment and clinical areas between appointments.
A really important part of my job is making patients feel as comfortable and welcome as possible. We always have a bit of a chat on the way up to the treatment room, which helps put them at ease.

Is it 9-5?

The job is almost 9-5. I start work at 8.30 am and finish at 5.30 most days. But the great thing about being a dental nurse is that no two hours are the same, let alone two days.
Each patient will have different needs and require different treatments. We do a lot of cosmetic work as well as more routine procedures, which means the work really varies every day.
The first patient is usually booked in at nine in the morning so I have to have everything set up and ready before that.
Before I finish for the day I leave everything clean for the next day. As well as nursing, occasionally I help out on reception which involves booking appointments and dealing with people arriving or leaving.

What are the biggest rewards and challenges of your work?

The best reward for me is the satisfaction I get from helping to complete a successful treatment that has a positive impact upon the patient. We offer cutting-edge orthodontic treatments, for instance straightening teeth without fixed braces. These treatments can positively change the way patients view themselves.
The greatest challenge is managing the concerns and expectations of patients. Our focus is on providing a high standard of customer service. We try to ensure that each patient has a positive experience.

Tell us an interesting fact about yourself

Last year I met Brendan Fraser, star of the *The Mummy* series of Hollywood blockbusters, at the closing party for the Belfast Film Festival. We had an opportunity to chat and he was a really nice guy, but once he found out what I did, he pointed to his mouth and asked if I could help out with his filling. I told him I knew a good dentist!

Adapted from: nijobfinder.co.uk

dental records	*gebitsgegevens*
let alone	*laat staan*
concerns	*zorgen*

3 Engineering and construction

THEME WORDS

arch
building plan
calculations
carpentry
construction site
control panel
expertise
license
mason
mechanical engineer
plumber
regulations
safety measures

sewer system
wiring
woodwork
workshop

to connect
to set
to weld

ready for use
refurbished
registered
trained as

A
WORDS

Cutting edge

B
DIALOGUE

Mr Thompson: Is everyone inside the workshop? Today we're going to find out how this CO2 laser engraver cutter works. Your homework was to study the first ten pages of the laser cutter manual.
Jessica, could you show us how you start up this laser cutter?

Jessica: Well, first you plug in these cables, like this. Then you turn it on. Right now it doesn't do anything, because you have to switch off the emergency stop first. You have to twist it to turn it on, or else nothing happens.

Mr Thompson: Well done. Now what next? Samir, can you help explain?

Samir: Next, I think we have to check if the air pump and water pump are connected to the machine. They are right there at the bottom of this panel.
This is where all the wiring is.

Mr Thompson: And what do you need those for?

Samir: I guess it's for cooling the machine down. After everything is plugged in, you can go to the control panel which is just below the emergency stop.

Mr Thompson: All right Jessica and Samir, that was excellent. Now the next step is how you actually cut out your design. I will show you...

C READING

How do I become… a superyacht builder?

Traditional skills such as carpentry and welding are useful, and you also need good sea legs.

Niels van Dinther, 48, is project manager at Pendennis shipyard, Britain's only superyacht builder and refitter. It's his job to plan and run the renovations of existing superyachts and to oversee the construction of new ones. He also supervises a number of apprentices who spend four years at the yard to gain experience in yacht manufacture and maintenance.

Van Dinther has built superyachts for billionaires for twelve years, refining and redesigning them according to their tastes. A lot has changed since he first started. Demand for superyachts has more than doubled over the past decade with over 5,000 currently sailing globally. As the wealth of the world's elite has grown, so has the size of their crafts. The largest currently in service is 164 m and cost € 340 million to build. 'When I started 12 years ago a 50-metre boat was considered large,' Van Dinther says. 'Now the average is 70 metres, and a lot of them are over 100 metres.'

Boats can take up to three-and-a-half years to build from scratch, by which time fashions have changed and technology evolved. 'Clients can be quite demanding and quite often change their minds or want a new building plan after seeing a new piece of technology or design,' Van Dinther says. One owner decided that his boat was too short and wanted an extra five metres added to the middle, so we had to cut it in half and add a central section.'

Currently Van Dinther and his company are building a lot of yachts with 'toys' – expensive extras ranging from water skis and inflatable water slides into the sea to running machines.

Bling apart, the superyacht industry, which is worth around € 24 billion worldwide, incorporates the traditional skills of carpentry, plastering and welding, and applicants with expertise in any of these could try their luck at a shipyard.

Pendennis runs a four-year general apprenticeship scheme and 70% of the 160 people trained so far are still employed by the firm. It's not easy to get selected for this apprenticeship. 'It helps if you can show an interest in sailing,' Van Dinther says. 'Get experience as a crew member by getting a job on a yacht. Or do a catering degree and find work as a steward or cook on board. If you can be versatile and turn your hand to painting or woodwork, that makes an impression.'

Adapted from: theguardian.com

refitter	*bedrijf dat boten herstelt en opnieuw optuigt*
inflatable water slides	*opblaasbare waterglijbanen*
plastering	*stuken*

4 Commerce

A
WORDS

THEME WORDS

availability
catalogue
delivery point
detection gates
fitting room
guarantee
launch
manufacturer
merchandise
responsibility
sales department
shift
shop window

stock
terms of delivery
trade fair
warehouse

to browse
to close the deal
to deliver
to gain experience

customer oriented
profitable
self-employed

B
DIALOGUE

New desk lamps

Julia Eccles: I'd like to order something that's not in your online catalogue anymore. Am I speaking to the person in charge of orders?
James Radford: Yes, I handle orders. My name is James Radford. Who am I speaking to?
Julia Eccles: My name is Julia Eccles. I'm with Mercury Incorporated. We have placed some orders for office furniture with you before.
James Radford: I see. I have your order history in our system here. What item were you looking for?
Julia Eccles: We are looking for some new PRIMAX desk lamps for our office.
James Radford: Unfortunately we no longer sell those. I can recommend the VORTEX. It's a new model, very modern and quite similar to the PRIMAX. We are going to add it to our catalogue next week.
Julia Eccles: That sounds interesting. I will consider purchasing them. We would need them by next week. How soon could you deliver them?
James Radford: We can despatch them from our warehouse within 24 hours.
Julia Eccles: Could you send the product details and terms of delivery to my email address?
James Radford: Yes of course. Is there anything else I can help you with?
Julia Eccles: That will be all. Thank you and goodbye.

C READING

A day in the life of a shopkeeper

David Meers is a shopkeeper for Kitchens & Dining at Ikea, Belfast. For the last three years he has worked in the sales team. He is responsible for the kitchens and dining department.

8am
On a typical morning I arrive at work and have a quick look at any new emails and check my planner for the day and week ahead. The store is open seven days a week, so I work a variety of shifts every week. For the past six months, however, I have been working on the very impressive rebuild of our kitchen department and the launch of our METOD kitchen range. We need to be able to answer the typical questions a visitor will have, such as the price, availability, guarantees, delivery, and assembly.

9.30am
The store opens to visitors for breakfast. At 10am the showroom opens so around this time we get ready for trade. We support the logistics team in filling the sales locations with stock. It's a busy start to the day.

9.40am
I take a break with colleagues from across the store in our co-worker restaurant. This is tradition across the IKEA world, and it is a good opportunity to catch up with people who I don't normally work with.

10am
We get a lot of questions in the kitchen department, and I enjoy the variety from someone looking to improve their cupboard organisation to someone who is planning a major design or refurbishment project. I have shaped the new kitchen department based on customer feedback and experience.

11am
Usually I have appointments with customers about their kitchen desires. Today my diary is filling up for appointments for the new kitchen range.

12noon
Lunch break is 45 minutes and is taken between 12pm and 2pm in the co-worker or customer restaurant.

1pm
The afternoon flies by and, as part of the large management team in the store, I share the duty manager role. This takes the form of a complete walk through the store and taking checks against our store standards. Where necessary we resolve issues promptly.

5.30pm
It's almost time to go home. We are encouraged to achieve a good work-life balance and I normally try to get home for an evening meal together with my family at around 5.30pm-6pm.

6pm
Home time. In the words of IKEA's founder Ingvar Kamprad, 'most things still remain to be done', but hopefully together with my fellow co-workers, visitors will enjoy our newly opened kitchen department.

Adapted from: nijobfinder.co.uk

rebuild	*verbouwing*
refurbishment	*renovatie*
duty manager	*eindverantwoordelijk manager*
promptly	*ogenblikkelijk*

5 Green

A
WORDS

THEME WORDS

agriculture
bottle bank
bouquet
bud
cattle
crop
factory farming
greenhouse
habitat
nature reserve
nutrition
orchard
permit

species
stem
weed

organic
sustainable

to breed
to combat pests
to dig
to maintain
to sow
to supervise

B
DIALOGUE

Classroom announcement

Colin: Hello everybody, could I have your attention for a moment? I'd like to make an announcement. To be honest, I don't do this every day but this is a special occasion. As most of you all know I've recently completed my countryside management course.

Leonard: Yes, you're Colin the countryside ranger now!

Colin: Thank you Leonard. That's a really funny nickname by the way... I did part of my work placement at the Wicken Fen, which also happens to be the National Trust's oldest nature reserve. While I was there I helped maintain the landscape and observed the wildlife. In short, I did a lot of practical work and it was a great experience. To celebrate getting my diploma, I thought it would be appropriate to return to that spot.
So, I'd like to invite you all for a nice organic lunch at The Fen this Saturday at noon. After lunch I'll give you all a little tour of the fen and show you some attractions. I hope to see you all there. Please bring some sturdy shoes with you, and don't forget raincoats of course.

Leonard: Nice one, Colin! Count me in!

C

READING

Neil Lincoln, fish farmer

My name's Neil Lincoln; I'm a fish farmer at the Environment Agency's Calverton Fish Farm. Basically we produce and breed coarse fish for the Environment Agency for restocking around the country – we do chub, barbel, tench, roach, bream, mainly the fish that anglers like to catch.

I've been working here for over 13 years; I came here after a work placement at college. I've always been a keen angler and outdoor work has always been what I've wanted to do.

I did enjoy school; I didn't think I was very good at school but I knew that I wanted to do something in farming and working outside. I loved fishing; I was always out fishing as soon as I'd finished school so working with fish was the ideal job.

After I finished my GCSEs at school I just wanted to go out to work, I didn't really want to go to college in the beginning. I spoke to a careers adviser at the school and they told me about fish farming. I got in touch with some colleges and I learned about the kinds of work you could do and thought I'd have a go!

I worked on a Youth Training Scheme at a local fishery and then went to college and did a First Diploma in Fisheries Studies, which included going on two work placements. One was up in Scotland at a salmon farm and the other was here. When my work placement ended they took me on and I haven't looked back since! I could have done more studying but I think I made the right move – I've learned a huge amount here from the people I work with and it's a really close team.

I'll still be here in five years' time, I'm sure, and we'll be doing a few more species at the farm and a few more projects. I'd like to progress and move up to the fish farm manager role, supervising the farm, but that role is more office based. I think this is my dream job – this is as good as it gets! Hopefully I'll still be here when I retire – it's just as good today as it was when I first came here, I love it!

Adapted from: gov.uk

coarse fish	*zoetwatervissen*
restocking	*uitzetten*
GCSEs	*eindexamen*
anglers	*hengelaars*
salmon	*zalm*

Bridging the Gap

havo

Brug van 4 vmbo naar 4 havo

TABLE OF CONTENTS

A VOCABULARY

accessible	*toegankelijk*	specific	*specifiek*
appropriate	*gepast*	to acquire	*verkrijgen*
defendant	*beschuldigde*	to adjust	*aanpassen*
exceptional	*uitzonderlijk*	to baffle	*verbluffen*
generosity	*vrijgevigheid*	to conclude	*concluderen*
government	*regering*	to initiate	*beginnen*
graduate	*afgestudeerde*	to resolve	*oplossen*
hardship	*misère*	to take charge	*leiding nemen*
humility	*bescheidenheid*		
improvement	*vooruitgang*		
intriguing	*intrigerend*		
lawsuit	*rechtzaak*		
litigation	*procesvoering*		
negligence	*verwaarlozing*		
plaintiff	*aanklager*		
preference	*voorkeur*		
prolific	*productief*		

B WATCHING/ LISTENING

Wannabe writer

Wannabe author Lucy talks about her writing ambitions. In this clip she tells when her passion for writing began, what literature she recommends and who inspires her. She also talks about her own short stories.

The Seven Stories

There are only seven stories in the world. I used to think there were a lot more than that, based on visits to blockbuster films and my school reading list, but my high school Creative Writing teacher, Mrs Post, corrected my ignorance. She said that all plots are a variation of one or more of seven basic themes: overcoming the monster, rags to riches, the quest, voyage and return, comedy, tragedy, and rebirth.

Mrs Post gave us the assignment to read a book and write a review of it. In this review we were supposed to make clear which of the seven themes were in the book. A simple assignment as it may seem, it turned out to be quite difficult after all. Why? Because I found out that the book I read contained more than one basic plot. Actually, all the seven stories in the world were in it!

I had heard a lot about The Hunger Games by Suzanne Collins. Luckily, I hadn't seen the film, so I could start reading it with an open mind. For those of you who don't know The Hunger Games, here's a short outline:

In the ruins of a place once known as North America lies the nation of Panem, a shining Capitol surrounded by twelve outlying districts. Long ago the districts waged war on the Capitol and were defeated. As part of the surrender terms, each district agreed to send one boy and one girl to appear in an annual televised event called The Hunger Games: a fight to the death on live TV. Sixteen-year-old Katniss Everdeen, who lives alone with her mother and younger sister, regards it as a death sentence when she is forced to represent her district in the Games. The terrain, rules, and level of audience participation may change, but one thing is certain: you have to kill or be killed.

After I had read the book, I started to wonder which of the seven basic plots were in the book. The first, overcoming the monster, was quite obvious. Although there are some real monsters in the arena, you could also regard the government as one. They are the initiator of The Hunger Games and cause all the hardships Katniss has to face. So for me it was clear that The Hunger Games has to do with overcoming some sort of monster.

From rags to riches, so from being really poor to being rich, is also a theme I was able to spot in the book. At first Katniss is penniless, but after winning The Hunger Games she can have everything she wants. She gets a house, and is rewarded with a large sum of money. Plot number three, the quest, was an obvious one. Katniss has to battle the other contestants in order to stay alive. More or less the same goes for story number four. Katniss goes on a voyage,

because she has to leave her village for the TV show, and returns a hero.

Then for numbers five and six. Although I didn't expect to have a good laugh while reading this book, on several occasions I had. Despite the pain, the suffering, and the brutality, there are a lot of comical notes in the book. And as far as tragedy is concerned, this theme is quite obviously present in the book. You get to know the contestants throughout the story, but most of them kick the bucket sooner or later.

Six down, only one to go: rebirth. If you take this literally, it's quite hard to find this theme in the book. Figuratively speaking Katniss is reborn several times in The Hunger Games. It often looks like she is going to be defeated, but she manages to survive every single time. When she goes off to the games, she is sure she won't return to her village. But what happens in the end? She wins the games and goes home a hero!

So, are there only seven stories in the world? As far as I'm concerned there are infinite possibilities by combining the stories. Really good stories though, like The Hunger Games, have all the stories combined into one.

Adapted from: lenwilson.us/seven-stories

D SPEAKING/ WRITING

Back Forward Stop Refresh Home Search Favorites History Mail Print

http://www.facesoflawsuitabuse.org/

'Hot Coffee' Redux: NC Jury Tosses Ridiculous Spilled Coffee Lawsuit Against Starbucks

A North Carolina jury has tossed a lawsuit brought against Starbucks by a Raleigh cop who spilled hot coffee in his lap three years ago.

If that story sounds somewhat familiar to you, it should. A similar 'hot coffee' lawsuit against McDonald's back in 1994 became a poster child for ridiculous litigation.

In *that* infamous ridiculous lawsuit, the jury awarded the plaintiff an astonishing $3 million in damages after she spilled a cup of McDonald's coffee in her lap, though the parties later settled for a reduced, undisclosed amount.

In this case, Police Lt. Matt Kohr sought $750,000 in damages from Starbucks for serving him hot coffee that was, unsurprisingly, quite hot. After receiving the cup, Kohr proceeded to spill the cup of java all over his legs and thighs when the lid popped off.

And all of this started with an act of generosity: Starbucks had given the officer the cup of coffee for free. That's right: Kohr sought $750,000 from Starbucks for spilling a gift all over his lap. It seems that no good deed goes unpunished.

More than 20 years after the original hot coffee lawsuit – once described as the 'poster child of excessive lawsuits' – it's ridiculous that Starbucks had to pay the cost of taking this case to trial to defeat this ridiculous lawsuit.

Acknowledgements

The Tonight Show with Jimmy Fallon, www.bu.edu/today/2015/writing-for-the-tonight-show-with-jimmy-fallon/
A professional prankster, www.thesun.co.uk/sol/homepage/showbiz/tv/4877500/jason-bent-man-city-stunt.html
Space colours your place, http://diply.com/creative-unusual/10-diy-space-saving-ideas-your-home/180521
The man who grows furniture, www.dailymail.co.uk/news/article-3033546/How-grow-furniture-Eco-friendly-designer-uses-special-moulds-guide-branches-ready-chairs-tables-lampshades.html
Dragon's Den, www.bbc.co.uk/programmes/b006vq92
The right person for the job, http://blog.firefishsoftware.com/bid/99293/10-Awesome-Job-Adverts
How Google started, www.biography.com/news/google-founders-history-facts
Jobs of the future, http://careers2030.cst.org/jobs/fashion-designer/
www.telegraph.co.uk/finance/personalfinance/9892011/10-well-paid-jobs-of-the-future.html
Understanding laughter, http://science.howstuffworks.com/life/inside-the-mind/emotions/laughter3.htm
Tiny street art, www.theguardian.com/lifeandstyle/2014/oct/10/tiny-art-miniature-street-scenes-slinkachu
www.theguardian.com/artanddesign/2011/feb/27/mini-street-sculpture-cordal-slinkachu
Why everyone loves to work in the UK, www.indeed.co.uk
http://content.wisestep.com/best-reasons-to-love-working-in-uk-united-kingdom
De teksten uit Exam Preparation zijn afkomstig van Cito, Engels CSE vmbo-gl/tl, 2015, tijdvak 1 & 2; vmbo-gl/tl, 2012, tijdvak 1 & 2; vmbo-gl/tl, 2013, tijdvak 1 en vmbo-gl/tl, 2014, tijdvak 1 & 2
InterPals, www.interpals.net
Skydiving, www.quora.com/How-did-it-feel-when-you-went-skydiving-for-the-first-time
Volunteer opportunities, www.safehavenhumane.org/volunteer-opportunities-kids
My daily routines, https://au.answers.yahoo.com/question/index?qid=20090813031056AA1FbLV
Learning styles, www.worldwidelearn.com/education-articles/how-do-you-learn.htm
Troy von Scheibner, the urban illusionist, www.standard.co.uk/showbiz/celebrity-news/magician-troy-von-scheibner-thandie-newton-kissed-me-on-the-cheek-i-ll-never-wash-my-face-again-10090853.html
Grocery shopping and ordering whoppers, http://wiredcosmos.com/2012/06/07/sociology-in-action-the-breaching-experiment/
Jamaica's three languages, http://reallifeglobal.com/jamaican-english-with-bob-marley/
Irish around the world, www.everyculture.com/multi/Ha-La/Irish-Americans.html
The power of the placebo, www.bbc.com/news/magazine-34572482
Life in Singapore, www.expatliving.sg
www.goabroad.com/articles/study-abroad/singapore-laws-to-know-before-you-go
My big fat cousin's wedding, www.poetrysoup.com/poem/my_big_fat_cousins_wedding_420627
I often contradict myself, Ken Nesbitt; My Hippo Has the Hiccups: And Other Poems I Totally Made Up (A Poetry Speaks Experience); Sourcebooks Jabberwocky (2009), ISBN:
Bottled up, www.robertburtonrobinson.com/2012/04/23/bottled-up/
The case of the lower case letter, www.eastoftheweb.com/short-stories/UBooks/CaseLowe950.shtml
Never Always Sometimes, Adi Alsaid, Harlequin Teen (2015), ISBN:
The Adoration of Jenna Fox, Mary E. Pearson, Henry Holt and Co (2008), ISBN:
Fun events ,newmindspace.com
The scavenger hunt , http://qz.com/15321/inside-the-epic-all-night-goldman-sachs-scavenger-hunt/
Why crime drama is good for your brain, www.telegraph.co.uk/news/science/11374598/Why-watching-TV-crime-dramas-is-good-for-your-brain.html
Just the job, First News, 2013

A good deed every day of the year, www.independent.co.uk/news/uk/home-news/luke-cameron-finishes-off-365-days-of-good-deeds-by-giving-away-365-in-cash-9952772.html
Whoa! An Administrative Assistant Does ALL That?, http://blog.aftercollege.com/whoa-administrative-assistant/
Working as a dental nurse, www.nijobfinder.co.uk/job-profiles/187/antoinette-simpson/
How do I become ... a superyacht builder?, www.theguardian.com/money/2015/may/12/how-become-superyacht-builder
A day in the life of a shopkeeper, www.nijobfinder.co.uk/job-profiles/298/david-meers/
Neil Lincoln, fish farmer, www.gov.uk/government/uploads/system/uploads/attachment_data/file/391911/15.01.05._UKCES_Career_Brochure_V13_reduced.pdf
The seven stories, http://lenwilson.us/seven-stories
Aunt Sues Nephew for $127k Over 'Negligent' Hug, www.facesoflawsuitabuse.org/2015/06/hot-coffee-redux-nc-jury-tosses-ridiculous-spilled-coffee-lawsuit-against-starbucks/
I often contradict myself, Ken Nesbitt*; My Hippo Has the Hiccups: And Other Poems I Totally Made Up (A Poetry Speaks Experience);* Sourcebooks Jabberwocky (2009), ISBN: 9781402218095
Never Always Sometimes, Adi Alsaid, Harlequin Teen (2015), ISBN: 9781848453906
The Adoration of Jenna Fox, Mary E. Pearson, Henry Holt and Co (2008), ISBN: 9780805076684

Bronvermelding foto's

Beeldresearch: B en U International Picture Service, Amsterdam

iStockphoto: p. 7, 16 lb, lo, 49 l, 60, 70 b, 72, 112
Getty Images: p. 9, 51, 81, 83, 97, 109 l, 178
ITN Source, Londen: p. 11, 25, 89, 103
www.ellisobrien.com: p. 13
Hans Kok, Amsterdam: p. 15, 29, 85, 99
Imageselect, Wassenaar: p. 16 rb, 23, 35, 49 r, 53, 54, 62, 68, 69, 70 o, 71 b, 73, 76, 176, 180, 182, 184, 185
Shutterstock: p. 16 lm, rm, ro, 21, 36, 44, 49 m, 50, 59, 66, 67 b, 95, 109 r, 111, 164, 174
Avar Furniture, Londen: p. 26
Hollandse Hoogte, Den Haag: p. 27, 37, 40, 56 lo, 57, 61, 67 o, 71 o, 77, 100, 110
Andrew Farrington / BBC: p. 30
INTedu, Londen: p. 39
Imagetower.com: p. 41
Johan Falck, Sayit: p. 43
www.artscape.se: p. 52
www.sfts.org.uk: p. 56 b
Rob Baar / Nimeto, Utrecht: 56 ro
Corbis: p. 55, 58, 172, 183
Natural World / bbc.co.uk: p. 74
Wikimedia: p. 86
MM Fotografie, Amsterdam: p. 90
Nationale Beeldbank, Rotterdam: p. 104
iStockphoto: p. 113, 158
Bookpage.com: p. 119
Booknuts.com: p. 121

Met betrekking tot sommige teksten en/of illustratiemateriaal is het de uitgever, ondanks zorgvuldige inspanningen daartoe, niet gelukt eventuele rechthebbende(n) te achterhalen. Mocht u van mening zijn (auteurs)rechten te kunnen doen gelden op teksten en/of illustratiemateriaal in deze uitgave dan verzoeken wij u contact op te nemen met de uitgever.

We have done our utmost to find the addresses of copyright holders from whose work we have borrowed extracts. Despite our efforts we do not always succeed. We kindly invite all those concerned to contact us.